# Young Song

## A Novel
## of Reconstruction-Era Korea

### by
### Richard Cavalier

ISBN: 0-7596-6954-6 (ebook)
ISBN: 0-7596-6955-4 (Paperback)

This book is printed on acid free paper.

1stBooks - rev. 03/14/03

Except for historical persons and places named herein, all names of all novelistic characters are invented, and any similarities to actual persons or places are therefore entirely coincidental.

# Dedication

To the memory of Peter VANDERPOEL, who understood, believed, and cared; and to all the ladies and others who form the composite characters of a fictitious book stewn with unhappy historical fact.

Special thanks to the Albert Lea (MN) *Tribune* for permission to reproduce the newspaper articles that first appeared there despite viewpoint contrary to the official versions of the time. Since then, time and Korean politics themselves have corroborated that viewpoint.

*M.W. —*

    *This one is kind of looney.*

*The Police blotter states:*

    *"Male body, age mid-60s, apparent suicide. No note. Presence of a manuscript that deceased was probably writing or reading. Handwritten notes, like a diary, are spliced in. They look like recent notes, although the manuscript itself seems to be older and kind of dog-eared. The body was discovered in a hotel room by a chamber maid. Loner or traveling? No known family."*

    *The manuscript could have some bearing on this case. What do you make of it?*

                                                  *J.T.*

Richard Cavalier

**17<sup>th</sup>**

*Even after the long trip, I couldn't sleep. So I dressed and went out looking for her. Most of the evening. Much of the night. She has to be here. Korea is her home. And if so, I'll find her.*

*18^{th}*

*It had to be Young Song! The same willowy walk. Her hair. Her cheekbones. If she had lived her life on the prowl...I began to follow. She walked down Nam Dae Mun Street, and I remembered that name. But it was so different from the street of how many? years before...the skyscapers nearby did a great imitation of an American city, with lithe skeletons and glassy grins, interlaced here and there with reminders everywhere in signs and lonely characters that this was, after all, still the Orient.*

*Korea. But wasn't she Korean? And isn't that why I was here? She turned a corner and was lost for a moment, but I hurried and soon was close behind her again. If she asked why I hadn't written more often, what would I say?*

*Certainly I couldn't mention that I'd been married and divorced as a lapse of memory of her. No children. Not for either of us? Had she married? Well, my married affair had passed, like so many other transitory pleasures. Best not to mention it. She wouldn't like the competition—not that it was, really. Young Song had never ceased to be special. That's why I'd know her walk and her cheek and her willow-like sway. Anywhere.*

*She turned again, and as I reached that corner, Young Song turned with no warning into a doorway. I ran. Without checking the sign outside, I charged through the same doorway.*

*"Yo bo sayeo," called the woman at the desk. "I help you?"*

*"No. I just wanted to say hello to Miss Kim, and he gestured toward Young Song.*

*"No Miss Kim." The woman came from behind the desk. "She Mrs Lee. You go now. Doctor come."*

*I stared at the woman Kim. It was not Young Song, now that he saw her face. It was not the nightly vision nor even the decades past. Nor could it have been. This woman was in her mid-twenties...as Kim had been too long ago. Young Song was now a middle-aged woman. I knew it intellectually, of course. But that was not my vision of her. I can't see a middle-aged face when I look into memory.*

*"I'm very sorry," I said with an almost-Oriental bow. I backed myself to the door and fled through it. I felt myself a fool. But where could I find Kim? What would she look like? Would she remember me? Would we both feel the same together after so many years? Decades...Would there be sparks or sputter?*

*Sparks were too much to ask, I decided. I had long since stopped running, but my slow walk had begun to aggravate my impatience—as if running would help me to find her sooner.*

**19<sup>th</sup>**

*I found myself on Nam Dae Mun Road again. Almost without thinking I turned south—toward the base. It was habitual. I didn't belong on the base anymore and hadn't—for maybe thirty-something years. And it doesn't look the same. That was my age telling itself. I felt depressed. Why had I come? Why hadn't I just waited for her answer by mail? It was so easy to be reasonable now that I was here, and it was too late. Well, I'll just decide to make the best of it.*

*Yet I've already been here for two days, and in at least twenty hours of walking, I had not seen her. Why should he expect to? Where did she work? Who were her friends now? She might be sick or invalid, for all I knew, and I would never see her again. Certainly not in her old neighborhood near the Army base. I had already asked around there. No one knew her. Or at least no one would confess to it. Friends are like that. Whether anyone actually knew her-who knows?*

*She had always loved American movies; I remembered that when I saw the marquee with Joan Crawford's name. Dear Joan. The dear unthinking, unfeeling Joan. How resilient she was. SurvivorJoan. How she would have advised Kim or anybody else against seeing him again!*

*Miss No-nonsense Crawford. But hadn't she herself made a nearly-too-late commitment and survived it? Well, she had almost survived him, anyway.*

*There was a tea shop near the theatre, and I decided to drop in for a rest. And maybe some tea. Hon cha, wasn't it called? Sticky sweet and somewhat weak. But a tall glass, and nobody minded if you weren't talking sense. The staff couldn't understand too much beyond the words of a restaurant order.*

*I must have given my order properly, because the tea arrive in a few moments. Sugarless. I motioned for sugar, and a solitary packet was delivered. Oh, well; not worth a scene because nobody needs sickly-sweet. She was never partial to tea, anyway.*

*Now there was nothing to do for hours but sleep. I dreaded even the thought of going back to the hotel. The hotel room was adequate but overly small. Certainly it wasn't room enough to gallop about in. Or even to lie in and think without constricting any possible dreams. But the Koreans were small people, even if the structure is purely post-War. Why had I come? Money to waste? True love? Of course not that non-existent but ever-sought dream. Without true love, what was there? With true love, what was there? So what was the difference? And the fuss? Besides, the trip had been long, but it wasn't that bad, considering. I was beginning to relax.*

*Sooner than I had expected, I turned toward the hotel after I had started to walk again, and I found myself in bed. Well, not exactly, of course, since I had removed my shoes but not my pants and coat. I might want to go out again; and*

4

*so it was just as well. I'm still tired from the trip. It was stupid, coming here. Really stupid. And a waste of money. And time.*

*I must have dozed because the watch had jumped. I got up; washed my face; brushed my teeth; returned to bed. This time I took off my clothes first. Why bother to go out? Seoul was big and had twisting paths that no one walked at night. It might have changed. But there wasn't a finding just for the looking. Stupid. Maybe sleep would help. I lay down again, fretting for a time, and slept again.*

# Chapter One

Gravel rang in the corridor of the darkened courtyard walls as Beaumont strode to the head of Hyo Jae Dong. There was no bus in the traffic circle, and he looked for a taxi. None. He glanced at his watch, waited for a moment to see whether the headlights approaching from Kyung Myu Dae, the street directly opposite him, would stop The car leaving the Korean presidential mansion passed him by, and he started southward along the Capital Way.

"Hey, GI! *Takushi?*"

A corruption of the familiar term taxi, but familiar to him. Beaumont signaled to the taxi. Quickly he confirmed the packet of seven one-hundred Hwan notes in the fold of his pocket. About 600 formed a dollar in Army Script, the substitute for the Almighty Dollar. So he had the price of the trip in a separate wad. The taxi completed its turnabout and stopped at the curb beside him.

"*0-baek Hwan,*" he offered as he opened the rear door to the cab. He extended five fingers. "To Eighth Army Post." An open door promises trip-money better than words can.

"*Ani!*" exploded the driver and his assistant almost together. "*Ku-baek Hwan* corrected the assistant. He held up nine fingers to prevent misunderstanding. Beaumont slammed the door and walked away, but all of them knew that the false exit was part of the bargaining system.

"GI—hey. *P'al-baek.*" Eight fingers were flashed.

"*Yuk-baek.*" Six hundred. Beaumont waited while syllables of rancor spilled from the car, while the driver and his second decided whether to settle at the standard rate. That was part of the bargaining system, too.

"*Ch'il-baek,* came the offer from the car.

"*Ch'il-baek, chossumnida,*" answered Beaumont: Seven hundred, okay. He knew seven hundred Hwan was the fair and acceptable price. Overcharging GI's was simply standard practice. He climbed into the car, and almost before he was settled—door ajar—the car pulled away. He put his foot against the front seat and braced himself against the cushions for the harrowing ride.

The gears complained as the driver shifted up in a haphazard way, and the entire body of the ancient and wounded car strained audibly as the trio swung sharply left onto Won Nam Dong, paralleling the bombed-out Capitol building. Though only a shell now, the structure had served the Japanese invaders long and well, and it seemed to offer him an outsider's view of itself each time he passed it. It imposed itself on the night. The Japanese had a talent for creating settings, and this shadow on the mountain rim was no exception. But now the building was a reminder of thirty years of foreign oppression...not counting the

Americans, of course. We as oppressors were not invaders in the traditional sense. Hadn't we been invited?

*A* sharp right turn put the car on Sei Jong Ro, or Capitol Boulevard. Leaving the Capitol directly behind, the taxi speeded southward. Almost immediately it slid to a stop at Chong Ro, a major crossway. As the light changed, the taxi leaped into motion again, protesting the abuse with mechanical screams.

Beaumont began to laugh. He drew a length of uniform braid from his pocket. Tapping the shoulder of the assistant, he held up the braid and indicated with gestures that the trio ought to tie the dilapidated car together. The assistant articulated the joke in his own tongue for his driver chief, and the three laughed broadly as the careened around potholes and pedestrians and ox carts.

Tae Pyung Ro, a lesser thoroughfare, proceeded directly from Capitol Boulevard. Beaumont sat back to watch the lights in the major buildings along the avenue. This was press row, government, and embassy way, all rolled out in one. Here there were the lights and sounds and confusion of a metropolis. Here was the commerce worth fighting for. Stupid reason, he thought. The horn blared, and Beaumont knew they had reached the traffic interchange with Ul Chi Ro—Main Street. Nearby was the Hotel Bando, where President Rhee, Syngman resided; he owned it. And his friends controlled much of Korea. Opposite, the American Embassy. It was a cozy and defensible arrangement—in all senses. Abruptly they stopped. The driver cursed at a peasant pulling a cart. With many threats and maneuverings, they rounded the cart and speeded past Duk Su Yuang, the last used of the royal palaces. Beaumont reminded himself to return there as soon as spring was official. If spring would ever be....In this March, spring seemed only a rumor. But the temple grounds seemed to come to life before the rest of the city. Maybe that rumor had started there. In a moment they had reached Nam Dae Mun, or South Gate. He knew this portal to the ancient walled city in this Land of the Morning Calm. The gate seemed to climb on itself to rise five stories on its pedestal of stairs. Carved animals on the swayback wedge roof posed tirelessly, and basked nightly in an electric sun. Maybe their culture could be saved. Maybe....The loop around Nam Dae Mun put them on Han Kan Ro, the main supply route for the military post. As they passed the Rail Terminal, they were ensnared in a web of traffic. They stopped.

"*Ppalli, ppalli,*" Beaumont said after a long moment's delay. "Fast."

"No can do," replied the assistant.

Beaumont took a package of cigarettes from his pocket. It was half full. He offered the package to the pair and braced himself again as the taxi swung into the center of the road. You can do anything for a package of cigarettes. It was wasteful to smoke cigarettes when they buy so much, he thought. He might even consider quitting. Again. There was an argument of horns, but they hurried on to the post, past the ramshackle and decrepit and malodorous and disgusting...and whatever else you could say about war's aftermath. The Koreans didn't have it

7

easy, even if the fighting were over—for now. But when would the North Koreans decide to come over the hill again? At the first gate of the compound the driver slowed, but Beaumont directed him to continue. They passed several other gates-like post boxes, keeping the male/mail sorted.

"Yogi," said Beaumont as they reached Gate Five. The car stopped instantly, and he stepped out. "Ch 'il-baek Hwan," he said as he handed the pair the agreed sum, seven bills. Then he took another one-hundred Hwan note from his pocket. "*Ppali-ppali. Komap-sumnida.*" The tip rewarded them for speed, and the driver honked before he started. They might try to cheat you, he knew, but they weren't inhuman. It was simply easier to oppress the country if your own government professed the opposite...and there was much profession.

Absently he waved a farewell to the departing car and dodged through the gate of the compound. He showed his ID, although that was *pro forma* to avoid garrulous guards. He turned almost immediately along a gravel road that paralleled the fence. In a moment he entered a Quonset hut standing among a row. It was the office building of the Adjutant General.

"Where in the hell have you been, Beaumont?

"I had a class, Lieutenant." It would do no good to say a friend should have covered the time for him-by arrangement gone awry.

"You had forty minutes of CQ duty, too, Soldier. Bargain rates for hauling ashes the night before payday—is that it? Well, you stay till the work is done! I could court martial you."

"I said I had a class." Clever, that Lt. Johnson; cherry-boy clever. The Army ground them out of Officer Training School fast and could chew them up in battle even faster. None had real experience—just rules and rank. And insufferable dispositions. All of them. Well, almost all.

"Now I'm going to have my class: Nookie one-o-one. Keep fritzing with those Koreans, Beaumont, and you're gonna get in trouble." The Lieutenant grabbed his coat and went out. Actually, Lieutenant Cherry Boy didn't belong there, except to bitch. Normally, he worked in the adjacent Quonset hut. Oh, well, the officers make personal switches, too.

Beaumont stood flush to the oil heater and tried to claim all its meager warmth for his frame. He put his hands near the metal flue-then on it. It was tepid. There wasn't enough warmth to go around in Korea, he felt. Not from heaters. There had been snow on the ground for days, but the Army's official paper, *The Stars & Stripes*, reported the temperature to be in the 40s. That meant officially that someone had *not miscalculated* the needed amount of fuel, and so fuel was *not* in short supply. Simple solution to the cold: Not enough warmth. Not from the heaters and certainly not from the people. Probably there were too many like the lieutenant, who lived his life as officers should in Korea, shuffling thoughtlessly from office to quarters to club-with never-noticed visits to the Chosun Hotel, where the expensive hookers met the officers. That rated as public relations contact in the press releases and therefore satisfied the Commanding General, who sometimes seemed merely to want to retire. Maybe that was unfair—he fought a decent war. If any wars are decent. And it set the pattern for the enlisted men. Admirable leaders, these Lieutenants Johnson; Sergeants Johnson and Privates Johnson followed such direction well. A few million Koreans now detested fifty thousand Americans...and were probably justified, Beaumont decided. With a feeling of disgust he threw his coat aside, wound a sheet of paper into a typewriter, and attacked the keys.

## *20^th*

*I awoke and adjusted rather quickly. I tried not to think about it...It was only a dream. Not that it mattered, whether I worried about it or not. Why do I bother?*

*Today was Sunday. It was a traditional family day in Seoul, and often people went up to Nam San Mountain or to the various palaces of the old royalty. They were state parks now and open to all. Young song had liked them immensely and went to Duk Su Palace at every opportunity. So I will go. But what would she look like? Can I really recognize her—her picture is gone from its treasured frame, too. But that was how long ago?*

*Of course I would remember her! And she, me. You don't give somebody a year of your life without remembering something. No matter how it turns out. So I went to Korea. And maybe we would meet. After a shower and a breakfast I felt less stupid than I did the night before. After all, if we had truly lost contact, there could be no letter, and searching for her was the only possibility. It seemed more reasonable again. But was I glad I had come? Well, maybe later. If the outcome were good. And why shouldn't it be? This was her home. She wasn't in prison, was she? Was I really enough of a threat for that?*

*I scuffed along, idly. It was late morning, but still before noon, and the park was not particularly crowded. But the day was bright, but there was still the crisp of March, and the tree blossoms were yet to become spectacular...a nearly translucent icy pink. Okay, admit it. I was glad I had come, stupid or not! I'd find her! Maybe even today! Easier to use "he" than "I. More objective. I'll switch.*

*Duk Su Palace was not as he had remembered. Or, rather, he didn't know what to remember. Yes, the water gardens and the rock gardens were there. And the temple was impressive with its fancy scalloped roof. For centuries the palace must have been terribly drafty with its thin walls and silk or rice paper dividers for walls. But the furnaces were still located under the floor level, with channels for the heat to cross under-floor to the chimney on the opposite side of the room. It's pretty much what the Romans had invented...or were the Romans imitating the Koreans while we imitated both? Wasn't radiant flooring the latest new invention in American modern comfort, post-WWII? Only a couple of thousand years. How quickly we learn!*

*He must have walked for hours, admiring the landscape, the handicraft, the history, and the contemporary awareness that made history so important. Well, it wasn't walking in the sense of going to a known destination. Rather, it was wandering in the sense of not knowing or caring when you had arrived or would leave. He tried not to repeat too many paths if there was an alternative. As Yogi Bera said, "When you get to a fork in the road, take it." But long before the afternoon was over, he had run out of alternatives.*

*He sat several times, but always the urge returned to do something. And he wandered aimlessly again. And sat. He stood instantly and wandered off again. The only change, naturally, was the people. Korean faces, yes...but so different and alive! How strange that I hadn't noticed them when I first came this morning. I'd come, after all, to find one among them. Well, you don't have to stare at all faces to recognize the wanted one when you see it.*

*Evening was sending hints when I decided that she wasn't coming today. I started toward the main gate, although I had only a faint idea of where it lay. There was no rush. Plenty of people spoke English, if pressed. And it was possible to follow the crowd in any language.*

*Then I saw her. Impeccably dressed in native garb, with a silk sash around the nunnish ground-length skirt—or habit. Much more mature than yesterday's mistake. Well, wasn't the whole trip about yesterday's mistakes? We make them and go on. Although he had come back to recapture the old—not truly gone on with life...No big deal. She wasn't smiling—at least not at him. Maybe she didn't recognize him.*

*"Young Song," he said as he approached. Do you remember me—Gordon?"*

*She didn't reply until one of the onlookers translated, and then she apologized because she did not know English. When they had managed to clarify everything, she apologized because she could never have known him—she was not yet alive in the 'Fifties.' They all apologized, each to the other, because it was not a most fortuitous meeting. Not all meetings are. They parted. He vowed to be less rash in the future. It would be better for everyone, himself included, surely. Especially for himself...and he was thinking like a soldier again.*

*How and by what route he returned to the hotel, he wasn't too sure, but he woke up after nightfall and stared out the window for a time. Would he go out again? Why should he? Yet there had been a time when he'd have moved heaven and earth to find her for a night. Nice to able to remember, but the capacity to do was going, wasn't it? There is definitely a hill in life. Forget it. The bed will be soft, and the night will be long and dark.*

# Chapter Two

"Tell me—what is it you will do when you return to the United States?" said Karl in his peremptory manner.

"Shout hallelujah," answered Beaumont with something of a laugh. He wasn't certain he had joked. "I don't really know, he said after a time. It's only three months away—next June. I suppose it depends mostly on what comes of the newspaper series I'm planning. If I can find an outlet.

"You hadn't told me about that."

"No?" he lied. "I thought I had. It doesn't matter, really. You know that I've gathered a lot of information from my students—and friends, such as you."

"But I didn't know about the newspapers." Karl set his shoeless feet squarely on the coffee table before the sofa.

"I've sent an article outline off to several of the metropolitan dailies back in the States. Now I'm just waiting. Maybe it'll hit. There's almost nothing accurate on Korea being published there. I want to find out whether this is a fault of the journalists—or whether something more is behind it.

"Some of each, of course," said Karl. "Reuters has a fair and impartial coverage, although I'm not sure that it's considered to be an important agency in the United States."

"Reuters is usually quoted only when one of our own wire services hasn't gotten a satisfactory story."

"Which is almost always," remarked the Swiss. He had virtually no accent. Maybe a hiss of sibilants or a stray and strangely used word. It was his legacy from school in America. "I'm always surprised that such rubbish is tolerated by you Americans."

"We believe in the silver lining."

"Unfortunately, world politics don't always have a silver lining—just folding green. Or a happy ending. You believe in those, too, not? And so you shouldn't allow facts to be toyed with by amateurs." He thought for a minute and took another swallow from his glass. "Maybe if your government agency people really knew what was happening, your newspaper reporters would have half a chance. If they talk only to the people in charge, they get only the official version."

"Back in the States, they haven't learned that everyone in the world doesn't share our passion for self-criticism, especially of the very public kind. United Press has a Korean reporter staffing their office. He can be disciplined by the government here. Or worse. And the Associated Press does the same. So what do you expect?

"True, true," said Karl.

"With things as they are, the local wire boys don't dare speak up. Even with a different internal situation, these men probably aren't going to send America the kind of copy that Americans should be getting back there."

"This regime has a lot of people frightened," Karl observed. "I don't know how it is that you Americans can support it so vigorously. Especially when it's making such bad publicity for yourselves all over the Far East."

"I don't know why somebody doesn't see. We have a zillion observers and government bigwigs crawling all over this place."

Karl sucked at his tobacco. "My Dear Boy. Don't you know that your State Department sends copy for verbatim return reports to its offices overseas? Local people here can't change a comma. And your CIA does the same thing. So when the obvious happens contrary to your independent and often Pollyanna public policy, it is always termed an unforeseeable shock: after all, the officials can say, there is never a single contrary opinion on record!" Beaumont must have reacted more than he expected. "A shock to you? The only shock for the rest of the world is that Americans don't seem to care."

"Maybe that's what I should say when I get back."

"Not likely. But luck. What will you say?"

"Tell everyone exactly what's going on around here."

"Are you sure they want to know?" Karl heard no answer, and he continued. "Americans put too much faith in government. It's the great god of your century. Too few people ask questions. No one acts. I've never known citizens to do so little when they have so much to do."

"It takes a reason *to do.* I'm not sure I have one. At least not yet."

"If you are jealous for your independence, you will make a reason."

"Whether or not I like to admit it—and I don't—I think you're right."

"I know I'm right. That's why your reporters can know so little and yet write so much. I think so I am right."

"As far as I know, only two Americans cover the Korean situation. And they come over a couple of times a year from Japan. A British guy comes from Hong Kong and looks at the surface. I know them—more or less. We meet at the bar at the Bando Hotel. It's the only place they know, it seems, except their own rooms. Maybe they also know the route from the airport. Or how to interview Rhee. That thief. They want only a handout from the head of government stating that everything is wonderful in this country. Parrots, not thinkers. Is that what your press really wants? They ask me questions, like 'Do I agree?' rather than 'What do you think?' That promotes the official view, of course. And of course I know nothing at all that would interest them. Why waste breath? They are a disgrace to their profession!"

"I hope it's their own carelessness—not an editorial policy. That would be hard to live with."

"Ach, *natuerelich*! Naturally you hope that. But what will you do if it is not carelessness?"

Beaumont thought a moment. "I don't know."

"I'll tell you what you will do: Nothing. Because you can't do anything."

"I hope you're wrong."

"We shall see, My Friend. We shall see." He took another long draft of coffee—no, tea. "Well, let me say that if the same thing happens to you that happened to other Americans that I met—then there's nothing to be done against the official view of two governments. Yes? Two or three I know—other places, of course—Hong Kong and Taiwan. Two or three other people told me they would go home and report—truthfully. They went home. And nothing happened. They die intellectually, perhaps. Or maybe they are burned by the contrary official versions and interests. Maybe? So they are as well dead."

"I think you're wrong. At least, I hope so. There's got to be a better reason."

"I think you are too intelligent to think me wrong when I have experience in the matter and you have not!" Karl was obviously piqued. "There is a time for national pride. But there is also a time for mental vigor. It is already 1959. There is no more time to waste. I won't permit you!"

"That is a proper manner to treat our guest, *ja? Shaden.*" Shame, said Magda Kauffmann softly from the kitchen doorway.

"I treat him the way he deserves to be treated. Stupid Americans."

"Give him no mind," she said to Beaumont. "You come to dinner with us, Gordon—ja? I found beef today. Little bit string. So I will make *sukiyaki.* We are almost Japanese, Karl *und* I."

"Then just try to get rid of me before dinner."

"Any more ideas to say I am wrong, and we will be rid of you very soon," said Karl, with a touch of seriousness.

"Karl!" Her voice said *for shame* without those words.

"This is a man's conversation. Go back to the kitchen!"

"In my town near to Bern we always thought those Austrians were barbarians," said Magda with exaggerated good humor. Karl is really Austrian, you know...I should have listened to my mother. She gave me warnings about Karl," Magda chuckled.

"You are very wise not to be married," remarked Karl quietly enough so that his wife had to listen carefully in order to overhear. She made a *hopeless* gesture and returned silently to work in the kitchen. Karl leaned forward to look kitchenward. Gone. "She is very fine, my Magda," he said even more quietly. "She is my good fortune in life. But not to admit. Now. To those newspapers."

"Karl, I often wonder exactly how far I can go with these articles. Little enough of what I know can be set down with unquestionable proofs."

"What do you expect of government people and lawyers?"

"Yet I have discovered much of what I know for myself. I know it's true. And I have sources I can depend on. I sometimes think I know as much of what is happening around here as the Ambassador does."

"In most places, that would not be difficult. His job is *not to see*. Didn't I tell you now that your State Department sends "reports" to be duplicated on local letterhead and dispatched back to Washington? The established policy is never challenged. But the appearance is that policy is always right. Until it goes all wrong, of course. You people are very foolish."

"This Ambassador is a good man, though. He's been sending back some rather graphic reports, it seems."

"And I hear that he is in trouble with your State Department because of it. His reports don't seem to jibe with current policy. Don't worry. He won't last much longer." He frowned.

"Where did you learn that?"

"From a friend. In the embassy. Of course," Karl laughed quietly. "The one thing I really can't understand is how we can permit the monetary system to function on two levels, as it does."

"Called Black market. It happens everywhere."

"The Ambassador reported that recently, too."

"Don't tell me about it. For a little business like mine I must pay three or five times the face value of *Korean Hwan* to get American dollars...to buy foreign exchange to keep up my operation. Hwan are worthless without America, and the dollar is still king. That's what you want, isn't it? *Natuerlich.*"

"I suppose. Did you know a closed hearing was held in Washington several months ago? The local government claims that the excess Hwan are being retired from circulation."

"Directly into a certain person's pocket. And then the President can retire."

"Somehow it sounds better the way it's stated officially."

"You are American, I see. Official things can always sound better than reality. That's the really fine thing about government pronouncements," Kauffmann said with elan. "Well, the Ambassador has been instructed not to think aloud or talk, even quietly. So the foreign-exchange club will have their excess profits. Maybe I will have mine."

Beaumont didn't answer. It was all too unsettling.

"Maybe we can arrange for you to talk for the Ambassador."

"That's what I've been hoping—if the articles click. I can start by saying nasty things about the proposed Status of Forces Agreement."

"Well, don't forget the Chinese and their scandals. After all, Madam Chiang, Kai Shek was known in an American college as the daughter of General Sun, Yat Sen, although she was really related to him as a sister-in-law. It hardly matters because there are only two major reasons for disguising a woman's past: first, if she was a Fallen Woman Lately Risen—which no one thinks; and second, if the

15

purpose is to disguise the family's attempts to create a political dynasty through marriage relationships. So the smart money thinks that General Sun was merely establishing a dynasty when his brother-in-law, Chiang, Kai Shek, ruled China after him. Together they took in all the gold and issued worthless paper script. A collaborator of Chiang was even worse as a corrupt individual who subverted the Chinese people's drive to independence and nationalism.

"Of course I heard that. It's common knowledge in Asia."

"Then do you wonder why the Communists came to power in China with so much public support? Do you suppose that Washington really couldn't discover why? Madam Chiang went to school in the U.S., after all. So many people knew. Even her sorority sisters, I am sure." He took another swill of beer. "Such information is bad for the morale of the soldiers, I know," observed Karl. "Your commanding General found it necessary to declare morale excellent on three different occasions during one month—around Christmas, I think. That should indicate just how worried he is. And we all know that if morale has been declared excellent, and if that's repeated by a Prince of the Church of War—then surely morale is Excellent!"

"And there is no corruption in the city of Seoul or in the nation. So why do we worry?"

"No corruption as far as any outsider can see officially. So the Americans here are doing work worthy of a grand reward. Which they take for themselves now, so that their officers at home don't forget them. Remember Gilbert and Sullivan: 'Stick close to your desks and never go to sea, and you all may be rulers of the Queen's navee.' *Pinafore*, yes?"

"Karl, I think I should let you write my stories for me."

"Not *stories*, My Friend."

"That's just slang for *article*. Besides, who wants to be corrected by a foreigner? Everything you say about us is from envy, you know."

"But you have so much more to say as an American."

"I don't know. You've been here nearly three years. I, not one."

"I've been here only briefly longer, myself. In the business world of ancient Seoul—but a newcomer."

"With a lot of connections."

"Natuerlich. But I don't know whether I can prove everything I know, either. I can show you evidences of graft on both sides of the national fences. And I can estimate that only twenty percent of all American appropriations are actually spent to buy something for this country's benefit. Eighty percent isn't a bad profit to be shared by friends."

"That's too wild. I couldn't make a statement like that."

"I'm sure you can't. Still it is true."

"We'd have to start small and work up to a grand tantrum."

"Fine." He thought for a time. "When you hit your high point, tell me. Then I shall introduce you to an engineer who has paid a handsome sum to certain people at the Office of the Economic Coordinator so that the projects he engineers will continue to be considered. Otherwise he is out of business. You already know, I think, that the really important people in Seoul have obtained large money grants just before going *bankrupt*." Of course the money is lost."

"That's on the street, too."

"One Mr. Loo received a loan to start a drug firm of some sort. They need it. But it seems that the business failed even before the plant was fully constructed. Now his son is taking out another loan of equal proportions to put the plant into operation for the first time. There were many percentages obtained."

"Nothing like that surprises me anymore. And I don't even get angry anymore. What comes next?"

"Profit!" He chuckled. "Maybe I should introduce you to one of your own countrymen. He really tried to do his job right. A consultant engineer. He is being extremely difficult and is causing problems at your OEC because he refuses to approve unsound projects. Those people at OEC are—you have a phrase—out to *get* him."

"Will they?"

"Eventually. I've seen it happen before. Actually I give him no more time at all."

"What about our embassy?"

"They have no control at all over the OEC. Even if State Department wanted some. Why should bureaucrats look for problems?

"I'd like to meet him—that engineer."

"I'll try to arrange it before you leave. Or before he does."

"Thanks, Karl. I'll need your help for this."

"It's my pleasure."

"Why are you doing it?"

"Suspicions. Who knows? Maybe because I wish I could have had the freedom to do something similar in my country. Old nobility still matters there."

"Karl has a sister in the United States," called Magda from the kitchen. "She ran off with an American soldier after the war in Europe."

"We said many unkind things to her. Then. She was very young. Even now not much older than you are. But it has lasted. Maybe it was love. Do you believe in love?" Beaumont spread his hands in a *who knows?* gesture. "Maybe I can look her up for you."

"We are in contact. No. You can help best by doing what you are planning to do. *That* even she can appreciate." After a time, "How careless of me—would you like another beer?"

"I've had more than my share already. No. Thanks."

17

"You don't smoke a pipe...and I'm out of cigarettes," Kauffmann said as he rummaged through his pockets and nearby table drawers.

Beaumont found himself reaching for his pockets. "I hope I didn't leave them in the taxi. Again."

"What is that? I didn't hear."

"Cigarettes. American. I brought you a carton."

"That was very nice. Please come more often." He laughed.

"If they are around."

"How do you say—a lifesaver?"

"I think they are maybe here," said Magda. "You left a bag down at the door when you came inside. "

He picked up the bag that Magda pointed at and pulled out a carton of cigarettes. He put the bag back at the door. "Some things I need," he said by way of explanation. Then, in what seemed a change of mind, he handed the bag to Magda. She took it immediately into the kitchen.

"Did you say beer—yes?" Karl asked.

"No. I've really had enough, Karl. Maybe too much."

"It doesn't matter. You can spend the night here."

"No. The post has bed check. So only on special occasions, when I've made arrangements with the CQ. Then I can miss."

"Do you have a steady?"

"No. Probably fortunately. Or maybe not so fortunately. That it's physical is—well, the object. But the casual aspect really gets me. It points up the lack of meaning in my life. Of which there isn't that much in my life. Certainly the Army isn't providing anything convincing."

"You'll get used to it. Or make your own meaning. Maybe even find it here."

"I might. Maybe that would be the misfortune. I don't intend to take one of the street girls home with me. I couldn't fit her into my plans—or my family—or into my life, for that matter."

"Never say *never*. I thought you were more independent."

"I am. She wouldn't have a picnic.

"Maybe you can fool even yourself—try."

"Not now."

"What about your friend and his friend?"

"Who knows? Camden is kind of torn up about one of our language students. If he did the Proper Thing, it wouldn't surprise me."

"I wish him luck," said Karl.

"Dutch chocolate!" Magda exploded. "Karl—Dutch chocolate he brought...and fruit preserves! What an extravagant friend we have, Karl. Even on the black market I can't buy fruit preserves. She went back to the kitchen, surely listening.

"Thank you," said Karl quietly. "I might be one of Magda's misfortunes, too. She asks only so little and I cannot give even that to her because she is willing to follow my work."

"*Schoenen danken*, Gordon," called Magda.

"You see. She is grateful for trifles."

"*Bitte schoen*," Gordon answered.

"I think you won't disappoint me," said Karl with no particular inflection. He busied himself at nothing. "There's a magnificent sun in this country. The winter hides it, *natuerlich*. But in the spring it goes down outrageously orange just over the Han River. Then I can appreciate this house, for which we pay so dearly."

"*Gouging* is the term we use," said Beaumont.

"Did you know that this entire new housing project on Ie Tae Wan is directly controlled by the Rhees, yes?"

"No, I didn't know."

"Look outside." Karl went to the door. "All these houses were built with American funds and materials, but they're in private hands now. Part of the money was probably stolen. Some of the properties were a give-away to the "highest bidder," no matter how low. We pay rent in American dollars to the Rhee interests. It is a vicious thing. So much rent, and just down the hill from us is one of the worst slums I have ever seen. Should I feel guilty or sick? I do not know. Such an accident is our birthplace. What did they do to deserve so much misery?"

Then, at a second call from Magda, they went back inside and readied themselves for dinner.

## 24<sup>th</sup>

*It was so vivid a dream. He hadn't thought of Kauffmann for years, and yet Kauffmann was alive in front of him with his many pronouncements and prognostications. He had believed in Gordon, and he had not lived to see whether Gordon had ever succeeded. That was fortunate, in a sense. Even at this advanced age, no one wants to be counted a failure. Not that Gordon must be. It's always a matter of degree. But Kauffmann's comments on the meaning of life. How appropriate that he should restate them now—just when they were most needed.*

*Kauffmann knew a lot, but he had been wrong about Camden, too, who had finally married his musame—fallen women scorned as moose in Korea. Isn't that a Japanese hold-over word? It didn't really matter. Scorn is scorn in any language. In the U.S. it had a different meaning, if related. Had he also been wrong about Gordon? Sure, Gordon had tried. Everybody tries. Or almost everybody does. On the other hand, it's not exactly easy to fight the system. The problem is that the newspapers are a part of the system, even when they permit criticism. For show? Apply that to TV, too. The appearance of catering to the public is important...yet when the chips are down, the paper or station is owned by the wealthy, who will not testify against themselves. How much freedom of comment is left? It reminds me of a newspaper writer from Wilmington whom I once met and who felt he had absolute freedom to criticize the DuPonts,...if ever he wished. Of course he never wished. Where does responsibility begin? Where does obligation end?*

*And why had he come here? There was no sign of Young Song, and he had looked for days and walked for leagues and miles in all the places he knew she— once—had frequented. Yet nothing. She might be avoiding him—except that she couldn't know he was here. Had her life and habits changed so much? Would I recognize her? If only I still had her picture. But the now-empty picture frame— surely she'd recognize that....*

*Young Song was a rollicking delight, with her verve and innocence. She was life and beauty and surprise. She smelled of spring with the flower she always wore in her later days with him. Together sounds better. Did she regret as much as he did? Would she be as willing as he to admit miscalculation? Was recovery possible? Or was Mann (was it he?) right in knowing "You Can't Go Home Again"?*

*He shifted the emphasis from the movie palace with American flicks to the tea rooms. Everyone goes to tea rooms—it's just a matter of when. She was sure to come in to one of them eventually.*

*Like a school boy, he was infatuated. Like a school boy he yearned for the next date, the next smile, the furtive touch. But in several days, she did not come. Was he feeling final despair or just an awareness that this was indeed a silly outing for no likely outcome? On this evening, he scuffed along the bases of business monoliths that hadn't existed when they were together. Korea had become rich. Well, at least some people had. Maybe she had become rich, too. Would she need to hide the past? But had it been a good past? Maybe she would be willing to give up the present for a taste of the past. It was impossible to predict her reactions—she was too pure of spirit.*

*A large crowd was leaving a hall—probably music. Did they still light candles during performance in anticipation of the nightly blackouts caused by the change of generators? Not likely—this was a re-made city. Skyscrapers replaced the shacks he remembered. But it would do no harm to mingle and search. So he went there. And looked. Of course she wasn't among them. Not that he saw absolutely everyone. But a good number of faces. And shouldn't luck be with him after so long a time? It wasn't for lack of his effort.*

*Tired, he'd come back to the hotel. He could use a shower to loosen some of the muscles, but it was very late, and the walls are thin. He didn't want an altercation with the manager or neighbors. A quick wash would hold till morning. But it'll feel good to flop on the bed and think aimless thoughts. And in his aimlessness, he would fall asleep, fully clothed.*

# Chapter Three

"Selfish," Mrs. Pak chided gently as she finished plaiting the strong black hair of her daughter. "You should be ashamed to live in this house." The throaty tones of the Korean language added to the harshness of the words. "Your father has no work. And your sister is hungry. Your brother—he, too. But you wear braids."

Young Song frowned. She knew seventeen years to be too old for wearing braids when one's family is poor, but she had not yet been made a woman. That was the meaning of braids. She decided that her mother was being unreasonable but didn't dare to say so.

"I don't want a soldier. Father said I must not," she insisted, adding quietly, "unless I wish."

"What should a father say? But you have a duty to him. He knows. And so should you."

Young Song watched her mother, who moved with an easy grace about the room. Her mother even looked severe, the girl thought. A great garment billowed from Mrs. Pak's breasts. The books said it was an imitation of the French Empire style, but it seemed likely that the Koreans had gotten there first. It hung in an unshaped skirt to her ankles, making her look like the very old American women whose pictures Young Song had seen. She was not old, her mother.

That was the reason her mother continued to argue after so many weeks, Young Song decided...because she was grandmotherly and finished with life, but still living. It was the war. It had changed everything.

"Soldiers want girls with American clothes," Young Song ventured after a respectful silence. "I haven't any. They don't want me."

"Your cousin-sister has clothes. I brought some things here for you to use. Your cousin- sister knows your duty, even if you do not."

"Her soldier will be angry if I use them. And my cousin is too large—here—for me."

I can put cloth inside the top to make you big. No one will know." The mother felt she might slowly be winning, because the objections were becoming more reasonable.

"Maybe I can go tomorrow, instead. Tonight I can't. I don't know how to—be—with a man." She flushed.

"They know how. Today the soldiers are paid. Go today," Mrs. Pak said sharply losing patience. Then she allowed herself to be a mother again. "Don't be frightened, Song That's the reason for women. Find a soldier. Soldiers know what to do."

Young Song stood up and began to disrobe. Her mother splashed water into a basin and set it on the floor mat in front of Young Song. Together they began to bathe her, taking care not to waste the new cake of Lux soap that a soldier had given to her cousin-sister, who cooperated.

Young Song dried herself and dressed in the borrowed clothes. But her feet slipped about in her cousin's heeled shoes, and she couldn't walk confidently.

"I can't go," Song protested hopefully. "No American shoes."

"Wear Korean shoes," her mother said impatiently"

"Everyone will laugh."

"It's already dark. No one will see."

Young Song went to the door and stepped down into a pair of flat rubber shoes with upturned toes. A heap of rubber footwear lay in the ground level of the ground entry. Disconsolately, she kicked the heap aside.

"I will have a bed ready," Mrs. Pak promised. "For my good daughter, who knows her duty."

Young Song put her hand to her mouth, to cover her smile. It was not often that her mother complimented her, although she thought her mother was sometimes very kind.

"*Annyong-i ke-sipsio*," Song said. Goodbye to one who is staying.

"*Annyong-i ka-sipsio*," answered the mother. Goodbye to one leaving.

Mrs. Pak escorted Young Song across the small open courtyard. A brass bell rang as she unlatched the tall wooden gate. She guided Young Song outside and re-latched it. The bell stilled. Mrs. Pak called a warning over the fence to children in the street. Perhaps they took notice. Then she felt the chill and went into the house.

Young Song followed a narrow street that went off toward the Army post. She walked quickly, her head lowered, so that she would not be recognized. She felt certain that the people in the streets would be waiting to see her come home in her shame. And they would talk among themselves and point fingers after her. But the war....

As she walked, she crossed often to the opposite side of the narrow dirt street, bypassing puddles of mud forming as the snow died in the spring sun. A ring of ice had begun to build in the small pools as the cold night came on. Young Song walked faster.

The roads changed very fast, she thought. A few days ago they were tumbled with snow. A few days more and they would be dusty and sick with the smells of urine and refuse. Then the rains would begin. She decided that everything was changing and unreal. Even the summer rains that clean. Even the spring that had started.

As she neared the Army post, Young Song stepped under cover of trees that flanked the wall of the camp. Someone told her that the trees, misshapened by

23

the war, still hid barbed wire strung on the brick wall. But it was already dark, and so she couldn't be sure.

"Hi."

She was startled by the voice and didn't answer. The soldier hesitated a moment and then went on. People loitered everywhere. Girls laughed and teased with soldiers between visits of the military police car making a sham patrol. As the car approached each time, everyone went in other directions, as if on urgent business. They returned immediately to the rallying point outside the main gates. Others went off in pairs and stayed away.

Young Song remained behind a fat tree and didn't answer the voices that came from passing groups. One time or twice someone offered to bargain with a soldier for her, and often another girl offered encouragement. An hour passed. Young Song started home. She planned excuses for her mother—such things as that soldiers don't like Korean girls with American clothes and rubber shoes.

"Hi."

Young Song pretended not to hear. The soldier was behind her and then beside her.

"I saw you waiting there," he said and continued to walk. To the MPs, walking signaled legitimate business, not that anyone really cared.

She didn't answer. As they walked, Young Song dropped a step behind, watching. He was very tall, she thought. All soldiers were very tall. She decided without looking that he had yellow hair because all soldiers have yellow hair—or almost yellow hair. She had hoped he would be good-looking, but he was not. Well, not exactly. It wouldn't matter.

"I said hello to you," he said. The soldier was behind her again, and she turned.

"Good evening," Young Song answered in her best book-English. She was proud of her ability, even if it was not wise to be so proud about anything. Humility was demanded.

"Good evening," he replied with the over-pronounced tones of a teacher.

They walked on together. Young Song carefully averted her face as they passed clusters of Korean people, who called shaming phrases after her.

"Where are you going?" he asked."

"I am going to my father house." She spoke slowly and distinctly.

"Is your father at home?"

"Perhaps my father is at home."

"Is your mother at home?"

"Yes, my mother is at home."

"Oh." After a time he asked, "Where did you learn to speak English so well?"

She flushed. Compliments should not be so direct. "I learn to speak English in high school."

"You speak it very well."

"I think I do not speak very well. I am sorry."

"Why sorry?"

"I did not agree to you."

"That's all right. Many people don't agree *with* me.

"Thank you."

"How old are you?" he asked.

"I am nine-and-teen years old."

"Korean or American years?"

"I am seven-and-teen years old American and nine-and-teen years old, Korean. How old are you?"

"Twenty-four. American." Of course he didn't believe her. It was common for teen Korean boys to taunt American men with claims that "My mother, she cherry," or to subtract decades from a compliant woman's supposed age as they bargained. Among some, younger was considered better.

"I am sorry," Young Song said.

"Why? Am I too old for you?"

"No. My father house is in this street."

A narrow alley shouldered its way through the low shops and featureless wooden temporary mixed with masonry permanent buildings and then disjointedly joined the main roadway.

"I'm sorry, too," he said, "because you're going home."

"I am sorry."

They laughed.

"I thought I could spend some time with you," he said.

"Spend?"

"To use. To visit with you."

"Perhap at my father house"

"Won't he be angry?"

"Yes, he will not be angry. He know."

"All right." The soldier hurried Young Song into the side street. "Off limits," he said carelessly. "Do you understand?"

"Yes, I understand."

"My name is Bo," he said when they were in the dark way.

"How do you do," she responded.

"How do you do. What is your name?"

"My name is Miss Kim."

"How do you do."

They splashed through crisping puddles in the dark alley. The soldier apologized for the splashing and the girl apologized for the street and the mud.

"Do you go to university in the United State?" Young Song asked after a time.

"Yes."

"What do you study there?"

"Many things. I'm a teacher."

"Do...are you teacher at Army? I am sorry. So many question."

"I like your questions. But I have a have a different job in the Army. Not a teacher."

"I am sorry. My father house is here."

They mounted a stone block that united the street and the gate. The high board fence kept the house from their view. Young Song shook the gate, and the brass bell sounded. She answered a low inquiry from inside. The gate was opened, and they stepped up into the court. Young Song re-latched the gate, because its keeper had disappeared from the court.

She watched the soldier appraise the area. There were still tufts of snow in the corners. Ice crusts, slipped from the tiled roof, lay in shivers against the chill board walls.

"I am sorry," Young Song said again as they reached the entry. "Please— your shoe. Korean custom." She kicked the rubber shoes from her feet and bounded inside.

"Yes, I know," he said, but she was already gone.

He unlaced his boots and stepped up to the floor level of the house. The entry was walled, with sliding panels to form a diminutive foyer.

"Please. Come inside," Young Song called from an adjoining room.

He moved a screen and went into the room. A half dozen faces shone in the glare of the electric globe dangling overhead.

"Sit down, GI," another young woman said to him coarsely. "Over there."

A place was made for him in the over-populated room, and he insinuated himself into the group. Then he lowered himself to the fire-warmed floor and brought his heels up to his buttocks. He knees sprang up, and he tried to push them nearer the floor. A child laughed. He edged closer to the glowing brazier in the center of the group. The added warmth was an extravagance for the occasion, and the pungence of charcoal had been softened with a stick of incense.

Young Song began to speak rapidly in her language, punctuating the address with the word *Bo*. Then she turned to the soldier.

"Here Mr. Kim, my father," she said with required formality.

Mr. Kim leaned forward from a squatting position. He bowed until both his head and his buttocks appeared to be pendant from his knees. His string goatee, nested on the white cotton robe, sprang back undisturbed as he lifted his head.

"Here Mrs. Pak, who is my mother." It was a Korean custom for a married woman to keep her own maiden name throughout her life. Mrs. Pak bowed, cautiously, the less to honor; and the soldier did his best bow.

"Here is my cousin-sister, Miss Choi. She speak English."

"Hi," said Miss Choi casually, at ease among her clan-family and its guest.

"Hi." He saw that she was more fully developed than Young Song and aware of her advantages. Maybe it was in her carriage, which was not humble, but flagrant in any language.

"Here my sister." Young Song touched the small girl hiding behind the cousin-sister. "Here my brother," she said, completing the circle. The brother was probably about seven or eight years old. American."

"Hello," the brother shouted. He showed ten fingers to tell his age by Korean count. So young; yet they already looked old. Is it only the war?

"Hello. How are you?" The soldier grabbed at the boy, who rolled away, but gamingly, not shyly. "Yes. Hello," the boy echoed. "Hello." He laughed. "Hello, hello." His mother pulled him aside.

"I am Bo," he said, opting for the shortest form, and he bowed slightly. The group clustered more closely about the clay burner, and no one spoke in an interval of minutes. Finally the father rose, bowed perfunctorily, and went outside. Mrs. Pak motioned, and the two children left.

Young Song hurried into another room.

"You pay now. Can do?" cousin-sister Miss Choi asked, translating Mrs. Pak's request. Simple business procedure among buyer and seller.

"Can do," the soldier replied.

"How much you can pay? You speakee."

"How much *you* speakee? he countered in her street-English.

Miss Kim never whore-girl. This first time. Miss Kim father not catchee job now. Need money." Miss Choi continued. To bargain successfully is an art she prided herself on possessing. After a respectable time lapse, the three agreed on a sum. The soldier pushed several military payment certificates toward Miss Choi. Miss Choi pushed them across the floor mat to the mother, who scattered the bills across the floor.

"Mrs. Pak does not like to do this thing," Miss Choi said. "There is too much tax. No work. Must eat. What can she to do?"

He decided he would have paid more, but what they required was enough for the start. Of course the amount would rise...if there were a future for the visits.

Mrs. Pak asked a question. Miss Choi translated. "You catchee—" She stopped. Sliding nearer to him, she whispered in his ear, effusively confidentially.

"Hava yes," he answered.

"No makee baby Miss Kim."

He rose, entered the adjoining room, and slid the panel shut behind him. Young Song was already seated on the floor in a mattress of quilts. The random patterns of the coverlet washed about her in the flow of light from the brazier.

"I am sorry," Young Song said.

"Don't apologize. I'm sorry." He sat beside her, and she stiffened. He made no further moves immediately, and she relaxed. More small talk. He began to caress and then to fondle her. They lay back.

He began to undress. Young Song took his uniform and hung it carefully on pegs along the outer wall. He hesitated at his underwear. She waited, and he slipped his T-shirt over his head and unsnapped his military shorts. Young Song took them with the lapsed concern of a wife and rolled back the coverlet. Then she drew the covers over him.

Young Song turned to undress. "Do not look."

He made a show of turning his head. Reluctantly she stripped herself of her clothing, hung it carefully near his, and, holding a towel in front of her, slipped into the quilts. He put his arm around her and stroked her arms and throat and thighs. After a time she ceased to tremble, and he raised himself on his side, kissed her repeatedly and grew urgent. Young Song touched his almost-yellow hair and his nearness over her; and with confusion and hurt she became a woman. He realized then that he had been first. He regretted it. But it was done, now. For a while they lay silently together. Then they dressed and went out among her family. Young Song sat apart. The cousin-sister indicated that the soldier was to sit near the mother. The father was still outside, but the children had been put to sleep on quilts in an end of the room.

"You likee Miss Kim?" Miss Choi asked.

"Yes."

"You likee to steady with her?"

"Maybe."

"Wife in States hava yes?"

"Hava no."

"You lie. All GI marry. All same-same."

"Yes, I steady with Miss Kim."

"You Number One Heart," Miss Choi said. She related the agreement to Mrs. Pak, who did not acknowledge the comment.

"How much you can pay?"

"We'll talk about that tomorrow," he said.

"Tomowwoh," she said angrily and made a spitting sound. "You nevah come here more. I know."

A siren intruded, a physical thing. They stopped talking at the blare. He checked his watch: eleven-thirty; civilian curfew, Police state. They relaxed again.

He went to Young Song. "I'll be back tomorrow."

"Thank you," she said.

He put his hand to her face, but she pulled away.

"No. My mother will see. I am sorry." Despite the whole of the evening, she was genuinely embarrassed by his unguarded show of affection.

"Do you like me, Miss Kim?" A pause, with no answer. "I like you very much."

She nodded. "My name is Miss Kim, Young Song."

"Young Song," he repeated softly, receiving the compliment of knowing her personal names.

"In English it spells Y-o-u-n-g S-o-n-g.

"What does it mean?"

"Do not mean. Is Korean name."

"In American it means you're beautiful with life."

"Thank you."

"Good night," he said.

"Good night," she replied.

He went to the darkened entry, found his boots, and began to lace them. That the boots were still there spoke well for the honesty of the family. Boots could be sold on the black market. Even used boots.

Young Song followed as he left. tentatively. "Bo?" she asked.

He looked at her in response. "Is it all right—I say Bo?"

"Of course it is all right."

"Tomorrow I will cut my hair."

"Why?"

She grasped a braid. "Now I am a woman." She turned away. "You are not angry to me?"

"No. I'm happy." In the truth among truths, she was a *find*.

"I like to be a woman." She smiled behind her fingertips and then blushed.

"Thank you, Young Song."

"Goodbye."

"Goodbye," he said, without wanting to leave.

Young Song crossed with him to the gate. Mrs. Pak reproached her husband from her place at the door. He ignored her. Holding the clapper of the bell, Young Song unlatched the gate. All were silent as the soldier stepped outside. The gate was bolted, and one muffled sound escaped the bell. Then Mrs. Pak cried out against her husband, who had allowed the evening to happen. He struck her.

"I am sorry," said Young Song to no one. In the quiet she felt the soldier desert her.

# Chapter Four

"Suggest something, Mr. Lee," Beaumont said distinctly.

Confidently, as befit the best student in the class, the young man answered, "I suggest that we meet together in the tea room."

"That's a very good suggestion, Mr. Lee," he commended. "But it's not necessary to say 'meet *together*' because it's not possible to *meet apart*. Therefore, the word 'together' is unnecessary. We say 'redundant'." To the entire class he said, "Mr. Lee suggests that we meet in the tea room. Who else has a suggestion?"

With a nod he recognized a young lady at his left. "Miss Ahn, have you a suggestion?"

"I suggest that we walk in the garden," she said.

"Very good, Miss Ahn. Miss Ahn suggests that we walk in the garden."

"We shall look at snow blossoms," Mr. Lee chortled.

"Do you suggest that we not meet there *together* to look at snow blossoms, Mr. Lee? The barb pierced—no criticism was tolerated from any other student regarding their follow students. Ideas were welcome—corrections, yes—but criticisms should come only from him. Beaumont moved on quickly to lessen the sting.

"Mr. Kim, what do you suggest?" He listened, corrected, and then called on a second Mr. Lee." There were two Misses Yu and a Mr. and Miss Chung. Only one Mr. Choi; one Miss Choh—their hostess; one Mr. Soh. Differentiating between them without creating ranks or orders was always a problem. Personal names could never be used. He damned those honorific languages with the artificial sensitivities they engendered. He decided that their lives would be much simpler if fifty per cent of the Korean population hadn't elected by custom to be called by one of four clan names. Worse, there seemed fewer than a dozen other patronyms, mostly derivations. It was a nation of Smiths and Joneses and Browns and Whites.

There was pedagogical conversation for a time. Then he found himself saying, "For the next time—Lesson Twenty-seven. Mr. Camden will be finished with special duty and will surely be here, because I cannot." He glanced at his watch. It was five minutes of eight. If he hurried, he could be back on the post at eight-thirty—or, rather, at *her* house.

"Lesson Twenty-eight will be mine again. We will discuss, in addition, the verb *to prefer*, which means 'to like more than.' Mr. Lee, it will be your turn to deliver the related one-minute composition. Any questions?" There should have been questions, he thought, because the texts were abominable; but tonight no one signaled for help, and he was glad.

"Quickly, the ordinal numbers."

First, second, third...the group began to chant. Somewhere near fifty-seventh a young woman servant entered with a tray of cups of tea. She set cups out for the several students. One cup remained, for their master. The end of his schedule, he thought, but he couldn't refuse without insult, and so he resigned himself to stay for tea.

*One-hundredth* marked the end of class, and with precise timing, a man of middle age entered the room. Bo rose and surveyed his host, the father of Miss Choh. The man bowed in his own tradition, even though he wore a strangely-proportioned suit of the West. His was not an altogether wise contrast to the garment of a reproving ancestor watching from a wall, but obviously he was trying to move with new times.

"Good evening, Mr. Beaumont," he said in accented, yet distinct, English. When Beaumont had returned the salute, Mr. Choh nodded to his daughter and then greeted the others. The servant set tea before him. Was he chaperoning or simply curious?

"Your English is wonderful," he lied. "Would you like to be the teacher here?" But the obligatory compliment had been paid and turned aside. There was no danger of being replaced.

The group was sitting in the living room of the Western style structure and made polite attempts at conversation. Each person tried to look as if he belonged among overstuffed chairs and divans, rather than floor cushions. He chuckled to himself. As if everyone *belonged* in Grandma's parlor back home over a century ago. He became aware of Dr. Choh again.

"My daughter and her friend have told me how much they enjoy your class, Mr. Beaumont."

Truth, or obligatory? "It is they, themselves, who make the class pleasant," Beaumont replied easily. A compliment turned aside—the class murmured approval. He was indeed learning the customs in his stay of not even a year. Mr Choi smiled. To disclaim credit when directly complimented was an art few Americans developed, he knew.

"In a manner of speaking, you are probably right," Mr. Choi answered in his combination of phrase book clichés. Yet he had an easy fluency that probably belied years of self-teaching. Dr. Choh repressed a smile...one shouldn't be carried away.

Then it was Beaumont's turn to be humored. Mr. Choi obviously knew English well enough to use clichés in all the wrong places. A stage in many developments, he knew.

"Do you think it possible that you will continue to conduct more class in the future?"

So that was the purpose of the tea? "Of course," Of course. "If the class wishes to meet beyond that time, we can possibly arrange that. But we don't have an additional textbook. We would need to create common experiences in order to discuss matters." He knew that *further classes* was not the object of the question. He, himself, didn't want to become tied to the English language book. Life wasn't lived *there*. And more, Chuck Camden wouldn't be too pleased to lose his only direct public contact with the very pretty Miss Choh, whose acquaintance Camden had very carefully cultivated.

"After the thirty classes of the book, who person will help you?" The father was implying, without ever stating it, that he was aware of and objected to Camden. Very efficiently and effectively accomplished.

"I have friends who will help."

"We shall discuss it again at another time," Dr. Choh said, placing himself in charge; and Beaumont knew that the matter was not closed. Dr. Choh rose, took leave of Beaumont and the others with a silent bow, and went out of the room.

There were desultory comments from the students. Each belonged to families as barely wealthy as Dr. Choh, although perhaps not so prominent socially as he. Then again, wealth itself was fairly new in Korea and implied political recourse. One shouldn't say *bribery.* It was not polite, even if true. These students were gaining status through their parents because of the American system that they now imitated. Certainly that was true of the import activities of the second Mr. Lee's father—or even of Miss Chung's dignitary father. He knew that the father of two of the other students were members of the one-house legislature. Who's left to challenge?

Beaumont set down his cup and rose; tea was ended. The others did the same but waited until he had left the room before they followed. That was proper. There was a scramble for shoes in the foyer, as sitting room manners evaporated. Before the group disintegrated, Beaumont managed to give Miss Choh the message that Camden would return her drawings at their next class session. She flushed and moved away quickly. Was she strangely shy, or did she believe that nobody knew? He decided that even that question was strange. They were all strange, he knew. A motley collection of ages and interests. *Nouvelles noblesses*! Together they could have supported a family on lesson expenses alone.

He decided to ask to resume the practice of meeting in their various households as soon as the winter's end made transportation more certain. It was highly informative...and usually away from Father Choh. They passed through the gate of the high masonry wall. Most of them called a farewell to Miss Choh and went in several directions.

Two students elected to walk him to the bus stop. It was both a chance to practice and a visual sponsorship that precluded theft by the ubiquitous slicky boys, who could remove any stretch-band watch in split seconds, toss it to a friend, and be found "innocent" if searched. And more slicky skills besides. So skilled were they with disguised pass-offs and fakes that some of the slicky boys made our American football plays look like comedy routines.

He glanced at his watch: it was nearly nine. And much too late to keep his appointment with Young Song. The bus was free to soldiers, and a cab was seven hundred Hwan. That meant no real income for the evening's effort if he was extravagant. He would be needing much additional income—all that he could get— if his personal plans succeeded.

He decided that the bus was an excellent idea, and the three set out for the terminal at the head of Hyo Jae Dong.

# **Chapter Five**

By six o'clock on the appointed next evening, Young Song had been waiting more than an hour for Bo's arrival. Miss Choi, her cousin-sister, had assured her that six o'clock was the hour for soldiers to arrive in order to take the girls back to the Army post for the early movie.

Young Song liked the idea of going to a movie. High school students had been forbidden by their superiors at school from patronizing the Seoul movie theatres. And although she occasionally saw a film with her friends, it was always with a feeling of guilt that they emerged, hoping that they would not see a neighbor or any other person who recognized them and could tell their parents.

Young Song heard the gate bell and started. She lay aside the book she was pretending to study and prepared to greet her guest. Mrs. Pak, her mother, returned with Miss Choi.

"*Miguk-saram kesimnikka,*" Miss Choi asked of Young Song.

"No, the American person is not here," Young Song replied in English, using her cousin's phrase in translation. But she expected him.

"Tough luck," Miss Choi countered. She removed her coat. "I know he lie. GI all time lie to Korean girl. GI all same-same." She prattled in the street English that she knew well.

"Bo not lie. He arrive soon." Young Song was adamant.

Miss Choi laughed patronizingly and translated the exchange for her aunt. It was enough, she said, that they must be associated with a soldier in such manner. Young Song should not be permitted further to shame herself by defending him, Miss Choi declared to the mother.

Young Song went back to her book. Miss Choi and Mrs. Pak began to recount their strategy if the soldier should arrive. After a time they began to discuss their alternatives if he should not arrive because the girl was already a woman. Nearly an hour passed; evidently he would not come, and they were wordless except for sporadic comments as charcoal was added to the brasier or as sounds in the meandering street might have signaled his approach.

Finally, Miss Choi reached for her coat. She explained to Mrs. Pak that there was no reason for their waiting. If she, herself, had never made a long-term liaison in three years, why should Song expect it of her first experience? No, she assured them, the soldier wasn't ever coming back.

Mrs. Pak shrugged. Maybe it was just as well. Perhaps they could manage without a soldier. And then maybe the first attempt would have to be repeated...well, not really the first, again. She glanced at Young Song. Apologetically she said aloud, in gutteral Korean, "It can't be helped." That was the Japanese invader speaking.

Both girls looked up as Mrs. Pak spoke. Her words hung on the silence, meaning something different to all.

Miss Choi buttoned her coat. "You likee come to post?" she asked. "I go post now. Wait at Post gate. Maybe I see GI I know. Some person, sure."

Young Song shook her head. Miss Choi pushed the sliding door open and went out into the cold foyer. Mrs. Pak followed her outside, saw her through the gate, and returned. For a long time there was no conversation. Then Mrs. Pak reminded her daughter that the father and the two children would be back soon. Mrs. Pak didn't want the children to become accustomed to seeing their sister in American clothes—or to see soldiers arrive.

Obediently, Young Song removed her cousin's Western dress and bound herself inside a carelessly-French Empire native gown. Then she took up her book and remained wordless for the evening. As soon as they came in, the children were put to bed in their quilts on the warm floor at the far end of the room.

Out of consideration for his daughter, Mr. Kim said nothing when he discovered her still at home. Gratefully, Young Song closed her book and set out her own quilts. She undressed and slipped between the quilted covers. Her parents went into the adjoining room, and after a long period of talking, they, too, tried to sleep. The board siding sprang nails with the cold, and the sharp sounds kept the older three awake. Young Song awaited morning impatiently. If she couldn't sleep, at least she could dress in her students' black uniform. Then she could go out unknown among people who didn't know that she wasn't wanted. With that admission she felt exhausted, and she slept.

35

# Chapter Six

Beaumont arrived at the outer gate exactly twenty-four hours late. Mrs. Pak answered the bell, and as he entered, Beaumont said quickly, "*Annyong hasimnikka.*"

With surprise Mrs. Pak answered, "*Ne. Komapsumnida.*" It was a perfectly phrased greeting with a respectful word of thanks in answer. By tradition it really enquired whether the other person had slept well. There was no *hello* or *hi* in the Korean language.

As he removed his boots in the foyer, Mrs. Pak slipped inside ahead of him and announced his arrival. He heard a rush of activity and entered just as the younger daughter was leaving. The young son saw her off through the gate. Beaumont returned the bow Mr. Kim made toward him and then turned to Young Song.

"Good evening, Miss Kim," he said formally, using the most appropriate form of address.

"Good evening, Bo." She caught herself. "I am sorry," she said hastily. "I do not know your father's name."

"My father's name is Beaumont. My name is Gordon Beaumont. But *Bo* is easier"

"Good evening, Mr. Beaumont," Young Song said properly.

"Good evening, Miss Kim."

They both laughed.

"I'm sorry I couldn't be here last night. But I drew a special duty assignment." To excuse by duty was far better than having chosen against her.

"Yes. I know."

He knew she probably had no idea exactly what the terms meant, but she did know that he was aware of his broken commitment, and that was sufficient.

"Would you like to go to a movie?"

"Oh, yes. I would like to go to a movie."

"Then hurry. We haven't much time.

"But I have Korean dress."

"That's fine. I like your Korean dress."

"Thank you." She spread the folds of the blue brocaded fabric and rearranged the white collar over the gold and scarlet stripes. She had in fact been fitting it for an occasion to come, but if he liked it, it would be sacrificed.

"Where's your coat?" he asked.

Young Song took a heavy garment from a row of pegs. As she did so, Mrs. Pak said something, and Young Song flushed. Mrs. Pak said something quickly, and the girl started.

"What's wrong?"

"I am sorry. My mother says I cannot go with you until Miss Choi come here."

"Where is Miss Choi?"

"Miss Choi at her house. My sister go to Miss Choi house. They come soon."

"Tell your mother I would like to go now. We have early curfews."

Young Song conveyed the preference, but her mother argued.

"I am sorry."

"Tell your father I will bring you home safely in two hours." The male head of household should determine, and he did, because Young Song repeated the promise, and her father smiled and nodded. The pair stepped into the foyer. Mrs. Pak passed them as Bo stopped to lace his boots. Holding the clapper of the bell so as not to signal the neighbors, the mother let them through the gate. As they started off, she called a farewell.

The two made their way to the Army post, paused momentarily while Bo registered his guest at the sentry box of Gate Three and went directly to the theatre. As almost always, the film was a Western, and Bo explained the principle of hero, badman, and sheriff to Young Song, who could not understand why they were there at all if Bo already knew how it would end.

Leaving the theatre, they made their way with the crowd past the lines of Quonset huts that had been erected temporarily several years before to supplement the Japanese buildings still standing on the post at the time of the major war. He calculated quickly from the civil war's truce in 1953. Five years had passed. There was little enough in the city to show for five years of reconstruction, he decided.

Without a conscious effort he guided them to the huge Quonset structure that served the post as a cafeteria-style snack shop. It seemed as if the entire theatre crowd had moved in at once, and there was a rush for tables and another rush for the service lines. They were long and slow.

Young Song marveled at the banks of stainless steel equipment and was visibly awed by the surfeit of light. In the city outside, electricity was still a precious and regulated commodity. When would wartime end? Or would it ever end?

Her first hamburger and malted milk overwhelmed her, and she told her pleasure anew between mouthfuls. She began to understand why her cousin-sister liked to go to the movies with soldiers.

From the Snack Shop they went directly to Gate Three, registered her exit, and turned west toward Young Song's residence. As they walked, they passed a number of girls loitering in the shadows of the wall. The whole process seemed to Young Song much like that of only two nights before. As they left the area of the post (where congratulations to her came from the other girls), city people began to call nasty names after her, but she pretended not to notice.

"If I see you often" he began, "people will know you and talk about you."

"I can do nothing."

"Don't you care?"

"Yes. I do not care. Do you not care?"

"No." Then he added, "Unless you become angry."

"I can do nothing."

"Would you like to stay with me for a while?" he asked.

"I do not know."

"We would have to find a house."

"My father has house."

"No. We can't stay there always. I'll think about it."

"I will think, too."

He laughed. "I'm glad. That'll help."

"Oh, thank you," Young Song replied, ingenuously. They made a turn from the wide street into the alley, and in moments were at the family gate. Young Song pushed the gate gently to make the bell ring ever so softly. Her cousin-sister admitted them.

"Hello, GI. Wuz new?" Miss Choi asked.

"Not much. What's new with you?"

Miss Choi darted inside without answering.

"Please don't learn street English like your cousin-sister," he admonished Young Song.

"I cannot," she replied. "There is not a book so good."

"Young Song, you are precious."

"I not understand that word."

"Some day I will tell you. Now it's a secret."

Their shoes now removed, the two went into the house proper. As they expected, the two children were sleeping. Mr. Kim was away from the house, and Mrs. Pak and Miss Choi kept company around the fire. Young Song and Bo were admitted and given a quilt to hold the heat of the warm floors about their legs.

"Good movie?" Miss Choi asked.

"We saw a Western movie," Young Song answered.

"Shoot-om-op, we speakee, *kurae*, Bo?"

"Shoot-'em-up is right."

"We went to the Snack Shop," Young Song said proudly.

"Why you didn't bring me hamburger, GI?" Miss Choi demanded.

"Because I hoped you wouldn't be here."

"Smaht sombech, you." Miss Choi related the insult to Mrs. Pak. Without looking up, Mrs. Pak gave an order, and Young Song excused herself from the group. She went into the adjoining room, leaving the sliding door open slightly.

"Miss Kim cry, you don't come last day," Miss Choi began after a while. She enjoyed berating him.

"I explained to her that I had special duty."

"What she know 'special duty'?" She spat. You come here next day again maybe?"

"Maybe so."

"You want to steady Miss Kim?"

"Maybe so."

"Why you all time say 'maybe so'? You want steady Miss Kim?"

"Maybe."

"You say yes—you say no. Not *maybe so!*" She was at her most officious, a survivor of shooting and non-shooting wars. She translated the exchange for Mrs. Pak.

"You catachee Miss Kim tonight?"

"How much?" If he acted too eager, the price would rocket.

"How much you speakee?" Miss Choi countered.

"Two dollars."

"Two dollah! What you think? Miss Kim not two dollah whore girl." Mrs. Pak expressed her contempt when the bid was told. "I speakee fifteen dollah."

"No."

"Last day, payday. You *takusan* money hava yes." She used the Japanese word for *large quantity*. All the GI's used it, too.

"*Takusan* money hava no." he argued.

"Wife in States hava yes?"

"Hava no."

"You lie. All GI lie." She was silent a moment and then made an appeal. "Mr. Kim no hava job now. All Korean—job hava no. Work govament for pay tax. No money he take he house. You understand, I speakee?"

"I understand."

"You speakee now. How much?"

"Five dollars."

"Ten dollah—catchee short-time."

"Five dollars—all night."

"Nevah hoppen, GI. What you think? Miss Kim not whore-girl. You no pay—you go post."

"Seven dollars—all night." he said.

Miss Choi thught a moment. "Bed-check hava yes?"

"Hava no."

"Nevah hoppen you stay all night," the cousin-sister mocked. "Seven dollah—short time. Payday last day."

"Okay."

"GI money." She wanted military scrip.

"Korean money," he said firmly. It was worth much less than the official value quoted internationally. He could offer more later, voluntarily.

"Korean money—Number Ten. GI money—number one."

"Korean money."

"Okay. GI money. Six dollah."

"Okay. GI money. Six dollah," he agreed.

It was illegal but common to give script, he knew. But military payment certificates—MPC's—were the accepted currency on the local market. He counted out six military payment certificates and left the bills in a thin stack on the straw mat. He went into the adjoining room. It was dark, and he called softly to Young Song. She answered from the corner, where she had already spread quilts.

"Did Miss Choi explain to you what it means to *steady?*"

"Yes, I understand."

"Do you wish to go steady with me?"

"If you wish."

"I wish it."

"I wish also," she said.

"When will you graduate from high school?"

"I will graduate from high school after five week." She didn't add that then she must make her own way in the world.

"That's soon enough." He squeezed her tightly. "You're very warm," he said. I'll get us a house when you graduate."

"Thank you," she said. "I have house."

He kissed her once again, smoothed her hair gently, and then went back to the other room. Miss Choi greeted him with surprise.

"Whaz wrong, GI?"

"No more catchee Miss Kim in Papa-san house."

Miss Choi relayed the message, and both women eyed the money still on the floor. Bo sat, reached for the bills, and handed them to Miss Choi.

He doubled the amount on the floor. "Miss Kim never catchee other GI. Understand?"

"You bettah believe I understand, GI." Miss Choi answered emphatically.

"You likee Miss Kim?"

"Yes, I like her."

"You no hurt she heart."

"Never." Then he changed the subject. "Where do you live?"

"I not far. I go one-one-one." She designated three directions, but they had little meaning on the map for him.

"On Sunday, I see Miss Kim at your house. Three dollars GI for you. Presento. Okay?"

"Okay—you say, GI. Presento."

"You write the address for the taxi driver."

"Okay. Pencil hava yes?"

He handed her a mechanical pencil and a card; she wrote her address on one side. On the other she drew a small diagram to mark the entry to the house and her room. She gave him the card with a flourish.

"Thank you. On Sunday—understand? At three o'clock. You go."

"I understand. Miss Kim, she come my house. I go."

He held out his hand for the mechanical pencil, and Miss Choi, with a show of surprise, discovered it in her pocket. She returned it apologetically, if resentfully.

Mrs. Pak was informed of the arrangements, and now she asked a final question.

"You likee steady Miss Kim?" Miss Choi translated.

"Maybe so. After Miss Kim graduates from high school."

"That long time. No can wait."

"Five week. Miss Kim must go to school. Understand?"

"Mama-san need money."

"I give *sukoshi* money." He used the Japanese word for *small quantity.* "When Miss Kim graduates, I steady her. Then I pay for steady. Okay?"

"How much you pay?"

"No sweat. We'll talk about that later," he said impatiently.

"Yes, sweat," Mis Choi argued. "GI—they stingy. All time say, 'next week, no sweat.' Not pay. I know."

"Don't argue with me. On Sunday I come to your house." A siren knifed them, and they stopped talking. A test, but on any night it could be a raid.

"How long you stay in Korea?" Miss Choi asked.

"One more year," he lied. His tour of duty would terminate in far less time, for eleven of the required fourteen months' duty had passed. But he offered the women no opportunity to seek a better prospect.

Told the duration of his stay, Mrs. Pak challenged him and demanded to be told how he could have greeted her so fluently if he been in the country only a few weeks.

"Tell her I have a special teacher," he said. Then he took his jacket and prepared to leave. "Remember," he said to Miss Choi. "Miss Kim never catchee other GI."

"I know," she said. "You Number One Heart, GI. Miss Kim, she lucky. I all time catchee different GI. I not lucky. Maybe I whore-girl—you think?"

"You're pretty tough..." he said.

"I pretty?...What you speakee, they listen."

"...but there's hope," he said, finishing the thought. He let himself into the foyer and began to lace his boots.

Miss Choi opened the gate quietly. As he passed her, she reached out and touched his face.

41

"You Number One Heart," Miss Choi said. "Number One." Then she went inside to relate the good fortune to her cousin-sister.

# Chapter Seven

On Sunday they were together in Miss Choi's room, talking about nothing in particular. They spent several evenings there; and then another Sunday arrived. The day and the room were spiked with cold, and neither Young Song nor Beaumont was tempted to leave the warmth of Miss Choi's bed, although they'd lain together on the over-aged mattress for several hours. It seemed enough to lie there—to talk or to indulge a recurring urge to fondle someone warm and responsive. They repeated themselves once or twice.

With amusing effort, Beaumont leaped from the bed and bolted into his shorts, splashed the wash bowl, and his uniform, in rapid succession. "Let's go," he said, mockingly severe. "We're working on a schedule."

He caught the corner of an Army blanket and slipped it off the bed. He held it up, and Young Song darted out from the nest of quilts. She wrapped herself in the blanket and padded down the hall to the privvy. Lacking plumbing, the private closet could hardly be termed a *bath,* but it was the appointed room, Beaumont reminded himself; and he gave up the idea of more than the earlier freshening splash of basin water.

As he laced his boots, he took inventory of the room. It was one of several which the retired landowner rented to such ladies as Miss Choi, who had the spirit of enterprise. The house was drafty, but so were all. It was reasonably well maintained, and only a short walk from the Army headquarters. In fact, it was ideal for joint purposes. And expensive, on their economy.

Besides the bed, Miss Choi had accumulated a bureau with a dressing mirror and two unsteady chairs of independent origin. Aligned on the bureau was a collection of empty perfume, cologne, and shave lotion bottles. He wondered how many visits to Miss Choi were represented by each empty bottle. No new and full bottles...maybe her time was already passing.

That was his first thought of Miss Choi as a person—not as a hostess— during that day, and he might have felt sorry for her, except that she herself seemed oblivious to the prospect of better matches; and so sorrow would be ill-placed. How flexible are social standards among men whose wives and mothers and sisters were not looking on during these brief encounters. Miss Choi needed little more than a rounding of her roughest social edges. Aside from that and her street English, he seemed rounded nicely enough to do well for herself in her— not necessarily *chosen*—trade.

He was startled when Young Song returned. She was fully dressed within minutes, and they prepared to leave. Young Song slid the screen shut and carefully snapped a padlock through the collar of the doorframe.

"Do you want to see a Western movie?" Beaumont asked as they found their shoes at the outer door.

"Maybe I would like to see Western—if you wish. Would you like drink malta milk?"

He laughed. "Yes, I would. How did you know?"

"Then we go to Snack Shop," she decided, and she opened the outer door of the house.

Beaumont stepped through. At that moment, the gate opened at the opposite end of the small court, and Miss Choi entered just ahead as a guest.

"How's the prices—good stuff?" the soldier asked.

"As good as the people who pay them," Beaumont answered coldly. Already he disliked the man, and his disheveled appearance and back-street grammar made Beaumont's dislike a probably-permanent thing. Teaching has its disadvantages, too, Bo thought to himself.

Miss Choi asked a question of Young Song in their language, and Young Song replied in that tongue. She moved on to the gate. She turned back to beckon to Bo as soon as she had surveyed the alleyway outside the gate; it was bare. To any person passing there was no noticeable difference between her and the cousin and their respective soldiers, Young Song realized. She would need to exercise care, or she would be too soon identified as one of *those*.

"Are you ready?" Bo asked her.

"Yes I am ready, she replied lightly, pretending to take no notice of the meeting. She waved to her cousin-sister and then shut the gate behind them.

From her preoccupied air, Bo knew Young Song was making and fighting comparisons, and he said nothing at all as they started up the narrow path between the stone and wood walls of the courtyards. The alley seemed hostile because of walls.

"Would you mind if we do not go to the Snack Shop?" he asked after they had walked a bit. "I forgot that I have much work at the office. I know it's Sunday."

"Yes, I do not mind," she replied. "I must study, too."

"Good. I'll take you home." He signaled for a taxi, and they climbed in. Young Song gave the street—not house—address.

"I'll be busy for several days," he continued. "But I shall come for you at your father's house on Friday evening."

"Thank you," she said softly. "I wait."

Wordlessly after that they waited for a driver to find the proper street, relieved that the night had arrived, and witnesses would be fewer. Given a good tip, the drivers remembered nothing. She was safe for now.

*30<sup>th</sup>*

*How long had he slept?  It seemed like moments, but the clock said it was well over an hour.  He was lying on the bed in all his clothes.  Even his shoes. And he didn't feel like going out again.  Whatever had possessed him to arrive in Korea without an address for her?  If he had written first, she could have met him.*

*How alive the memories were!  How certainly he had been with her only moments before.  To be with Young Song again seemed almost too good to be true.  That's what people said of good deals, too.  "If they seem too good to be true..."*

*He put on a coat before he left, but a real spring had arrived, and he really needed only a jacket.  So he walked again toward the gardens at Duk Su Palace and went inside.*

*As always, there were people around, but it was not as crowded as on Sundays.  He surveyed the crowd, although he didn't expect her to be there.  And he started to walk on the familiar paths.  Eventually he realized that he would not find her there—at least on this day—and so he left.  He went for dinner, but what he ate, he didn't remember.  Several hours had passed, but he felt he needed sleep more than exercise, and he went back.  Alone.  What else is there to say?*

# Chapter Eight

Reluctantly Miss Choh agreed to join him at the tea room, but only on the condition that they sit at the rear of the shop and that she be allowed to face the back wall to lessen the danger of recognition—by anyone.

They started up the stairs to the second floor level of the building and entered the White Deer Tea Room. It was quite ordinary, as tea rooms go, with plain wood floor and under painted walls, but it was not frequented by soldiers. Four or five tables were crowded together, and they were shown to one.

Charles Camden had asked for a location that served all her prerequisites. Having seated themselves according to her plan, he ordered *hon cha*, a red tea served overly sweet with a floated nut. Absently he stirred his tea and held a finger in the eddy of vapor that wafted from the glass. Then he held his hand aside for a moment, and the droplets died in an instant. Then he set the bouquet of tea-scented flesh before Miss Chohs' nose. She lowered her head slowly and inhaled.

"That is a very good way to try tea," she said.

"I'm glad you think so," Camden said. "Invented especially for you."

"I do not understand *invented*, Miss Choh said.

"It means *to make for the first time*. Or to create—do you know that word? he asked.

"Yes, I learn word *create* in Bible school. My father want. It is important word, I think." She looked pensive. She had used the new words in a phrase, and that was the best way to remember. "If you create way to try tea, is that important thing?"

"Not so important as you." He turned his hand and gently framed her small chin between his thumb and forefinger.

She drew back. "Not permitted to do in Korea," she reminded him in a tone that was gentle but yet insistent.

"I should have remembered," he said. "But in the States we are allowed to touch a fragile thing if we are careful not to break it."

"I do not understand many new words."

"They mean that I like you very much."

"Please do not tell me. It is not good luck."

They were quiet for a time. Miss Choh made an engrossing talk of her tea. Camden toyed with his and finally pushed it aside, nearly full.

"Tell me about your family," said Miss Choh with a new animation. It was the prescribed way to begin a serious visit in Korea. She wanted the visit to be proper.

"My parents live in Chicago," he said, "In a part of the city nearest to the water in Lake Michigan. It's just north of the business district. And it's a very nice place to live."

"That is very convenient," she said slowly, emphasizing each of the syllables of the word. "Do I pronounce correctly?

"Correctly."

"That is very interesting. Where you live. Who is your father?..."

"My father is a doctor, and my mother is a secretary. He thought. "Actually, my father is a very busy doctor. My mother is a busy body. And at home we all go round-for-round together in a very busy way." He laughed.

"So many words," said Miss Choh.

"And what do you want to do in life," he asked.

"Maybe I can be secretary, too. Will you become doctor?"

"Once I thought I might. That's what was expected of me, anyhow. But I changed my mind. I left school, and here I am in Korea. Nothing to it."

"I am very sorry you will not be a doctor," she said sympathetically.

"Forget it. I'm not sorry. I don't know what I'll do when I go back. But it won't be in medicine. No big deal."

"If you could be a doctor now, you would not must go back home. In Korea we need many doctor."

"Yes, I know. There's purpose there."

"My father is doctor, too. You know."

"Yes, I know. I'd like to meet him."

"Many year ago he wish for to go there." She thought for a time. "To the State for to study. But he did not go. Not good to be doctor in Korea, my father tell me. Here is not enough medicine. Not enough hospital. Many people die. Not good."

"We send medicine from the States."

"Not enough, my father told me. Besides, some slicky-boy steal medicine and sell it for black market. You know black market?"

"I know about it. Is your father a good doctor?"

"Oh, yes! Good, good." she said with enthusiasm. Then her face lost its glow. "He is not important in Korea. He is wrong party. He is best doctor, and other politics party must to let him teach. Best medicine from States is save for doctor of best party."

"Where does your father practice?"

"He see people at house. Sometime at Yongsei Hospital."

"Yongsei Annex—near the railroad station?"

"Yes. Do you know Yongsei?"

"I've heard of it. In fact I pass by each time I come to class, but I have never been inside. Never invited—so no matter."

"Some time he is there, my father. Other time he stay at house."

47

"Can I talk to your father some time?" he asked.

"Oh, not. I not take GI to my father house. He will angry."

"Maybe I can help him get medicine. Maybe my father can send it to him."

"Not possible."

"All right. Some other time."

"Do you angry?"

"No. I understand. I'm just a dog-faced soldier. Not much different here from on the bases back home. So we'll just forget it. Okay?" She had no answer, and they sat silently for a time. "Tell me about you," Camden said after a time.

She shook her head.

"What's wrong?" he asked.

"In Korea, not polite say nice thing about this person."

"Then tell me all the bad things about you."

With that they both laughed—he first, but even in laughter, his lantern jaw and turned-down mouth gave his expression a dour look. Even so, she laughed, too. And she shielded her fine smile behind a screen of fingers. To show teeth— eating implements—was considered rude.

"When will you be finished with school?" he asked.

"I am study at Seoul National University. I will be graduate after two more year."

"Then what will you do?"

"I wish for to study art in the United States."

"That will be very expensive."

"I am sure. Already I save more than five thousand Hwan."

He wrestled with a laugh. Small amounts of currency could be a fortune here and a pittance in the States. How could he explain to her what her approximately $10.00 would buy?"

"I think to win a scholarship."

"They're difficult to find. You must know that."

"Yes, I know that thing. I must hope for something." She looked down at the scarf she had folded and refolded on her lap. It had taken all of her attention and yet none of it. "It is difficult, to be Korean. If I wish win scholarship, my father must be from best politics party. Now he is not. After two years, maybe he is. Best party sometime must change. Sometime Liberal party not win election. People not happy."

"Or someday Syngman Rhee will die."

"Ie, Sung Man," she stated, giving one Korean form of the name, "very old. Many thing can happen."

He was beginning to understand how transliterations of written characters helped the Koreans to confound the West: the letters *R* and *L* sounded much alike in the Korean language and so could be substituted in any combination that the

48

writer chose. Therefore *Ie*, *Ee*, *Rhee*, and *Lee* were merely different but acceptable Roman-letter spelling variations for the same original name. Ie-Lee-Rhee had traded on that fact in order to lose his past.

"Maybe. All the same, it's probably a good thing that he's been around so long. At least the country is getting established again." His was the typical American understanding.

"Not is good thing. Only American people say so good thing. Korean people never say. Very difficult. If Japan soldiers still here, is same."

She believed it, he felt. He scowled. Subjunctive modes seem easy in literature, he thought, but, if ignored, they play hell with ordinary conversations in an unfamiliar tongue.

"When you brought me some of your drawings, I thought you were already studying art. You are very good."

"I would like, art study. Is better for be doctor. Korea need doctor. No job for artist."

"I hope you are not angry, but I showed some of your drawings to my friends." She made no reply, and he went on. "One friend is an artist. Another friend is Mr. Beaumont, who teaches class with me."

"Yes, I know Mr. Beaumont friend. He tell me you return all my drawing."

"Of course I will. Soon. But my artist friend is still studying them."

"Does he like them?"

"*Sukoshi*," he said in Japanese, and instantly he was aware of his error. He made a slight bow over the table and continued, "He likes them a little. You must practice very carefully. He says you have talent that you must develop."

"I must to be doctor."

"I will be very proud of you if you try."

"Already I try."

"Already I am proud. Will you visit my home when you come to the States—even if you will already be famous?"

"Not, I think. Not possible."

"If my mother and my father and my sister are all at home, then will you visit me?"

"Maybe, is possible. But I not leave two years. Maybe you not want see me."

"Of course I will want to see you. I will always want to see you."

"You wife like see me, yes?"

"I don't have a wife."

"But two year...

"You let me worry about that."

"I will visit for you."

"Good. We'll paint the town red."

"Is permit, paint?"

49

"When you come to take over Chicago, anything at all will be permitted."

"So certain to tell me where you live."

"When it's time for me to go home. Now, I must know your names if I'm to introduce you to my mother."

"I not tell you my name, first visit."

"But it's not our first visit. You've been in my class for nearly four months. How often have we met?"

"That is not same. This, first public visit." She looked at his wrist. "What is correct time, please?"

"Almost perfect English!" he complimented. "And I understand perfectly.... It's ten past nine." He thought for a moment. "Tell me your names—no excuses!"

"Miss Choh, Ai Ja," she said as if it mattered not at all, although it surely did. Improper!

"That's better."

She fidgeted. "I must go my house now. Is very too late."

"All right." He took a thin fold of Hwan from his pocket and slipped four one-hundred Hwan notes from the fold and left them on the table. A waiter arrived instantly...not that this particular GI would leave without paying. Obviously, some of the oppressor-liberators did.

"Are you ready?" Camden asked.

She nodded and stood. As he helped her out of the narrow booth, she began to adjust her head scarf. The ruse kept her hands before her face throughout the time-consuming crossing of the tea room floor. Once outside, she relaxed somewhat.

"Thank you for fine invitation to tea."

"Thank you for accepting," he said. Then he asked, "Would you show me around the temples sometime soon?"

"Chang Duk Palace, very pretty in spring," she said.

"Will you show me Chang Duk this Saturday?"

"Maybe not possible. I do not know."

"Just for a little while. Maybe Mr. Beaumont will bring a friend, too. We four can have a sightseeing tour."

"Very well. I would like."

"Good. On Saturday. At one o'clock. Where shall we meet?"

"Chang Duk Palace gate," she said, as if there could have been no question. "I will be there. Sure."

"Good. Now, let's get you a taxi."

"No. I will take bus. Please, you go now."

He moved off—far enough so that they would no longer be considered a couple, but he could provide protection. He turned away from her exact direction and waited until she was safely boarded onto the bus. Then he hailed a cab and went back to the post.

# Chapter Nine

It was Camden who had worried about Miss Choh's reaction to Young Song, who had no social pedigree. But after a few minutes of the venerated game of *who-are-your-family,* the girls developed an affinity for each other and, as was customary with friends, went off arm in arm through the palace grounds.

"You are not exactly the sexiest date I've ever had, Beaumont," said Camden to his friend as they trailed the girls.

"Ah, so; but I speakee Number One English, GI. I speakee that count *takusan* Number One good."

Their laughter brought a reprimand from Miss Choh both for their delaying the excursion and for their not venerating the many generations of ancestors who were present here in spirit. They continued as a line of four down the narrow paths. Several Korean couples were walking about, and the two girls kept their faces averted as they passed all of the others.

They passed a line of small buildings splendorous in a persimmon-colored lacquer. That color was the designation of the major structures in the enclosure.

"Chang Duk is the best palace in Seoul," lectured Miss Choh. "Americans not come here because they not know. This house not important," she said, gesturing toward several outbuildings nearby. We see important house only."

"*These houses,*" Camden corrected. "Don't forget your plurals."

"Yes," she replied, and the lesson was unceremoniously ended.

They passed an arched stone carriage bridge over a small stream, gargling with the newly melted snow. The girls, each embroidering on the other's narrative, retold a fearsome and imaginative account of the attack and murder of an emperor at that very point in the garden by assassins who lay in hiding under the bridge, awaiting his passage.

"When did that happen?" Beaumont enquired.

"Long time ago," said Miss Choh in reply. Having answered the question to her own satisfaction, she started off.

"I am sorry. We must go here," said Young Song quietly.

She guided them from the broad walkway into a narrow passageway between two massive wings of the structure that resembled blockhouses of a fort. She played with a latch, and the gate opened. As the door closed behind them, the common approaches from the garden paths were left behind a sturdy wooden wall, and they found themselves in a cloistered walkway fronting on a private garden.

The first building was an ancient court chamber with an adjoining throne room. The throne was barricaded, but even at a distance they could observe the infinite craftsmanship of the huge tassels that hung from the canopy. The royal insignii of two phoenix-counterposed were still visible on the billowed silk, although the gold coloring (substituted by someone for the true gold) had been corrupted by age into a musty brown. The mahogany beams overhead were intricately joined, and they still shone with a luster that subservient hands had coaxed from them in some century gone.

From the throne room they proceeded into an adjoining room that might have been a meeting hall. Now it was a museum, and glassed cases protected remnants of royal decrees, garments and personal effects.

A writing quill, a pair of stirrups, a breast plate, a dagger, a feathered cap, pottery. Each treasure drew an exclamation of wonder from the young women. Some of the items were named and dated in English with hand-lettered cards put there for the benefit of American visitors some years before. Now the cards had yellowed, as if to be worthy of the dates they bore.

Pausing to straighten and compare their Western garments in the huge court mirrors, the girls called their charges in hushed voices and led them into the private apartments. Each apartment stood alone—one or several rooms, depending on rank—either partially furnished or bare, and always in a square pavilion design, like islands cropping up in the flow of the garden stream. They were moored by an enclosed causeway to the throne room. Climate control was not a new idea.

"Why are we so high up from the ground?" Camden asked.

"The apartments seem to be on stilts."

"Floor is high for fires...under," said Miss Choh. She found a door and took them outside. At one side of the pavilion she found a sunken area with a metal door set in the stone base.

"Servant go inside to make fire. Floor hot for winter. Also cool for summer."

"Radiant heating—the newest thing back home," remarked Beaumont to his companion. "The Romans had it, too. Only a few centuries ahead of us—we learn fast!"

"I guess the Orient has been around a while," said Camden.

They tried to return to the apartments that they'd just left, but the exit door had swung shut and latched itself. Or a disapproving co-visitor had distanced them. It didn't matter which. The inconvenience was small.

"That not matter," said Miss Choh. "We can go to secret garden." She led the way around the square apartment and approached a long wall created by a series of oversized stone steps. Shrubbery and herbs rooted in the massive planters reached eight or ten feet high. A lattice fence topped the rise. Had war ever touched this place of peace? Or was it first to be reconstructed?

"Please come this way," directed Miss Choh, and she walked far to her right, where the stone planters angled into a boundary wall in a thicket of pine. Miss Choh climbed a sweep of stairs, located a gate in the lattice, and let the party inside the prayer garden.

They walked through the planting of pines that shielded the inner garden. From their entry point, the meadow flowed away and ran into a pond, and from there, into a reed bed. Perhaps it was the source of the stream that had helped dispose of an emperor. Intrigue floated in the air. Beside the pond, pitched in the farthest corner of the enclosure, was a prayer house. Its scale seemed miniature, and were its compartments filled with dolls, it might have been a plaything of a child. There was exquisite calm. Only an occasional and seemingly improper tree looked over the stone walls into the garden. The winter had matted the suppliant grasses, but green tips had begun to push through the matting, encouraging the sun to a sheen.

The four walked wordlessly through the meadow. At the pond they paused a moment to offer condolences to the metal heron perched one-legged beside the fishless pond, showing its wound to sympathizers. Then they turned back, ambled up the incline to the pines, and set themselves outside.

Through a series of convolutions and passages under the causeways linking the apartments, Miss Choh returned them to the main council chamber. The Americans inspected the cast lions that lay sunning themselves on the stair abutments. Young Song pointed out first one and then another of the intricate carvings of jungle creatures swarming over the spines of the wedge roof. And then, surfeited with royal trappings, they set off toward the entry gate.

"Over," said Miss Choh, indicating the fence, "for zoo. We can go there. Some day. If you wish." If was difficult to know whether she were inviting or recommending or being available for invitation.

"We'll plan that," replied Beaumont to his buddy. "We can pretend to be old and disdainful, and then secretly enjoy everything."

"I feel insignificantly young among these antique relics," replied Camden. "I'm not sure I need the zoo. We're already being stared at."

"If you not wish go there, we must not," said Young Song with great consternation.

"Of course I wish to go. I meant something else."

"Very well. We will plan." Miss Choh started away. "We must hurry," she warned. "Soon the gate will be closed." They took up a serious pace and soon passed over the bridge of the assassins, left the persimmon-colored buildings of imperial import behind, and emerged through the columned gate into the broad avenue of Won Nam Dong.

"I must to hurry," said Miss Choh as soon as they reached the outer walk. She made several brief comments to Young Song, who seemed to understand perfectly.

"Thank you for lovely visit," she said primly to either and both soldiers. "I see you at class." Entering the afternoon traffic on the avenue, she deserted the group.

"Miss Choh house very near," said Young Song, and no further notice was given the abrupt departure.

Camden hailed a taxi. Soon they were passing Compound II of the American legation, and the Capitol Building loomed just beyond. The taxi turned left onto Sei Jong Ro, and, with the gutted Capitol squarely behind them, they settled themselves into the ancient car for the trip to the Army post.

"Drop us off at the traffic circle," said Beaumont. "I think she'd prefer not to attract too much attention with the taxi in the alleys. You can take this thing all the way in. We'll split it straight up."

"I can walk as easily as you."

"All right." He thought for a moment. "Do you have Hwan?"

Young Song said nothing, although she didn't particularly want to be seen walking with two GI's near her own home.

"I think so." It didn't matter, because military script was the preferred currency, but if taken from GI's it was counted at the official rate— approximately half of black market value. He had sufficient Hwan.

"Good," said Beaumont. "I'm low. Do the honors, will you?" he asked Camden. "I'll cover it on payday."

"Sure."

And as if Young Song were not present, they conversed.

"What do you make of the day?"

"I don't know," Camden said. "Nothing complete in itself. But maybe it's a prelude to something."

"As dear Lieutenant Johnson says, 'Keep fritzing those...'"

"Stop. I've got a weak stomach." Officers were not much admired among the enlisted men, especially the draftees. All enlisted men resented the dichotomy that ran even to health. All the officers who contracted VD got it in cold contact from a toilet seat; the enlisted men always got it in warm contact in bed. But the enlisted men didn't use the same toilets as did the officers—so how did it happen? One of the wondrous mysteries of the military.

They traveled the remainder of the distance in silence. Beaumont called a stop, and the three exchanged courtesies. Young Song walked ahead for a half block and then turned toward her alley, The two men went together to the post. The day of visits had ended.

# Chapter Ten

One weekend afternoon, only Miss Choi was there to greet him at her house. She admitted him without ceremony and tended to his comforts as if little else could have been expected of her.  Or was it just busy work?

"Where is Young Song?" Beaumont asked.

"*Opse-yo*," replied Miss Choi absently. Gone.

"*Opse-yo*, hell.  Where is she?"

She study she house. *Mo sukoshi* school hava no.  Now you steady her. Now you pay."

"I'd forgotten about that."

"GI alla time forget pay," Miss Choi taunted.

"All right.  What do I owe you?"

"Sevenee-fi dollah."

"You're crazy."

"Sixty dollah."

"I don't want to play games now!"

"Today you Number Ten, GI."

"And you'll be Number Dead if you don't wise up."

"Smaht sombech, you."

"How much?"

"Fifty dollah.  Sure, Mama-san say."

"Fifty dollars is too much," he argued.  That was half of his monthly pay, allowing for little discretionary spending, such as the house he had promised Young Song that he would rent.

"Not too much.  Miss Kim—she must have room.  Me understand, GI."

"I understand.  Too much money.

"Papa-san, Mama-san, two baby-san-cost thirty dollar-one month.  I know."

"Miss Kim, she not catchee other GI.  Must have room.  Must give money to she Papa-san.  Papa-san job hava no.  All Korean, job hava no.  You no pay— Miss Kim she catchee *takusan* GI.  Maybe she same-same whore-girl.  You want she be whore-girl?"

"No, I don't want."

"Miss Kim not butterfly.

"Same-same whore-girl, you, Miss Choh? No!"

"I Number Ten Heart."

"You can be Miss Number One if you try."

"True?  You say true?"

"I say true.  Why don't you catchee steady GI?"

"Nevah hoppen. When I cherry-girl I catchee GI first time. I just friend, he say first. Then, you know wha hoppen. No more friend. All GI lie. All GI same-same. Want one thing. I know."

"Did you like him?

"*Ne. Takusan*, I likee he. *Takusan.* He go States. I cry. Cry. Cry. He not care. He say first we go States. He marry Miss Choi. He lie. He say 'So long, baby. Hava fun.' She made a guttural sound to express contempt. *"Kasuk!"*

He was startled by her imitation of the foul slang term but found himself wondering how it might be spelled. It was not the sort of word to ask to polite people, even translators. "Don't say words like *kasuk*," he instructed. "Only whore-girls say *kasuk*."

"I not care. I same-same whore-girl now. *Kasuk* GI! Nevah hoppen I catchee other steady. *Kasuk...kasuk!*" She jumped up from the edge of the bed, where they sat, and paced the room. Abruptly she stopped and rejoined him. "You want marry with Miss Kim?"

"I don't know."

"You lie, GI. You not marry with Miss Kim. I know. You nevah hurt Miss Kim heart—okay?"

"Okay. I promise. I never hurt Miss Kim's heart."

"You Number One Heart, GI. She hesitated a moment. "How much you can pay Miss Kim?"

"Can you get her a room in this house?"

"Nevah hoppen. This house whore-girl house. I catchee Miss Kim other house. Same-same nice. Same-same you likee."

"Everything included—including room?"

"All, all, all."

"I pay thirty dollars—one month."

She debated. "Maybe Miss Kim butterfly."

"Thirty-five dollars."

"You buy Miss Kim United State dress?"

Forty dollars—no more."

"Okay. Forty dollah. GI money."

He agreed to pay the forbidden Military Payment Certificates, and the bargain was sealed.

"When I see Miss Kim next time?" he inquired.

"Nex time Sunday. You pay now—Miss Kim room hava yes nex time. You come my house first, nex Sunday."

He checked his billfold and extracted twenty dollars. "Pay day in two weeks. Two weeks is twenty dollars. I pay Miss Kim twenty dollars now. The rest next Sunday."

He handed the money to Miss Choi, and she counted it several times.

"I trust you. You don't trust me?"

"I Korean girl. You GI."

Almost affectionately he put his arm around her. "Miss Choi, you're too much."

She was openly suspicious. "Whaz wong—you hot pants, maybe, GI?" She made a point of backing away.

"No. I like you; that's all. You're one of a kind."

"GI all like same thing. I know."

"Next time I bring you a present. A bottle of perfume from States. You likee that?"

"What you want, GI?"

"I want to be your friend. Okay?"

"Maybe yes, maybe no."

"Okay. Maybe so. Now I go post. *Annyong-i ke-sipsio.* You Number One Heart, too."

"*Annyong-i ka-sipsio,*" she answered. Then she remarked, "You speakee Number One Korea speakee. *Mo sukosh* you go States. I know, GI."

"You go Ie Hwa University—you Number One Smaht Teachah. She laughed and followed him outside and saw him through the gate.

"Hey, GI," she called as he left. "Miss Kim, she *takusan* lucky. Maybe."

Bo made a solemn bow to acknowledge the compliment and hurried away.

# Chapter Eleven

"Thank you very much for the very kind invitation to dinner," said the class in unison. Then each in turn repeated the phrase to Miss Choh, Ai Ja, who had without ceremony conveyed her father's decision to have the class meet at his home for its next appointed lesson. Beaumont accepted with effusive thanks.

*Ch'on man-e malssum imnida,"* Miss Choh answered very softly: A thousand time it matters not.

"We have no phrase in English that is as beautiful as "*Ch 'on man-e,*" said Beaumont thoughtfully, "but if you are talking to an American you would probably say, 'You are welcome'."

"Then we should prefer to say *Ch 'on man-e yo,*" said the studious Mr. Lee with a grin. "It is better."

"Better, yes. But not understood by most English speakers. We're learning to speak English understandably, aren't we?"

A note of hostility escaped him, and possibly the other caught it, because Lee acquiesced with an almost imperceptible bow of his head.

Given a choice, Beaumont reminded himself, he would have moved the troublesome Mr. Lee out of the class months ago. But that might have cost him the entire class, and Beaumont thought the group as a whole compensated for the one member. And so the lessons had continued.

The class was dismissed, and immediately Miss Choh was surrounded by the other members, who exacted details of time and place—an oversight, Beaumont admitted, that would deprive him of a personal comment to Miss Choh. And so he took leave of the class as a group, thanked Miss Choh for her invitation to meet at her home, publicly asked her for an address he already knew, and departed, very much pleased with prospects—on Camden's behalf.

On the appointed day, planning to visit with their host before the class period began, Camden and Beaumont arrived at the home of Dr. Choh, Tae Man somewhat ahead of schedule, but several members of the group had already assembled. The two acknowledged the class members with a nod as a woman servant admitted them to the living area on the second floor of the frame building. Taking Camden's package and the men's caps, the servant went away.

Dr. Choh entered momentarily, and just as the three men had concluded their mutual greetings, the doctor's wife appeared behind him. The Americans greeted her, and she bowed and withdrew immediately.

"I wish not to disturb the lesson," said Dr. Choh carefully. "Therefore, please conduct class. Afterwards, please remain yourselves for our guests."

"The doctor does us great honor with an invitation to his home again," said Beaumont easily. "We can only try to be worthy to remain as guests."

59

Dr. Choh pretended not to be surprised at the answer, which was suitable and proper but yet unusual for foreigners. He made a slight bow to Beaumont and then to Camden. Both returned the courtesy, and the doctor left the room.

Beaumont greeted Miss Choh and the others and inventoried the group. The two Messrs. Lee were present, as were Messrs. Chung and Soh. Miss Ahn and the Misses Yu—together with the hostess, Miss Choh—almost a complete class. Beaumont inquired after Miss Chung, and after a moment Mr. Chung (her brother) replied that possibly she would not attend. He recommended that the class begin.

The two soldiers seated themselves on the rice straw mats that covered the floor. Miss Choh gave them woven cushions, and those added another quarter-inch of straw base to the spare resilience of the floor.

The lesson from the text was only superficially a lesson. Responses were mechanical, and no questions were raised. Beaumont glanced at Camden, and the latter closed his book.

"Because this is a special occasion, maybe we can review the social amenities," said Camden. "Does everyone understand that term 'amenities'?"

The class repeated the word and Camden followed and corrected toward standard. The group continued with the book, but Beaumont wasn't listening; he turned his attention to the entry and soon rose to greet Miss Chung, Byung Mil, whose brother had said would not arrive.

"I am sorry. I must have special permission for leaving job," said Miss Chung self-consciously. Thank you."

Beaumont didn't ask for an explanation of the remark, which could have meant almost anything. He guided Miss Chung into the group, and with a remark in her own tongue, she apologized to the class.

"Good evening, Miss Chung," said Camden. "We have finished our lesson from the text and are now discussing manners."

Miss Chung made no answer. Then, as the class became more spirited, she seemed to relax and then to take up the lighter mood of the gathering.

When the group had heard the accepted manner for extending and replying to invitations, for greeting one's host and hostess, and for conducting dinner conversation (in the American casual form), Camden pronounced the class ended.

Miss Choh touched a small bell, and the woman servant entered with a tray. Cups, tea, and appetizers were set before the group. Beaumont tried one delicacy. Using chopsticks, he lifted a small cluster of newly-hatched fish from the serving bowl. He tasted. The fish were crisp-fried in an oil mixture and tartly seasoned. He took more. Camden sampled the other plate. He lifted a leaf of glace seaweed and, with an agreeable expression, passed a portion to Beaumont.

Dr. Choh joined the group, seating himself at the head of the low table. Instantly the light conversation stopped, and the few comments grew stilted.

"I think it wise to continue speaking conversation English," pronounced the doctor as he poured himself a cup of the aromatic tea. His diction was forced, and his action was a direct rebuke to the servant woman, who should have seen to his cup. "Therefore please continue in English."

"I think we should discuss international policy," said the disagreeable Mr. Lee. "I wish to know why the American government does not permit South Korea to liberate the north part of our country."

"Liberation of North Korea is a matter for the United Nations to arrange," said Camden. "And when the Republic of South Korea has developed a mature government that the North Koreans wish to have for themselves, there will be a liberation of the northern areas of your country."

"It will not come without conflict, maybe, but it need not be international war," Beaumont said. "That was very near, already."

"Unless war is necessary." Mr. Lee persisted.

"If that's necessary, is it wise to proceed now?"

If the meaning of the final comment escaped Mr. Lee, it did not escape the doctor. He said nothing, but he watched Beaumont through half-averted eyes.

"Then why do you not give us atomic weapons and new military equipment?" Lee insisted.

"That's part of the same question," answered Beaumont. "I have already answered it."

"Why don't you grant us a Status of Forces Agreement?" snapped Mr. Lee, cutting short a comment begun by Miss Ahn.

"Because American soldiers are very unpopular in Korea today. We have already been deprived of most of our rights as an American citizen when we entered the armed services. If we are then subjected to a prejudicial foreign civil trial—and I believe that is the only kind to be expected—we will have been cheated of everything that we are already committed to protect. Our country can't permit it. And I don't want it." He was obviously angry, and whether or not Mr. Lee fully understood the answer, he made no reply.

Dr. Choh smiled. "You have very direct approach to these problem, Mr. Beaumont. "Possibly at another time we can to discuss them further." He turned his head, uttered a single sharp word, and turned his attention back to his guests. Immediately the servant entered.

"I do think that the problem is a difference of cultures. Our is very old, and you, very new," the doctor began. "It is surely best that the people of those culture do not mix unnecessarily." The comment was intended as his indirect message to Camden, who pretended not to understand while yet remaining silent.

The servant kneeled to the left of Dr. Choh and apportioned a clear broth. The cups were passed around the table. Bits of meat were settled in the cups, and cubed bean curd—a soft white substance—had been floated. The guests drank the broth from the bowls and lifted the solids with chopsticks. Kimchi—the national dish—made of fermented cabbage, fruits, and vegetables—was served. It smelled horrendous but tasted...okay. Camden took enough of the malodorous course so as not to offend. He passed it to Beaumont, who did the same. The others ate heartily.

"Some of us are agreeable to Japanese foods," said the doctor as he interpreted the soldiers' reticence. "We offer *sukiyaki,* also."

The servant uncovered a chaffing pan and passed servings. She departed. Everyone noticed that the Americans preferred the Japanese beef recipe, but no one commented.   Slights are best left unnoticed...or surely unremarked... especially when not intended.

The dinner progressed almost without conversation.  From time to time, Choh, Ai Ja glanced her father's way to see whether he approved of the proceedings. He gave her no easy, unwitting indication. He had had his say, for now.

Abruptly the servant came to the door and called to the doctor. He went out instantly. The group continued with dinner after a comment from Miss Choh that an unannounced visit from a patient was a frequent occurrence and did not mean *grave emergency.* "My father wishes us to continue," she concluded.  There was an undeserved excitement in the group, and Beaumont turned the conversation to poetry and to the ideographs hanging at various points throughout the room.

The doctor had not returned by the time the fruit course was served.  Before long, the dinner was completed.  Miss Choh called to have the dishes removed and tried to lead a forced conversation.  But without a host to urge them to stay, several of the guests made the obligatory gesture toward leaving, and two did. Within moments, several more followed them, and within moments, only Miss Choh, the insistent Mr. Lee, and the Americans remained.   When Beaumont refused to be drawn into another political discussion, even the talkative Mr. Lee paid his respects to his hostess and left the house.

Choh, Ai Ja jumped up as soon as she recognized the impropriety of her situation among two men not her relatives and ran down to consult her father. She returned with her mother.  Having no command of the English language, the doctor's wife sat apart.

"My father will return very soon. He is sorry."

"We'll wait for him," said Camden, and he was granted a smile in return.

Then with her mother present to guarantee her reputation, Choh, Ai Ja became very communicative.

When I go to United State after graduate Seoul National University, I study medicine very good.  Then I help my father to make well charity patient, too. He have many charity patient."

"Is that what he's doing now?" asked Camden.

He not tell me, but I think yes. He is wrong politics party...he know many poor people."

"We say, *political* party," Camden said gently.

"Political?...Political." she repeated in slow syllables.

"Where is he?" asked Beaumont. "Here or at the patient's house?" It was a matter of time estimates.

"He is under," said Miss Choh with a gesture.

"We say *downstairs,*" said Beaumont. Does he have an office there?"

"Not office. A room like Yong Sei Hospital. Many people come there."

"We call such a place an office, also." Camden advised.

"That very nice," Miss Choh said. She smiled behind ready fingertips. "I learn many thing from you."

"Wherefore art thou, Romeo?" laughed Beaumont.

"Screw you," said Camden with a scowl.

"My friend Camden showed me your drawings, Miss Choh. Many of them are very fine. You should study art."

"You can not truly think so, but this person thank you."

"I agree with you that many Miss Choh drawing very pleasant to see," said Dr. Choh, entering. "If she would not be study medicine, then she would be study drawing." He was in charge of the situation.

"She told me she preferred to study medicine," said Camden. To help you."

"I did not hear Miss Choh say that," said the father.

Camden made no answer. He felt guilty. "Miss Choh told us that only a few minutes ago."

"And left us suddenly." said Beaumont for retrieval. "To get her mother."

"Perhaps that so," said the doctor. "Thank you."

"Besides, I think we can infer that from her general attitude," said Beaumont. "Many times we think people have said a thing when actually they have not."

"Perhaps that is so," repeated the doctor.

"I'm sure it is," said Beaumont. "I had the same impression."

"Mr. Beaumont and Mr. Camden are extremely friends. I am pleasure to observe." He smiled. "You pleasure me to wait until I have done with patient. She rest now."

"We have enjoyed our evening in your home so very much that we could not depart without thanking you," said Beaumont. "We would have waited much longer for you."

With his supercilious courtesies turned back to him, the doctor smiled. "Thank you."

"Miss Choh told us it was probably a charity patient," Camden said.

"Perhaps. That is not important," replied the doctor.

"I have been told by others that medicine is not easy to get," said Camden. "Is that true?"

"There is not much medicine. That is true. Also all medicine not good medicine." He sighed. "Many time something not medicine put inside bottle."

"Can you use Japanese medicine?" Camden asked.

"Japanese medicine good. Sometime use. Difficult for getting."

"In two days I am going to Japan on R&R," said Camden. "If you like, I will buy medicine for you, there."

"That is not permitted," said the doctor.

"I won't pass through customs, GI's never do."

"When you return to Korea?" asked Miss Choh with somewhat disguised alarm. Did her father notice? "Please. You bring medicine for my father. Yes?"

"Yes, if he gives me a list."

"I write such list, Mr. Camden," said the doctor. Abruptly he changed topics. "What will happen to English lessons when you return to United State?"

"We'll finish the book before then," replied Beaumont.

"Perhap another teacher?" Dr. Choh asked. "More learning."

"Perhaps." Beaumont.

"Miss Choh, I gave a package to the servant when we arrived. Could you have her bring it here, please," said Camden when the conversation lapsed.

Dr. Choh called out, and the woman appeared. He said something in their language, and she went out. In moments she returned with the package and set it on the table before them.

"This is a gift from my father to you," Camden said to the doctor. "My father is a doctor, also. In Chicago." He pushed the package toward Dr. Choh."

"I am very pleasure of your father gift," said the doctor, but he made no move toward it.

Choh, Ai Ja reached for the package and stripped the wrapper. She set a large medical volume on the table before her father. "For medicine," she said. "Book without drug."

"A recommendation, but no practical help," Camden said with disappointment to Beaumont. Beaumont noted that the very recent title included the words *preventive medicine,* and he remarked to Camden that it seemed most appropriate to conditions here.

The doctor bowed and stood up. "Please," he said as he started out of the room. He motioned and waited until the Americans rose to follow him before proceeding to his home office downstairs.

The office was sparsely appointed. An operating table derived from the American military campaign stood against one wall. Several chairs, a table, and a cabinet of apparatus and medicines filled the small space. At the far end, just off the main entry to the building, was a small anteroom, now a waiting room, with a woman seated. An overstuffed chair and divan made up its non-medical furnishings. There were books by the score.

As the two wandered through the office, the doctor sat at the table, took writing paper and pen, and created a list of needed supplies A string of numbers evidently detailed price, for when he had totaled the columns, he went back and struck several items. Then he folded the list and handed it to Camden, who vowed to himself to get even the struck items.

"I saw that it's only fifty bucks on the open market," Camden remarked to Beaumont. "I can probably manage without missing a meal."

"I'll cover it if you can't," said Beaumont.

"I am on special duty tomorrow," said Camden to the doctor. "I cannot come here. But it is not necessary for you to buy American money. I will return with the medicine. After ten days."

Dr. Choh looked from one to the other and back again. What was he compromising? he wondered. He said nothing. Then he turned away.

"Do you need instruments, Doctor?" asked Camden.

"Perhap," he replied. He lifted the glass on a single shelf and withdrew a battered pair of forceps.

"How many do you need?"

The doctor shrugged. "Possible, two."

Camden knew his father ordered by the dozen. He put his hand inside the cabinet. "Those scalpels wouldn't butter bread," he commented to Beaumont. "The man is in pretty bad shape. My father throws away better equipment than this because it has outlived its usefulness."

"We'll come back after ten days," Beaumont said to Dr. Choh. "Mr. Camden will have your medicine."

"I will have American money," Dr. Choh replied.

"That is not important," said Camden, and the doctor hoped he meant it.

The doctor led them into the entry. He clapped his hands twice, and the servant brought their military caps. Without speaking they laced their shoes and bowed to the doctor.

"Please say goodbye for me to your wife and to your daughter," said Beaumont.

Dr. Choh nodded.

"Thank you for the invitation to dinner," said Camden.

The doctor bowed again. "You are welcome." Then he extended his hand and clasped theirs in turn. With no further word he saw them through the outer gate and bolted it behind them.

In the street outside, the pair hailed a taxi. As it started off toward the post, they were silent. After a time, Camden spoke.

"I'm going to bring back everything on that list. And more besides."

"Can you afford it?" asked Beaumont.

"Not really. But I think maybe I can scrounge a few more bucks back in the barracks."

"Good luck."

"I mean it," Camden insisted. "There are a few other guys around who have a feeling for the people here."

"Feelings don't cost money."

"I'll get the cash. Don't worry."

"Starting with me?"

"Thanks for volunteering."

"How'll you get the stuff back into the country?"

"How many guys do the MP's actually check after their R&R? Back to you right here."

"Go ahead," Beaumont said after a time. "We're in this all the way, I guess. And we can always count techniques of smuggling among our Army benefits. We're already up to *one*."

"I feel rather good about this," Camden said.

"Are you doing this for the father or the daughter?"

"If I thought you were joking, Bo, I could be goddamn ugly about it."

"But I'm not joking. And you are already ugly."

"The truth is, I don't know." Ai Ja has been in our classes for four months. For nearly half that time I've been seeing her in out-of-the-way places. Then suddenly she went to the teahouse with me. And then with us to the temple. Now the dinner invitation. Do you know what it means?"

"Don't blame it on me."

"Do you want to know why I didn't go to Hong Kong on leave?"

"She begged you..." Beaumont said facetiously.

"You stupid bastard! My parents wouldn't send my birth certificate. I'd written about Ai Ja to them, and they were afraid I intended to marry her. I just wanted a passport."

"Did you? *Intend marriage*, I mean?"

"I don't see that it concerns them. Or you."

"Neither do I. Which is probably why I hadn't mentioned it sooner. It's noticeable, you know."

"Perceptive bastard, aren't you?"

"You're a fauning schoolboy in some ways. And you haven't fooled her father, either."

"Then I shouldn't have gone there tonight. Maybe she'll catch hell."

"Maybe. I don't think Dr. Choh is anybody's fall guy."

"I thought the same thing of myself once. Now, for a bunch of dirty, hopeless people whose names I didn't even know a year ago, I'm risking a couple of years in the guard house. Just whose fall guy does that make me?"

With a loud clang, a Los Angeles cast-off trolley challenged the taxi. They halted abruptly and then leaped into motion again. They went back to the post without further conversation.

*April 1:*

*If he doesn't keep tabs on the dates, he'll soon be duplicating numbers. It'll be a mess. But this business should not be taking so long. How long should he continue?*

*It's amazing how that recollection of of his quartet at the palace triggered so many memories. The remembrances of us alone would be logical. But Miss Choh's sincere dismay at the political horror—aided by the U.S. collaboration with the schemers—began to tug at my memory.*

*He doesn't think he'd be able to discuss Word One about those events so many decades ago if asked; yet the memories that well up by themselves seemed so fresh and tangible as to be real and now. Probably it was Miss Choh's comments then that forced him to look at realities, because it had previously been so easy just to accept the status quo. Now he was becoming immersed in them again. Am I glad about that? Was he?*

# Chapter Twelve

"Good evening, Mr. Jerome," said Chung, Kyung Tae, almost graciously, as he received his guest at the booth he'd reserved in the nearly empty lounge off the Bando arcade.

Hello, Chung," returned S. Martin Jerome casually. "Sorry to be late, but I was very pleasantly detained, if you get what I mean." Jerome laughed broadly.

"I'm sure I do," said Mr. Chung unemotionally, showing the good taste to be non-judgmental. "I hope she had the good taste to be clean."

"Jerome tried another laugh meant to be jovial. "That's very good, Chung. I'll have to remember that." He carefully avoided conferring the status of *mister* on Chung, who usually made an issue of formality. Jerome prided himself on taking every advantage shown in business arrangements.

"Will you have a drink with me?" Chung asked dutifully.

"I don't know why not. Make it a scotch—double."

Mr. Chung gave an order in his language to the waiter he presumed was standing just behind him. In a moment the double scotch was set down before both.

S. Martin Jerome lifted the glass. "To a mutually advantageous business arrangement."

Mr. Chung raised his glass indifferently and drank. S. Martin Jerome gave the impression of having just over-indulged again, Chung, Kyung Tae observed. He felt almost as if he himself should belch to relieve Jerome. He interrupted the appraisal of the American long enough to reply that it was indeed a pleasant evening, if too cool for the season. Jerome refused to pick up on the small talk. Silence.

"How are thing at OEC?" Mr. Chung asked, referring to the Office of Economic Coordinator. OEC was an American agency in Korea that conferred economic aid on the fortunate, defined as those politically connected or otherwise sponsored by the more *cooperative interests* there.

"Like always, we're pretty busy. Especially me, with the Chief back in Washington for a while. But I sign now. Business as usual, you know," commented Jerome.

"Surely you aren't busy only when the Chief is gone. I know that is not true. I've heard much about how you run things your own way—always."

"People are inclined to be over-complimentary," said Jerome with mock humility. "After all, the Chief isn't *entirely* incompetent."

"Not at all *entirely*," Chung agreed laughingly as he drifted with the new mood. "Not *entirely*. S. Martin Jerome locked his pudgy fingers together and saddled his belly. "You're all right, Chung. "You're all right."

"Business associate should be agreeable to each other, I think" mused Mr. Chung.

"Definitely," said Jerome. He drained his glass and signaled for another round. "Maybe you told me before, but where did you go to school?"

"Yes, I have told you, but these things are not important to a man like you, are they?"

"Oh, I wouldn't say a thing like that..."

"But if it's true...I studied at the University of California in Los Angeles. There is a student exchange program there with the University of Seoul."

"Yes, I know. We need more of such programs. For international relations."

"Yes. And for some of us, the first chance to see freedom."

"But you came back..."

"I belong to the political party in power. So I have a few privileges. That's something you must have learned during your stay in the Army. You were a sergeant, not so? Better than dog-face GI."

"You've done your homework. But we don't have to review ancient history to get our work done, do we?" A directive, couched as a question.

"A few years ago, only. If you know how a man stays out of trouble in the Army, you know how he stays out of trouble in government service. How can you be surprised when it happens here?"

"I'm not at all surprised, but I didn't expect to be discussing it." Was Chung pushing too hard? And would he be difficult to deal with, as a logical extension of this moment.

"Surely two such good friends as we are can speak in confidence." Mr. Chung recognized his mistake, but he determined not to back paddle. That would be to admit a tactical mistake that feigned ignorance should not cover easily.

"Of course."

"Do you regret you stay in Korea when your Army tour was up? It is not as comfortable as the States." Mindless.

"Of course not. I love this country and its people." It was a rote statement courtesy the OEC but it usually worked.

"Naturally," said Chung. "I love it, too. And it does offer unusual opportunities to foreigners."

"So I am a foreigner," said Jerome. Do you think me a powerful one?" The reminder wouldn't hurt. "Even he"—indicating the waiter setting liquor before them—"even he makes me aware that I am a foreigner."

"But he pay for his show of bad taste with not knowing you, and so we'll just ignore him. This turnabout is difficult for people to understand. After all, the Japanese were in control for many years, too. Now different people matter more."

"Too?" Jerome exploded. "We're not in control here, Chung. Syngman Rhee is!"

"A bad choice of words, possibly."

"Or maybe that's how we want to feel, regardless of the facts." Chung wondered whether he had gone too far this time, but he felt he had to show independence.

"Then maybe you'd better tell them who is in control. That's what makes this possible." Jerome shifted for comfort. "But you're a Ministry of Justice man. And a big man, too, I might add."

"Now it is you who flatters," said Chung. "I have an insignificant position at the Ministry."

"Maybe. But if I ever get the police chief's daughter in trouble, I'll know who to see to fix it up."

"Please. I would expect it of you."

Jerome blinked several times and decided he had not been bested; he sat back. Then he said, "Buy me a Bando chit book, will you, Chung?" Jerome pulled his book of bar coupons from his pocket. "Nearly gone."

"Surely." Chung ordered a booklet of cash coupons and counted out four thousand Hwan. He slid the booklet toward Jerome.

"Thanks, Chung. You know, if I'd ordered this, I'd have to pay eight good greenbacks. You pay only four or five MPC."

"Greenbacks are good for the economy. Stable."

"And good for the waiter, too. If I paid greenbacks at the legal rate, he'd go out on the market and double or triple his money, pay the bill in Hwan, and pocket fifty percent."

"In the best Western fashion. This is one of the tricks the Occidentals have taught us. I don't think it was the same double economy under the Japanese." He raised his glass. "To the home of the brave and the land of the kickback." He drank.

"You know, Chung, you could talk yourself right out of a business deal."

"Except that the deal is so *mutually* advantageous."

"Any project that promotes the objectives of my office is advantageous to me. And there are more than enough applicants who'll take the good old U.S. cash, Chung. I don't really need you, do I?"

"Of course not. But if I were to discover certain *irregularities* in the procedures that your office follows.... What then?"

"Suppose you tell me again—just why should I approve loan for a cosmetics factory? Obviously cosmetics are not strategic material. And they won't contribute to the food supply or ease the housing shortage."

"Indirectly, it will work. Cosmetics make jobs. And there aren't many jobs." Chung was sure he had the fish on the line.

"Cosmetics make almost no jobs. It's all packaging. You know that as well as I do. Better, even. But they make profits higher than almost any other project. So I'm sure your interest is not in the job market alone."

"Also we have that special method of profit sharing that interest you. I think that's the phrase you Americans use."

"For giving bonuses to employees—yes."

"For giving bonuses to *somebody*. That is still profit sharing, yes?"

If Chung were tough and aware, they could work together. "How much money will you need?"

"I have a few figures," Chung said, and he took a packet of papers from his breast pocket.

"Is this plan expensive enough to qualify for a U.S. loan?"

"I have two fire sprinkler systems, two electrical generators, extra heavy reinforcement."

"We can justify that as a military precaution," Jerome interjected.

"Of course. I have spent a quarter of a million dollars, U.S. That should qualify me." Chung insisted.

"We can't ask much more of you, can we?"

For some minutes, the two traded comments about general plans and financing. Finally the business plan costs seemed reasonable to them both.

"Do you have the cash reserve we require?" asked Jerome. "Remember, it's twenty per cent of the total loan requested."

"My engineering firm will give me the use of such a sum for the day of deposit. Therefore, I expect to have a bank statement of deposit to enclose with my form proposition."

"Now, you don't plan to go bankrupt with our money, do you? I must ask you that."

"Tempting, but no. The cosmetics are too profitable."

"Probably I can get this approved."

"I certainly hope you can. Otherwise I might have to ask several of my friends to get the loan approved through their good offices with your Chief." Too much independence? he wondered. "That, of course, would deny me the privilege of paying—tribute—to your business sense. I would like to remain a good friend, surely."

"Send a finalized proposal and a request for loan. We'll take care of you...providing that the construction of a cosmetics factory is found to be of benefit to the economy of the Korean Republic.

"You are very generous."

"I hope it's contagious." Jerome thought for a moment. "You're on the level, aren't you?"

"I don't know that term."

"You really plan to stay in business?"

"Naturally."

"We've had a lot—too many—bankruptcies lately. It's getting hard to explain. A lot of money is going out and nothing to show for it. Unless we count hidden bank accounts...and we don't want to show those. We can't report those to the U.S. Audit office and still survive. They don't seem to understand the *politics* of finance," said S. Martin Jerome, OEC officer extraordinaire.

"I'll be most cautious," Chung promised solemnly.

"I'll drink to that," Jerome roared. He banged his fist on the table in a new show of joviality and took up his glass.

Mr. Chung took up his own glass. They drank together without specifying the object of toast.

"This is a good place to relax after a long day, isn't it?" asked Jerome. "The casino upstairs helps, too."

"I like it. Of course the Hotel Bando is very Western. I'm sure that several other hotels such as this would help to increase the tourist trade."

"I don't think so. Besides, the town is too dirty. No real sanitation. And we can't have our people eating in the open restaurants."

"I'm sure they would survive."

"Survival has nothing to do with it. People travel for pleasure or gain. If there's no pleasure, they'll stay away. If there's a fast buck to be made, they'll come along no matter what. Besides, do you expect Rhee to welcome his competition? This hotel is *his*!"

"That's an interesting theory."

"I have a number of theories. They work out real good, if I do say so myself." He looked around. "Can we get a check?" Then he searched for pockets for a newly-purchased coupon booklet.

"Please permit me," said Chung, Kyung Tae without conviction as the check arrived. He tore several coupons from his own booklet.

"Then I must pay for my chit book." They both knew it was a formality.

"Consider the coupons a form of thanks for your inestimable assistance with my planning. I'm sure you've had better offerings. But then, I'm only now beginning to enter the business world—internationally."

"Gifts are neither expected nor required, Chung. I'm simply doing my job in the best way I know how." Pro forma.

"I'm very glad. We can use many more such honest people in this country."

They arose together, and as they did so, Jerome's eye caught the busy colors of a silk screen that filled the entire upper area of the long wall beside them.

"Very nice," Jerome said. 'I like stuff like that. Pagodas and palaces and stuff. Real Oriental, if you know what I mean."

"If only the management were in need of more American funds, we could have the screen sent to you as tribute. Strictly speaking it should not be here—it's a museum piece. But you know how things are."

"That's not a bad idea, Chung. Work on it!"

"It's a national treasure."

"Work a little harder."

"I'm afraid that's impossible."
Jerome laughed loudly. You never know how to take a joke, do you?"
"I take jokes for what they are."
The two left the Bando Hotel building and separated.

## April 9<sup>th</sup>

*While he was walking about the downtown area of Seoul, he began to study and to reminisce about how it looked in the old days of his memory. The city had indeed remade itself. From a town center of ramshackle sheds, plastered shacks, and the highly Westernized Hotel Bando, owned by the Korean President, the center had always been an amalgamation of very old, old, and somewhat-antique modern. Well, the palaces still stood, and so the very old was secure, but the then-new was older and the then-modern was now too-old—and it had gone down. Now there were sleek skyscrapers in the best American tradition and Japanese-style neon and concrete everywhere else, with flying buttresses for the highways.*

*It was a beautiful city; beautiful to look at—now—but what did it really represent except the triumph of underhandedness? When he looked for (and couldn't find) the Hotel Bando of old among the welter of new skyscrapers downtown, he thought about the hotel's strange and unenviable past—and of that Jerome person. Will that first name still come back to him? Jerome was a sorry symbol of decay and imperialism, all in one untidy rolling-waist-banded bundle. And what had he been able to make of all that? How interesting it would be to have a final report. But that seemed as unlikely as finding Young Song had begun to seem. But the stories—abundant stories....*

*Looking back, it was clear that the North Korean communists had miscalculated...but not in the manner usually ascribed: simply regarding the American resolve to fight another foreign war. That was a convincing argument to us, but the likely fact was different and deeper—much deeper. It probably involved Chinese miscalculations based on their own history, because, as we discovered, the Chinese were supporting the North Korean invasion. We didn't know why, other than to credit the communist threat worldwide. The two histories were not identical but were surely influenced one by the other.*

*From the first days of the Twentieth Century—causing the Opium Wars and the Boxer Rebellion—China had been dominated by foreign individuals and governments, including the West and America, all of whom were partitioning that country into spheres of influence in order to support colonial markets abroad. China was forced to accept opium in exchange for tea and the foreigners imposed ruinous taxes on the locals, ruining the national economy in the name of international profits. All foreigners supported the recall of gold in exchange for paper money, which was soon debased. So the Sun, Yat Sen contingent, including Chiang, Kai Shek and those who followed, made fortunes while the general population was being impoverished.*

*When he succeeded General Sun, Yat Sen, General Chiang, Kai Shek ultimately made himself hated by the general population of China because he insisted on fighting the Chinese communist patriots instead of the Japanese invader of Manchuria. By fighting other Chinese first, he was supporting Western interests, which, in return, supported him. But the scholar Mao, Tse Tung, whom we saw only as a communist, became the savior of the indigenous people and the Chinese students abroad, especially when he began to fight Chiang and the Japanese openly.*

*Chiang, as the brother-in-law of Sun, was committed to the policy of protecting the interest of their family, the political clique, and the Western nations, including Britain, France, Belgium, and the USA. Formosa/Taiwan was a Chinese province when Chiang retreated to it—why should we be defending its independence now? Oh, yes, communism—which the mainland Chinese then preferred and want to extend throughout their country. The Chinese people as a whole preferred Mao, who had the best interests of an independent and more benevolent China at heart. Had we won the economic war only to lose the moral war? We're still fighting the latter.*

*And that was the key: we Americans had ignored and opposed the wishes of the Chinese people—just as we've done in countless countries around the world—supporting strongmen, no matter how dictatorial they might have been at home. Rhee was a dictator, a deposed provisional president with no legitimate prior claim to rule.*

*Therefore, when the Chinese promoted an invasion from the North in Korea, they were likely expecting that the Korean people, like those of China, would join the nationalists against the foreign powers and rise up against the corrupt regime of Rhee. But at that time, Rhee's corruption was still not yet widely known to be massive, even in Korea because history books were not allowed to be published; the official version was taught verbally and audited when taught. Life under the Americans, by contrast, was aided, even if uncomfortable. Better, Americans were guaranteeing that the Japanese invader would not return. There was no immediate need to revolt against anything.... Unfortunately, need would follow later under "democracy."*

*So there was no popular uprising against the "fearsome" nationalists, known to us as communists. How fortunate that these views are so much corroborated by the books of Han, Suyin...hers published after we had visited (and so, confirmed) and before we write this (and so, corroborated). She grew up in China but knew the Western-induced corruption in her country and also knew the Chinese communist students in Europe, where she, herself, had studied. They were communists in the French tradition—which the U.S.A. learned to live with. But much later, having no help from the West, Russia ultimately dominated, helped Mao with warring, and then succeeded him. After all, it was we, not the Russians, who were double-dealing on a pact: Russia was bribed into joining us in WWII partly by the promised partitioning of Korea, although our State Department would rather forget that. Well, we can easily forget a nasty century, but China's memory is 5,000 years long!*

*We didn't know all of that then. But later in my stay there, the Tale of the Ancient made things very clear—in a foggy language. But The Ancient no longer lives. Neither do most of his friends. And the younger people who knew, now aging, were either direct participants in corruption or are still afraid to speak They are safe here, but they have families in Korea, and.... When Rhee was deposed as the first President of the Provisional Government in Shanghai, he refused to surrender his chop, in effect, the seal of office. He presented that to our State Department, which presumably had never heard the truth. So the memory of the First Provisional Government in Shanghai might still survive in scattered places—but for how long?—in the memories of a few patriots and their families or in the very old political refugees. And then? Fiction will become fact. Or as the Romans said, "History is the victor's version of what happened."*

*Young Song, do I really want to be here? Do you?*

# Chapter Thirteen

"Come in, Specialist Beaumont," said S. Martin Jerome from the far side of his desk. He sorted a few papers, covered a sheaf of manuscript, and pushed back his chair.

"Thank you," said Beaumont without conviction. He slipped his military cap under his belt but stood uneasily.

"Make yourself comfortable," said Jerome. "Were not all in the Army."

Beaumont sat in a chair placed directly opposite Jerome, shifting his seat slightly so that he had a view of another man who shared the room with them.

"My assistant here is Lim. John, this is Specialist Beaumont, who's here to ask us a few questions."

Beaumont shook hands with the Mr. Lim, who was called John. Many Koreans who worked for the Americans adopted American names for business, though probably not used beyond. They exchanged formal comments of greeting before Jerome mentioned the name of his secretary, a buxom Miss Moon, who had just entered the office with a sheaf of papers.

"After all, I understand," began Jerome with a deliberate emphasis on the syllables, "that you asked to see the Economic Coordinator."

"Not knowing whom to ask for, I decided on the man in charge. I expected to reach someone else, as I have."

"The Chief is a very busy man. Ordinarily such requests as yours are referred to the Reports Officer for OEC. But unfortunately he isn't in the office today. And so you have me. I'm—well, call me an assistant of sorts."

"I hope I haven't interfered with your plans for the day. I made the appointment several weeks ago. But what I want to ask shouldn't take too long."

"Good," Jerome said. He laced his fingers together and saddled his stomach with his hands. "Why are you here? Exactly what can I do for you?"

"You might tell me a little bit about the function of the OEC—no one seems to know much about the organization."

"You've inquired already?" Jerome asked quickly.

"Not formally, as now. Just a few questions here and there so that when I go home in a few weeks, I'll have something worthwhile to say to people who ask me what I've been doing for fourteen months of my life over here."

"Then this is just a parting visit?"

"We could call it that, although I expect to work in journalism."

"There isn't much I can tell you that isn't in some way confidential, you understand. Maybe that's why so few people know exactly what we do. We have an important task, but there's nothing mysterious about our operations. In fact we publish an extremely comprehensive report each year. The report summarizes our official activities for the fiscal year just ended. That should answer your questions."

"To whom are the reports distributed?"

"To authorized agencies and offices."

"But they're not published—or made available to people not directly concerned?" Beaumont commented, in what he hoped was light-handed pursuit.

"I'm not sure that would be prudent."

"Maybe not, but it would give the people back home some indication of where their money is going, wouldn't it?"

"What kind of work did you say you do?" Or are you a student—of the military?" An easy interruption can change gears.

"I'm a teacher—social studies. Foreign affairs is a special interest."

"We who are concerned with various aspects of foreign relations look askance at people who toy with the subject."

"I don't consider intelligent inquiry a plaything," countered Beaumont. He was rising to the challenge. "But perhaps intelligence doesn't enter into your definition."

Jerome shifted his bulk—the man opposite him would not be easily dismissed. He drew his chair nearer the desk and thumbed a letter just then laid down by Miss Moon. He assumed a critical air as he scanned the page; then he initialed the sheet, and turning it over, set it within reach of the secretary.

"You understand that I don't mean to be hasty or harsh with you, Specialist Beaumont."

"I'm sure you've had experience with many holiday experts. You really can't know whether I'm just another."

"You're right. Although there are ways of telling. One develops a sixth sense about such things after having served in responsible capacities for a time."

"It's obvious that you have."

"Oh, yes. I've been in most places where our government has seen fit to establish aid programs."

"Then you've seen a lot of money spent. I'm sure you know how things are done."

"In terms of dollars—perhaps. But in terms of all the things that we would like to do, really not so much. There's so very much left to do."

"Have operations always been as difficult as they seem to be here?"

"Difficult here? I'm not sure you mean that. We find the Korean government most cooperative."

"Is that right? I've heard conflicting comments during the year I've been here."

"Some people will say just about anything to get a little attention for themselves."

"I should have guessed," Beaumont said amiably.

"Now, if there's nothing more you wanted to talk over."

I have a few notes here. I did want to ask about the amount of money that went into the OEC in the last year."

"I couldn't answer that question. There are too many sources contributing to the economic rehabilitation of the country."

"For instance?" Beaumont made notes.

"For instance, the OEC itself. The military procurement program for another thing. Then there's the United Nations contribution through UNKRRA, which will be discontinued after June 30. And OEC funds are given to the military for its own distribution outside our immediate budget."

"What is your budget?"

"For the fiscal year 1958, appropriations are expected to be substantially more than thirty-four million dollars."

Beaumont made another notation. "Under the circumstances, shouldn't an audit agency be required?"

"We have one—the Office of the Controller supervises all funds."

"That's an OEC office, I suppose."

"Of course."

"Nothing outside the agency?"

"I don't think it's necessary."

"And for auditing the financial stability of a Korean firm that's applying for a loan?"

"Normally a function of the Bank of Korea—outside the jurisdiction of OEC."

"How does one determine the financial stability of applicant—for the purpose of making a loan?"

"A financial statement is part of the prospectus submitted.

"Assuming that I were a Korean National, how would I obtain a loan?" Beaumont's voice betrayed impatience at the avoidances.

"For what purpose?"

Beaumont search for something appropriate. "A cosmetics factory?"

"Why that?" It was a sharp tone."

"A thought...high profit," the soldier replied.

"You could submit plans and specifications in your prospectus," replied Jerome. "Collateral in the amount of twenty per cent of the proposed loan is also required."

"How does one determine that the applicant has the twenty per cent of the total sum?"

"That is a function of the Bank of Korea."

"Do you ever verify the report through other sources?"

"That is not my responsibility."

"Suppose I submit a prospectus. Then will I obtain a loan?"

"Definitely not. We must know your technical ability to operate the firm you propose."

"I assume that the OEC has testing facilities."

"No, but technical competence is a required part of the prospectus."

"Is that such ability as the applicant claims?"

"Yes. It's usually reflected in the technical specifications submitted to the CEB—that's the Combined Economic Board."

"Then all members of the Combined Economic Board are twenty engineers who might be creating work for themselves?"

"Well, uh...no. We have other boards of engineers that review the particular type of industry which is proposed."

"Then all members of those boards are engineers."

"Yes...well not actually." He forced a laugh. "You understand that we would have a difficult job in obtaining them. Good engineers can't be brought in fast enough. It's a handicap, of course, but we manage."

"How do you manage to hire men who are not engineers to act as engineers?"

"We take what we can get." It was snapped.

"Army personnel and drifters included?"

"Is there something wrong with Army personnel?"

"Masquerading as engineers if they are not—yes."

"We have engineers. A consortium of U.S. engineering firms—is our technical consultant." He mentioned a firm name.

"How does that organization function for you?"

"As the government's watchdog. No project is granted final approval until it has been approved by the consortium." Jerome laughed uneasily. "Do you really think the people back home are going to ask you so many questions?"

"They're inquisitive, I hope."

"Probably you should take one or two of our publications. These should answer just about all questions. As you can see from my crowded office, we're very careful of the taxpayers' money."

"I'll be glad to tell them what I know. And I'll take those publications."

"Fine. That'll give us both a little more time for completing the day's schedule." He reached forward to the booklets that had already been lying on his desk.

"Oh, before I go, I *would* like to know about the overall program."

"It's discussed in the pamphlets."

"Fully?"

"I believe so."

"Well, in case it's not—we can save me another trip by my asking now. Has a master plan for the Korean economy been established?"

"You must understand that OEC was an emergency program when begun; and all things were necessary."

"Does an individual, in applying for a loan, construct any plant he chooses, or does he select one already determined to be of benefit and necessary to a sound economy?"

"Business practice automatically provides a balance."

"Does everyone *manufacture?*"

"Many plants are subsidiaries of American companies—they merely package such things as pharmaceuticals."

"Is there a limit to the size of loan that can be requested for a packaging operation?"

"Do you suppose a limit is necessary?"

"Suppose I were a Korean National and wanted to obtain an OEC loan to construct a cosmetics plant even though other industries are more urgently needed. What then?"

"Yes. I don't see why not, if you're qualified."

"If, for example, I could produce all the lipsticks the economy could absorb, does any OEC policy prevent another Korean National from obtaining a loan to build a similar plant to produce lipsticks?"

"It is not our job to prevent competition. Besides, such a situation isn't too probable. We encourage competition."

"But if this is fact, does a written policy exist?"

"Not that I know of. But you must admit that the example is rather distant."

"Of course." Beaumont felt that he had proved his point.

Jerome began to shift. He played with a pencil; he looked up as if to receive something that was not handed to him. Finally he caught the eye of Mr. Lim.

"As soon as you are free, Mr. Jerome, I have something important to discuss with you. It is a matter that requires your personal decision." Good form for terminating a conversation.

"I don't want to hurry Specialist Beaumont, Lim. Try to hold off just another minute or so."

"This will take only a minute longer," Beaumont volunteered. "Just terminology...how do you break down the monetary category of loans?"

"I don't recall exactly. Maybe I have it here." Jerome sifted through a stack of papers without locating his item.

Up to fifty thousand dollars is small," said John Lim finally. "Up to five hundred thousand dollars is medium; above is large."

"Do the large loans go only to the national government, or can individuals borrow that much?"

"That depends on their project," Jerome answered with undisguised irritation.

Lim tried to be personable. "Government, mostly."

"But individuals can get a million dollar loan under OEC policy?"

"That is possible," said Lim. "Usually it is the national government."

And they need show only a single bank deposit receipt?" Beaumont looked to Jerome, who nodded.

"That Chung Ju fertilizer plant," said Beaumont. "It's cost us about thirty-million dollars. Is this a private or national project?"

"Originally it was a government project," said Lim.

*"Originally?"* Beaumont caught an exchange of glances between Jerome and Lim. The latter turned away.

"Is the Chung Ju plant to be sold?"

"We don't know yet. That is possible." Lim.

"I don't think Specialist Beaumont is vitally interested in fertilizer, Lim."

"At what price would the plant be sold?"

Jerome shrugged. "Well, I can't say. We haven't received the bids, yet."

"Is there a minimum bid price?"

"Not that I know of. But I'm sure there will be."

"Is this sale in line with other projects of the type?" Beaumont persisted. Finally he had found a route for the transfer of small fortunes from government into private hands of the politically influential. That was the rumor, now confirmed. Now provable fact.

"Yes. The dam, for example," said Lim.

Jerome blanched. "Specialist Beaumont is not authorized to have information about the fertilizer plant. You understand our concern, don't you, Beaumont? We can't just chatter."

There was complete silence.

"Then you feel that the sale of the fertilizer plant merely promotes private enterprise."

Jerome sank back in his chair, relieved. right."

"And that's the object of the program itself?"

"Yes, that's it," Lim stated quickly.

"We'd like to think so," Jerome mused.

"Of course OEC has been successful during its years of operation," Beaumont said emphatically.

"I'd say so," agreed Jerome jovially.

"Just how many projects have we established?"

"I don't know exactly—offhand. Maybe I can find the figures." Again Jerome shuffled. "It's a whole lot, I know."

"And they're all still in operation?"

"Oh, sure. "He took up two booklets that had lain aside on his desk and offered them. "Here's the report."

"Have there been no failures or bankruptcies—no mismanagement of funds?" Beaumont took the booklets.

"None! These people are wonderfully capable!"

"An enviable record. I hope I haven't taken up too much of your time, Mr. Jerome. But I hope you agree that we taxpayers should know more about what's happening in the world."

"And we're certainly glad to tell them our story."

"It's quite a story you tell.... Of course you speak for the Economic Coordinator—in what you've told me."

"Yes, that's right. I can usually handle routine inquiries." He was being indirect.

Beaumont sense it: nothing remarkable about his inquiry. "Then I'm glad I didn't disturb your Chief. Thank you for your time."

"And if the Chief wants to know why you were here, what shall I tell him?"

Beaumont knew he'd been too forward, and he covered himself. He'd decided to drop the idea. "I was going to send a friend. For a job."

"Your moose?" said Jerome, sensing a request. "I thought so." The Korean slang and most Americans used the Japanese word *musame,* but soldiers could corrupt virtually anything...and, evidently, so could some American governmental officials. Beaumont shrugged.

"Sorry to disappoint you—my student."

"Send her around. What's her name?"

"Miss Kim Young Song." If she was interested in corruption, here was a master course.

"I'll look her over when she gets here. But she'd better be able to type." Jerome rose from his chair. Awkwardly he took the hand Beaumont stretched out toward him. "Good luck on your trip home," said Jerome.

"Only a few weeks left. I'm already half packed." To Lim he said, "Thank you. You've been most helpful."

"Fortunately you're too far from home to go over the hill," Jerome added for no apparent reason, unless implying that desertion could be bought for a price.

Beaumont released his clasp of Mr. Lim's hand.

"I wouldn't give it a thought. I've found a home in the Army, you know." That was the laughable cliché, but not now meant for laughing.

"So many do," said Jerome without humor. He rounded his desk and opened the hall door. "Good afternoon."

"And goodbye," said Beaumont. He stepped outside quickly, and the door was close firmly behind; interpret that as you will. A voice floated over the transom. "Lim, call your friend at the Provost Marshall's office. See if there's anything we should know about this one."

Beaumont smiled. Then he took his cap, slapped it formlessly on his head, and bolted down the stairs, past a Korean guard, and into the graveled lot. He turned right as he reached the winding alleyway and almost immediately was in a main thoroughfare. He hailed a taxi and directed the driver back to the command post.

Inside the fence, he went directly to the library. In a moment he had convinced the Korean library assistant that although he realized that personal calls were not generally permitted, yet this was urgent business. He dialed. After a long wait, he had an answer.

"Karl...Gordon."

"Good afternoon, Gordon. Are you off duty so soon? What a life! I envy you!"

"I've just come from sick call."

"Is something wrong?"

"I was downtown. We might have spoken about it."

"I'm not sure. You can tell me about it sometime."

"Now is better. Have you heard anything about a new cosmetics factory?"

"Not details, because it's not competitive. But I can ask details. All engineers know each other here. When must you know?"

"No hurry at the moment. Whenever it's convenient." Both were silent for a moment. "UNKRRA is being discontinued this summer," Beaumont said. "Had you heard?"

"Yes. The United Nations is cutting back its operations over here. Funds will be disbursed by your own OEC here after May. That should be interesting."

"Do you know why the change?"

"No one knows exactly. Except possibly that reports sent to New York have indicated that Korea is very nearly rehabilitated. Forget the squalor. Forget the corruption. In such circumstances, *natuerlich*, the change is to be expected.

"I thought there was a UN observer team over here."

"There is. Three men...one American. Two of the men are members of their embassy staffs. To send anything but innocuous reports would violate diplomatic practice. Your American must have some interesting observations. And possibly opinions, too. Maybe you should see him."

"You're certain about the reports?"

"Yes. Of course they don't clear everything through my office."

"Do you know anything about a dam?"

"Hydro-electric project—yes. There's one planned without enough water to keep it running, It's the special interest of the man who gives away all the money for your government I hear. Dams are the special funnel for all the big money."

"Do you know anything about the sale of a dam?"

There was a long pause. "You're keeping me away from a client. Why don't you come to dinner tomorrow evening?"

"I can't make it. Shall I call you later?"

"Not by telephone...I'm busy."

So the phones were tapped, too, Beaumont understood. "I'll try to stop by late tomorrow. Briefly."

"Good. Magda will be glad to see you. Good day."

They both hung up. Beaumont was irritated at first that he had caused concern for Kauffmann. Then he decided that nothing in the conversation would condemn either of them, sauntered out of the library, and went almost eagerly back to the barracks to deposit the day's booklets and notes.

But it was chilly. Cold. There was snow still on the ground, but the *Stars & Stripes* listed the temperature at the forties. Then it must be warmer than the snow itself realized! He stripped. A hot shower in the Quonset barracks hut rewarded a day's worthwhile effort.

# Chapter Fourteen

"You are very kind," said Dr. Choh in an unusually low tone. For the first time he seemed to be dispossessed of himself. Then he began to refold the tissue papers about the medicines and instruments that had been unpacked before him.

And although they had been appraised of the non-class purpose of the visit from the Americans, the several Korean gentlemen (including two of Miss Choh's uncles and a neighbor) gathered around the table in the main room of the Choh household were even more uncertain than Dr. Choh, for they had no logical explanation for the gift from soldiers.

It was Mr. Choi, the eldest of the five guests of Dr. Choh, who suggested that certainly it was an excellent idea of the Doctor to invite his Korean family and friends to meet the American soldiers because certainly the contacts between the two groups of nationals were too few and of unfortunate nature.

Several other comments passed before Mr. Kim, who had not spoken since his initial greeting of the pair of Americans, stood up and moved away from the group. There was no sound between the re-wrap 'thank you' and Kim's move.

"How fine it would be," said Mr. Kim from his place at the window, "if all gifts of the American people could be medicine and food and clothing and building materials to help our people. Instead, we have been given dams that have no water and fertilizer plants that make no fertilizer and castor plants that have no beans and make no jobs, and glass factories that cannot make good glass. And money to turn us into thieves." After a moment he continued. "Always big things these Americans offer. Korea is a country of small things, small shops, small crafts. Make jobs now...make big buildings after our people have enough to eat."

"I am very pleasure," said Dr. Choh, agitated, "to have first gift of medicine from my American friends. We are not necessary to speak unkind words."

"Friends must be permitted to be honest," said Camden.

"Yet we must not blame friends for mistakes in things that are not in their control," answered Mr. Pak.

"Perhaps they can do to repair," said Mr. Kim.

"Certainly they can repair their government agencies as much as you can repair our government agencies. Pak speaking.

"But America is democracy," insisted Mr. Lim. "Why cannot these Americans make repairs? If our Korean government had democr——" He stopped. Such conversation was dangerous.

"You have a constitution—much as we," said Beaumont. "Paper," said Kim. "A license...written by people who use it best." He returned to the group. "Help must first come from Americans—now."

"Don't you get any help from our embassy and OEC?" asked Camden.

"To school teacher? Loans?" asked Kim.

"I expect that the Ambassador is a very fine man. Since 1956 he is here. Very intelligent. Every time when he go back to the United States to report anything, always he return with warning to say less. Why that happen?" It was Choi who continued the thought that Kim had originated.

"I don't know why it happens," said Beaumont. "I'd heard that he has been squelched by Washington.

"You know these thing?" asked Kim.

"Some of them, yes," said Beaumont. "Others I'm still learning about."

"You come to good school," said Mr. Kim.

"Why don't you tell us exactly what you think?" said Camden.

"There is much—much—to tell about," said Mr. Kim.

"Tell me about the OEC," said Beaumont.

Mr. Kim turned his face to the floor and made the sound of spitting. "Now I have told you about OEC!"

"I cannot write a newspaper article about only that," said Beaumont evenly. "If you have nothing more to say..."

"They turn American to fool—OEC," said Mr. Kim. "Do you not know it some Koreans steal from you by take money for large plants they never wish to build? Only get money. Then bankrupt. Money disappear. Korea people still hungry."

"Yes, I've heard that. And I've heard that some engineering firms and local banks cooperate to make that possible." That drew an involuntary reaction from each of the Koreans. They hadn't guessed that common knowledge was *common* to all.

"You've been holding out on me," said Camden quietly.

"But I can't yet prove that these things are true," Beaumont continued after a time. "I'm trying to collect proofs."

"Perhaps I should take you to home of cousin," Mr. Kim said. "He already start for bankrupt chemical plant. Now he have much money for do what he wish tomorrow. Not give money back."

"Did he ever intend to build the plant?"

"Chemical and gold and mud are same for make money, my cousin." Mr. Kim laughed. "He use very good engineer firm. He know how to buy important people. He is American mind, not Korea."

"Including Americans? Buying...?"

"What you think? I can give you name these people."

"Do you think Americans were given money?"

I know yes or no. But no name.

"How can I *repair* those faults," said Beaumont, using Lim's own word, "if you will not help me?"

"Tell your people that many American not now less rich than when they come to Korea."

"What if I write that I suspect *collusion*. Do you know that word?"

"I know. I have use it," said Mr. Kim.

"Could you use it now?"

"It is excellent word for purpose. Perhaps I could say it is a word invented especial for talk about OEC."

"And also tell your American friends that some of my friends buy job with America agency," said the very reserved Mr. Choi. "Not fortunate, some friend women. They have no money...so they pay other way. I see some baby."

Does the OEC Chief know about these things?" asked Camden.

"Certainly he know. Everyone know," said Mr Kim.

Possible is not," contradicted Mr. Choi. "He is very stupid person. I am not surprise if he know nothing about these thing."

"Many people at OEC are stupid," insisted Mr. Lim. "Some honest. Many people clever at OEC. These not honest." He thought for a time. "Clever also honest...I do not know of such person powerful."

"There was person," said Dr. Choh. "He chief consulting engineer for U.S. Government. He know what happen. He try to stop. So OEC and some people say he make trouble. They say many not true thing about him. So he must go back to United States. OEC Chief truly must know about that thing."

"It is fault by OEC Chief that we have dam and no food. He like dam," said Mr. Pak. "So Korean government must to pay for such thing it not afford, no need, at this time."

"You will need electricity for industry," said Camden.

"Other way we make electricity. Dam not necessary. Some day atomic electricity...already in United State."

"Soon government dam give to important people," said Mr. Choi. "Sell cheap."

Beaumont started. The cover! "Which dam—sell to whom?"

"Not sure. When sure, I certainly tell Dr. Choh."

"Please remember to do so," said Beaumont. "I am especially eager to learn about that dam. I heard that some time ago."

"How could you hear this thing?" asked Mr. Choi. "No person know very much."

"I have a friend in an engineering firm. Also I was at OEC a few days ago. I talked to one of the key men there."

"He not talk about dam." Choi insisted.

"It was an accident that I learned."

"Certainly. It is secret thing. Even much important political people not sure for Korean people permit such thing to do," Mr. Choi continued. He knew a lot about not knowing.

"Who, your friend at OEC?" asked Mr. Kim.

"Martin Jerome."

"He very powerful man," Mr Choi said.

"Mr. Jerome," said Mr Kim, "was American soldier—sergeant for Adjutant General file. He take easy job for more money at OEC. If he somewhere else in world, was for Army. He know nothing else. Mr. Kim was emphatic as he made each point. There was no doubt that he knew Jerome's history.

"How do you know that?"

"This person on committee, related."

"How did he become so powerful?" asked Camden.

"Adjutant General file have much important information. Mr. Jerome know more name and much important thing than OEC Chief. Chief know nothing at all."

"So Jerome become very important man."

Mr. Kim sighed. "That all."

"He soon become more powerful still," added Mr. Pak, "because of after June in this year UNKRRA will be discontinue. Soon all money for Korea by United State through OEC.

"Jerome told me only half that story."

"*Half* all he permit people know, no matter what topic." It was Mr. Kim, again. He would not give up.

"Forgive me about to say thing not kind," said Dr. Choh. "We say these thing to Mr. Camden and Mr. Beaumont. They must to think money what we want repair only. That not so. Money terrible problem for Korea. American money not so wise for terrible thing that America help for doing in my country."

"I am sorry," said Beaumont.

"Not be sorry. Be do something," said the doctor.

"I have already begun to do something. I am learning."

"You learn," said Mr. Choi, "then you tell whole world. Communist already do that. Radio Pyongyang in our north of country each day tell Korean and China and Japan people to see corruption in Seoul. Everybody look; everybody believe. Is so. Radio Peiping say to Asia people: democracy corrupt whole nation. Look South Korea; look Laos; look Taiwan. Everybody look; everybody believe. Is so."

"In Asia," said Mr. Pak, "already you lose face. Must to make important change. "Certainly Communist not then able for tell so much true to win. Then Communist no more say Seoul corrupt and other country corrupt. Then Asia people know these thing lie; then come democracy to Asia. Never before."

For a long while no one said anything. A rustle came from one end of the room, and Camden looked up in time to see the doctor's wife slip from the room. He heard a fragment of conversation and knew for the first time that evening that Ai Ja had been listening to them.

"Naturally are many Communist in South Korea. More come south each day to create problems. But people of South Korea will never forget war. Here very little danger that Communist come into power here. Don't need police state. Communist try very hard but gain nothing."

"Then why has the government established the Anti-Communist Center on Sei Jong Ro?" Beaumont asked.

"A little to fight Communist," said Choi thoughtfully, "but most to control political people who talk against present Administration and so, popular with the people. Now is very easy for discover that political enemy is Communist agent and put him in jail until Korea people forget."

"Has this happened recently?" Camden.

"March this year. Cho, Bong Am jailed as Communist. He popular with Korea people—he challenge rule of House Speaker Ie, Ki Poong. Ie, Ki Poong very powerful Korean person. He tell President what President wish hear. President no more good here." He tapped his head. "So in May election come no opposition for House Speaker Ie. Him honest. Many police. Where democracy?"

"I saw a British intelligence report a few weeks after the election," said Beaumont. "They said it was reasonably honest. Maybe with Cho out of the way, it could afford to be."

"British very good intelligent, but not know all thing. We believe Cho, Bong Am could for challenge President Rhee in 1960 election. Not more possible. Must discover new man."

"Possibly Cho is a Communist," said Beaumont.

"If misfortune not come to every man oppose Administration, we believe one man Communist," said Choi. "But in 1952, opponent kill by army general before election. General was vacation few years in Japan for this crime. Opponent for 1956 suffer cerebral hemorrhage while rest in his railroad car in campaign. Seoul people vote dead man into office. Do American people know that?

"That isn't the version we heard," said Camden. "If we'd heard it told your way, I hope our activities here would have been completely changed by now. Someone has got to make changes pretty soon. Rhee's strongman tactics can't remain."

"You pleasure me to make change," said Dr. Choh quietly. "Perhap we can give you other information that make many thing different."

"I can't promise that I'll succeed."

"Promise if you will try," said Mr. Choi.

"I will try," said Beaumont. "I can't promise more."

Instantly the six Korean gentlemen were enveloped in a rapid conversation in their own language. Once or twice the name *Kim* was mentioned. Abruptly the discussion was ended. Dr. Choh clapped his hands twice and directed a phrase to the servant as she came into the room. The woman departed, and Dr. Choh called out once more. This time his daughter came into the room with a tray of small cups and a bottle of spirits. Without a word she left. But her social graces had been shown. Dr. Choh filled eight cups and left a ninth cup aside. He also observed Camden closely when Choh, Ai Ja was in the room. Sidelong glances probably gave Camden away.

"Korean fruit-brandy," he said as he passed cups to Beaumont and Camden. "You must very surprise."

"I am surprised," said Camden as he tasted. No only good. "Fantastic."

"We think perhap that why drinking against military regulation." It was Mr. Pak speaking, infrequently.

"Everything is against regulations," said Camden. "We follow the few rules that make sense. Actually, we're supposed to know the rules and also to break them. If we're caught, it's our ash on the line."

"And those few rule stay forever," laughed Pak.

"Then you must have been in the American Army, Mr. Pak," said Beaumont facetiously. "Congratulations on your civilian uniform."

"For first time. It fit me very good," said Mr. Pak. "I borrow it from my son. He now use my military uniform. My son is KATUSA on main post." He used the common pronunciation of the acronym designating the Korean Augmentation to the United States Army. He laughed too jovially at his own joke.

"What does he think of the idea—your son?" Camden.

"You not wish hear. American people forget Korea people also very proud."

"Probably it is not so much that we do not remember as that we have never known," countered Beaumont. "How can we hope to learn about Korea when I can't buy a language or history textbook? I cannot even buy a Korean-language textbook easy enough for my students to translate for me. How can anyone hope to learn about Korea—truthfully—when there are no history texts at all?"

"History teach verbal by teacher everywhere in Korea. Many year more before book to allow. Many people must to forget true thing first." Mr. Lim speaking. "History change now."

"If that is so, why haven't any of the thousands of Koreans abroad already told about it?" asked Camden.

"Family here," said Mr. Lim. "This book for travel. Say talking people family be punish."

"Can I see it?" asked Beaumont.

"I get one for you," said Dr. Choh.

"No people talk. Family hurt. Also do never return to Korea," said Mr. Lim.

Beaumont felt that Lim had spoken more than he should have under the circumstances. Yet he was the lawyer among the group and should have been apprehensive. He must know he is among friends. Dr. Choh identified the sources of the information by group, without identifying the individuals. That left an office in the Ministry of Home Affairs. Mr. Pak seemed to have those facts. And the internal security force—that had to be Mr. Choi. An interesting image of sources. Even more important because the men obviously exchanged facts to determine complex meanings. And to discover plots and plans. That's sedition? He wondered. Under Rhee it certainly was.

"Korean Army not be first people forget. Fortunate for Korea people, army control now by America people." Mr. Pak reestablished the subject.

"What is that?" Camden inquired.

"My son—he pay sack of rice and few thousand Hwan in month. Maybe five American dollar. If family, they starving. When he release? Son officer not know when release. Officer, he family hungry. Must steal for live. That why police so strong."

"We are pleasure to be visit with Lum, Ki Yu," said Dr. Choh. "I think he know many interesting thing for tell you. First, for know something about Korea." He said something in their tongue to Mr. Choi, and the latter nodded.

"For thousand year, dynasty of Korea maintain great empire," began Mr. Choi. "Happen many struggle inside country and also many difficulty with other country. Always Korean people fight for free. Then coming Japan people. First conquer our country. Then go with Korea dynasty for annex Korea with Japan Empire. Happen in 1910. Many patriot try create freedom but not fortunate. More thing worse. Patriot read declaration of independence in Seoul in 1919. Many not-happiness happen when town and village burn by angry oppressor. Some patriot escape. Some kill. In Shanghai, some patriot establish provisional government for to keep alive Korea spirit when true independence must come. Ie, Sung Man *first provisional president*. Many problem happen even so because some not honest people in provisional government. Even so, Ie sentence by court of provisional government. Anger. Keep paper and stamp. After, Ie go Hawaii. Japan soldier catch new President Ahn, Chung Ho when he try secret enter Korea. Kill. So Ie, Sung Man show America people old paper and stamp. He president fast." Transliteration problems, both men realized: Choi meant this of President Rhee, Syngman, and both Americans knew that immediately.

Mr. Choi stopped reciting long enough to survey the look of shock he had produced in the Americans. Satisfied that they understood, he continued. "Ie now say he *only* president. He say wish help. He no care about Korea country. No. Japan people own all important thing. Korean people all servant in Korea. Soon end of war for world. Not Korea."

At a sound, Dr. Choh rose. He went to the door and greeted a new guest, an extremely old man. As the guest entered, all the Koreans go to their feet and bowed deeply. The Americans did the same. The old man bowed to each of his countrymen.

"Camden—*sonsaeng*...Beaumont—*sonsaeng*," said the doctor to the Ancient One. To the Americans he said, "Here is Lum, Ki Yu...Lum *sonsaeng*. Ancient One—he patriot."

The two Americans returned low bows to the old man. He had a great dignity in his native costume—white blanket breeches, a black outer coat, a woven black horsehair hat that was as tall as, but skinnier than, a chef's cap. And the pervasive string goatee. The Ancient One took his place at the head of the table, assisted, as he lowered himself, by Dr. Choh. When he was settled, the others sat. Dr. Choh found a seat at the side.

Rapidly, in his own language, Dr. Choh related to the Ancient One the story of the gift of medicine. He told how Camden had smuggled an entire case of medicine past the guards. Even more medicine than the doctor himself had ordered had been delivered, he emphasized. Some fine medical instruments were totally unexpected. Then, he said, the Americans had refused to accept money for the purchases because Camden and Beaumont and their friends had collected enough money to make a gift. The doctor expressed his gratitude again in both languages, and then he waited.

Lum, Ki Yu spoke a few words and paused. Dr. Choh translated rapidly, and the Ancient Once spoke again, pausing while each phrase was rendered. They made a unique team, the doctor and the Ancient. Yet more fluency was needed, and the group decided that all should contribute however he could. The force of the old man's words came fluently through the doctor and guests, who anticipated enough of the Ancient's words to supply occasional verbs in English before they were spoken in the original...the group knew both their language and their mentor well. They had obviously heard the material before.

The Ancient One declared himself highly favored to know Americans with warmth and feeling for human dignity. On condition that the Americans act on its meaning, the history of the Republic would be told by him who was once a *fox at the yellow water*. That had to be the original Rhee provisional government in China. The Ancient One was indeed a patriot!

"Everyone has said that we should help," said Beaumont. "No one has said what you will do for yourselves. Or even what it is that I could do to help."

The doctor related the comment to the Ancient One. First he listened to a few words of the elder's reply (agreed in translation by the others), and then, in phrases that hung in the cool air while the Ancient One advanced another thought, and the doctor translated a plea:

"Please to send home your civilians here; please to send to Korea America people who wish first do much good for Korea, then you help. First to tell America people no freedom in Korea; America people must to know no freedom in Korea; America people must to know difficult thing must to happen; American people not think difficult thing a crime, you help.

"Create public sympathy for a reform movement," mused Camden. "Correct our agency practices.... A tall order. But fair, I suppose. Among our people more concerned with TV."

"We'll try," said Beaumont in a low voice. "We have to."

Dr. Choh relayed the answers, Mr Kim prepared to translate...
The Ancient One began to speak.

### Fable of the Ancient One:

*On the private green*
  *where the crimson head of empire had spent its seed in passing*
  *wandered tether-willed a doe,*
  *white in color like the flustered cap of water,*
  *and the deer was the favored thing*
  *and jealousied of a dynasty of foxes.*

*Rare and flitful*
  *even as a pleasured glance of empire*
  *stepped the White Deer*
  *to the resort of its tether*
  *on the private green*
  *in the desired eye of a jackel.*

*'White Deer*
  *no longer shall be jealousied of blooded foxes,'*
  *said the jackel,*
  *'but shall graze in the public green';*
  *and set the jackel himself to snap the tether*
  *and lead the White Deer*
  *until the keeper set upon and sorely did the jackel.*

*Quick from under a morning sun*
  *fell the wolf pack upon the green*
  *in the manner of the jackal*
  *and undid the keeper fearfully*
  *while the White Deer was torn from tether*
  *on the private green*
  *and closeted in thickets unseen.*

*Nine snows settled with night in the thicket*
  *till a gathering of foxes*
  *took in the night callingly a jackal for its leader*
  *and snapped at wolves; they were hunted*
  *from the public green, the foxes,*
  *by the wolves,*
  *to scatter joylessly and crimson-led*
  *to the yellow water.*

And then it was that foxes
    *in the morning light along the yellow water*
    *saw among their kind stealingly*
    *the jackal nightly called their leader and set upon him*
    *and bonded him in shame;*
    *and quietly among the gathering called they a new leader:*
    *fox among foxes.*

*Snapping at wolves*
    *stood the gathering along the yellow water*
    *until the jackal unbonded set out upon the blue water;*
    *and making him a sign*
    *who was almost of their kind*
    *did the foxes send a jackal hopefully*
    *to the nest of the gamecock.*

*Snapping at wolves*
    *did the leader of the foxes of the yellow water*
    *with his kind*
    *spring upon the public green*
    *and run the thicket,*
    *seeking White Deer.*

*Finished with foxes of the yellow water*
    *went the wolf from its den*
    *to stir a water nest of the gamecock;*
    *and then the gamecock went with angry cries*
    *to its water nest and scattered wolves*
    *and went to the public green and scattered wolves*
    *and to the private green and thicket*
    *to the White Deer;*
    *and called the gamecock*
    *fairly for the leader of the foxes.*

*In the night*
    *was I callingly taken*
    *for the leader of foxes,*
    *said the jackal to the gamecock,*
    *and in the night did he become the keeper of the White Deer.*

And for a sign and night callings
  did the gamecock turn its head from the foxes
  along the yellow water and set a jackal and its kind
  to the keeping of the summer side of the public green
  and of the private green
  and White Deer;
  and did the gamecock set dogs
  to the keeping of the winter side of the public green;
  and set itself to watching from a pavilion on the summer green
  did the gamecock.

Danger, barked the jackals,
  and caused to rise around the White Deer
  a stout wall with careful spaces
  that caused the White Deer to be seen from time to time
  only by the gamecock
  as it preened
  in the pavilion on the summer green;
  and behind the stout wall began to fail
  the White Deer.

From the winter side of the public green
  then came dogs hungrily;
  ran the jackals fearfully;
  to the farthest side of the summer green
  went the failing White Deer
  of foxes.

Spurning dogs went the gamecock
  until the summer green was open
  once again for foxes and the White Deer;
  behind the stout wall bare of careful spaces
  went the White Deer at the resort of its tether,
  pulled by jackals.

Behind the stout wall
  on the private summer green
  went the jackals
  to tend the ailing White Deer;
  while the leader of jackals
  barked in the voice of dogs
  at the gamecock
  preening in its pavilion.

*Then slew the White Deer*
*the jackals*
*and sat outside the stout wall*
*calling upon the gamecock*
*to hear the flailing of the White Deer*
*that was called the sound of life.*

*And to the gamecock hearing and preening*
*went the jackals hungrily to the stout wall*
*on the private summer green*
*and ate their fill;*
*sent the jackals to the stout wall an amber doe*
*rutting and making the sounds of life of the White Deer*
*for the gamecock.*

*Preened and secure*
*in its pavilion on the public summer green*
*sleeps the gamecock*
*standing.*

*   *   *

The Ancient One lowered his head, crushing his string goatee on his chest. He said nothing more, and there was full quiet. Ringing quiet. Clanging quiet.

After a long silence, Beaumont stood. He looked at the Ancient One, the doctor, and the others; and still no one spoke. He bowed, turned, and with Camden just behind, strode from the room and descended the stairs. The two scuffled into their shoes at the entry and hurried into the street.

"Embarrassing, isn't it?" Camden remarked after a time of silence. Camden hailed a taxi. They climbed inside, and as the machine lurched forward, Camden leaned over the front seat and tapped the shoulder of the driver's second.

"To the Pavilion of the gamecock," he said, and the driver's second seemed to understand.

# Chapter Fifteen

Five weeks till going-home-time had become a longer part of his life than he had anticipated and more shapeless and disunited than it should have been. From the time of his first meeting with Young Song until the day Miss Choi, the cousin-sister, had extracted the price of a permanent liaison—that had been five weeks. And three more weeks had gone, counting from the time the party of four had rediscovered Chang Duk palace.

Now, only four more weeks remained, Beaumont realized. If the boat sailed on time…. Then he would be home. Home in the States, that is, because Young Song kept reminding him that her new room was his new home. *Their* new home, to be precise, is what she insinuated, but she never verbalized the thought.

Camden had even less time in Korea, Beaumont recalled. Besides, the situation of Camden was much less complex. Camden was taken with Choh, Ai Ja; but she had risked as little as possible by meeting him only occasionally in unlikely places. Her father, if he knew, tolerated her clandestine affair. *Affair* was hardly the word for such tentative meetings. Choh, Ai Ja probably would be shaken up a bit when Camden left, but, since it couldn't be helped, the end would be relatively painless...not an outright rejection. Lucky, Camden. Unlucky, Choh. Luck, Camden; you'll need it, he thought.

He couldn't say the same for Young Song's situation. She was out of her father's house…. Jobless. Dependent on a soldier now and maybe for some time. Unless she took to that secretarial course. A week—ten days, maybe—she's been enrolled. Business English and typing. Martin Jerome—damn his kind!—expected a Miss Choh but would have to *make-do* with the various Misses Kim as they graduated. Finally that would be Jerome's contribution to an *unimportant* person, if only accidentally. She would finish the typing course almost as soon as Beaumont left the country. Reasonably good timing. And except for the original deception about time yet remaining, there would be no extravagant hurts. It was business, Bo said again to himself. Even from the beginning, she knew it was not love. Somehow, that thought was not consoling to him. To her?

A jeep dusted past him. He set his mind on the jeep and followed it by eye down the hill and onto Hoo Am Dong, just north of the post. The neighborhood of shacks was not really less desirable than the others surrounding the post, and the stone buildings that lined the drainage canal (left by the Japanese invaders) gave an almost substantial look—a facade for news-reel cameras. But the location was acceptable to Young Song, and that was the real consideration.

There were kids in the street. In the gathering dusk, they began to look alike—the chubby ones with straight black hair, who belong there; slim kids with wavy or kinky hair or freckles, who were just passing through while looking for their fathers. It was one with freckles who called out, "Hey, GI. You wan twimin?" He was a big kid-about ten or eleven years old and over-sized, as Koreans go. He should be growing up into a blue Marine uniform or khaki green one, like his dad.

It was a lousy way to run a world. He put his arm around the kid, who had fallen in step beside him. "No, I don't want women.... Why don't you go home?" He hunted for a bill that made up for a night's work undone.

"Ya, GI. Ya. You wan twimin?" The kid really didn't understand his own words.

Beaumont handed him a hundred Hwan note. *"Ka-da, chogi."* Beat it, bum, he said, and the kid vanished. He cursed everything in sight...and then the people who kept it so...us!

Within minutes he had reached the weathered wooden structure where *she* stayed. From the path he stepped into the door-stone, pushed open the door, and stepped into the large empty room. Perhaps someday there would be enough to have something to sell, and the room would make a fine shop. But for now.

A child pushed its head out of a door in the hall directly ahead. As soon as the child recognized the soldier, he popped back inside and slid the door shut. Through the paper doors Beaumont heard a few childish words and the epithet *GI.*

Removing his shoes, he launched himself up the stair, which climbed from beside the hall, passed one or two sets of sliding doors, and stopped before still another. He rapped.

Young Song slid back the door, and he stepped through. She slid the door closed and then turned to him, puckering her lips.

*"Tulyo-yo,"* she said softly. I give to an honored person.

He bent down and kissed her in return. "An honored person gives to me."

"I am sorry," she said with alarm. I am not honored person. You honored person."

He ran his hands feelingly from her shoulders to the small of her back to her firm buttocks to her sheened hair. He tipped her head up and kissed her again. *"Chup chuse-yo,"* he said and put his fingers over her mouth to scotch the protest.

"Will you stay at your home tonight?" she asked.

"Maybe," he answered lightly. An honored person hadn't made a promise.

"Bed check at post?"

"Maybe." He knew it didn't really matter—no one was ever reported, except to reinforce a different infraction. Another silly rule—a formality in case you were caught egregiously and could easily be tagged with wrongdoings of various sorts. Discipline from the Army's heart.

"You arrange. I know it possible."

"Then probably I'll stay at my home tonight."

"I happy," she said, smiling behind fingertips.

"I'm happy, too," he said. "Surpassingly."

"Syrup-ly?" she asked.

"No. A different word. Not important."

"Would you like to go to the movie," she asked. "Or do you like to stay at your home?"

"Tonight's the last time we can see a Shakespeare."

"Bang-bang?"

"No...pfft." Simultaneously with the sound, he made a sword-thrust motion and pushed his finger into her stomach. She was delighted with the joke and returned the action.

"Okay. Get ready," he said.

"I am sorry. I ready for go now."

"Then let's go. We'll be late."

They let themselves out of the room, and Young Song snapped a padlock through the latch.

"Will we go to the Army post?"

"Shakespeare at an Army post?" He laughed. "This is a very important play—a drama. Do you understand?" When she nodded, he added, "So we must see it at Myungbo."

"Myungbo Theatre is very nice," she said. I have been there once." She hesitated. "School girls not permitted to go to movie theatre. Wicket."

"You're a very wicked person anyhow; so it doesn't matter."

"I am sorry. I do not agree to you."

They climbed into their shoes at the foot of the stairs. When they reached the street, Beaumont signaled for a taxi.

"I am sorry. We must not take taxi."

"Why not?" He was perplexed.

"So much money—we spend secretarial school. No more."

"That doesn't matter." The taxi stopped and he opened the door. "Get in."

"I am sorry." She refused to leave the walkway.

Beaumont closed the car door and waved it on.

"You think you're pretty clever, don't you?" he asked in a gruff tone that she knew was false.

"We must to save money," she answered. Two dollars was quite a sum on her economy.

They began to walk the long span to the next thoroughfare. Lights glowed from small windows in the frame structures. They passed shacks with light between the panels, shelters made of canvas and tin and wood haphazardly mated. More wood frame buildings...more tents and hovels. Such was the city of Seoul. Of course it was the fault of the recent shooting war, but *fault* didn't change reality. At the first major intersection they took a snub-nosed bus that jangled to the stop. There were few riders, but the pair took a seat toward the rear, where they were least likely to be stared at and discussed. They jogged along wordlessly, and before long the bus passed the teeming Railway Terminal and rounded the bend to Nam Dae Mun. The clay animals still basked in the electric glow high on the sway-backed gate. Their century never really changed.

Downtown, the city scrambled with activity. There were calls from everywhere as street peddlers hawked wares. Bells, horns, oxen-clatter and cart-callings. Babies scarved to a woman's back. And more bus horns, with drivers' curses to match. There were short people and hungry people; angry people and resigned people; people burdened with "A" frames for dragging their large bundles—or just burdened. There were custom suits in the Western fashion and pieces of school or military uniforms oddly combined. There were rent fabrics and dirt everywhere. More than a year after arrival, he seemed to be hearing and seeing it for the first time. The events of the past few weeks were acting up now, he was sure.

"Here," said Young Song suddenly. "We must to change."

They left the bus, moved to a far corner, and waited for a trolley. Young Song flashed the transfers as they entered. The dilapidated car trolley car clattered eastward, lurching and swaying over the uncertain trackage.

Suddenly there was a piercing whistle. The trolley car stopped, and an irate policeman stood in the entry, shouting at the motorman. As the warning became a harangue, the riders became impatient. Someone made a comment, and the policeman directed more words in that direction. Police were never wrong.

One of the elderly men stood up. Taking a note of currency from his pocket, he dropped it into the officer's hat. He carried the hat through the bus, and most of the riders dropped something in, even if only a few coins worth pennies, to prevent a ticket for the driver. So would this be our legacy to the newly-free Korea? Only time would tell.

"Courtesy S. Martin Jerome," said Beaumont as he dropped a note into the heap.

The elderly gentleman shook the bills into a manageable heap, folded them, handed the folded bribe to the policeman, and returned to his seat. The policeman got off almost ceremoniously, and the trolley moved on.

"When you must to return to the United States?" asked Young Song with great deliberation after a time. Both perceived at once that she would not be simply *left*, but rather, *abandoned*.

"Maybe soon." He corrected himself: "Sooner than I expected. I'm not sure, yet."

She said nothing more until the trolley had reached their stop. "Here," she said and stood.

Beaumont braced himself in the aisle, helped her out of the narrow seating area, and they alighted. A sharp voice reminded the girl that she had not proved a paid a fare, and absently Young Song surrendered her transfer.

"Only *sukosh* distance to Myungbo Theatre," she said and hurried off. "Very soon," she murmured as he drew nearer..."Pfft." She made the motion of the sword toward the belly of the night, and the night died.

But other nights yet lived, and she had so much enjoyed the Shakespeare that he decided on a night at a legitimate theatre to hear *La Traviata,* Verdi's tear jerker that had become the Koreans' National Opera. It was only a concert version (replete with candles lighted against the nightly changeover of electric generators) but Young Song was enchanted. But was he really doing her a favor to introduce her to things that she could not afford to enjoy in the future? Or was he simply, as he told himself, making memories that could warm their evenings? *And why did it matter?* he asked himself. *Really....*

*April 11*<sup>th</sup>

*Because of the son, he thought of them—Miss Choh and Camden. He hadn't really thought of them seriously for years, it seemed. Decades? That was probably more accurate. He hadn't seen Camden since their meeting at Chicago's O'Hare airfield, although they'd talked on the phone occasionally.*

*Bo was at the airfield in Pusan, having gone there in the off chance that this old naval port cum resort area might have attracted Young Song. Then he saw the man.*

*He was airfield staff, wearing a badge with the name 'Camden,' and was obviously a Eurasian in his prime-about thirty years old or so—no, possibly early forties. He had his mother's straight black hair and his father's lantern jaw. It seemed like a sure thing.... And few enough things had, recently.*

*"Is Charles your father?" I asked him.*

*"Yes." Shock. "Yes, he was. Did you know him?"*

*"Maybe. Was Mrs. Choh your mother?" Bo remembered that women kept their maiden name, merely adding the Mrs.*

*"Yes. So you did know them! How wonderful to meet their friend."*

*"How are they?*

*"They are not. Both have died...although not together."*

*"I didn't know. I'm sorry." What did I expect after more than four decades? It's all right." Quickly he changed moods. "What is your name?" He seemed genuinely interested in this ghost of the past. Fair's fair.*

*"Beaumont is my name," he said. Gordon Beaumont."*

*"You are? I remember your articles. My dad showed them to me when I was still in high school. We expected you to come back to see us. Did you never come back before?"*

*"I tried but couldn't get back into the country. Persona non grata, they said. There was too much trouble before I left the first time...But I tried, at least. I actually made the trip. Fool that I was—it was predictable, I suppose, to be refused."*

*"Good for you. You might have done everybody some good."*

*"It's too late now, isn't it?"*

*"Yes. It's committed." But things are not what they were. Better." He looked around nervously and said a few words to a co-worker in Korean. Then he said loudly, "Come with me, Sir, and I'll try."*

*I followed without question.*

*"My grandfather spoke of you, too."*

*"How is Dr. Choh?"*

*"Well enough but very old."*

*When they had moved off a few steps, he said, "You can't be too careful. Many people understand English in Korea these days. Luckily this passenger needs assistance and instructions; luckily I can point them out." He laughed ruefully. "Some things never change."*

*How can they? Even the son of a recent President was convicted of bribery, following a succession of convicted presidents. Could corruption possibly be deeper into the system that we helped give them? Bribery was not unknown in the Orient before we arrived, but did we have to shelter it? And even extend it? Shades of Chiang, Kai Shek! Later he'd read a book by Sterling Seagrave, called The Sun Dynasty, or something similar; it had more of China's real story. Probably Kauffman was right. Or might State finally learn? Apparently State is learning how to link aid and justice in Bosnia. It's much too late for Korea, of course, but Go, Madeleine, go! But Madeleine is already gone!*

*"Are you married?" Bo asked. It was curiosity more than concern, and both knew that. Small talk needs a topic, and it was too difficult to broach the serious things that needed to be known.*

*"No." He was quiet for a moment. "How could I? Except maybe to a Eurasian girl. Half-breeds aren't much admired here. Even after all this time: Half something/half nothing. Marriage never happened to me." Jeffrey was on duty, and so we couldn't spend much more time together, and we talked of many different things cursorily; although he was truly pleased to meet a friend of his folks. They exchanged addresses but knew they might never write. Bo gave Jeffrey both his Korean and U.S. locations although he had already forgotten his father and mother as a matter of practical life—though never in memory. It seemed not too likely that Bo would remember Jeffrey, whom he'd never before known.*

*"Did you know a Miss Kim, Young Song?" I ventured.*

*"She was a friend of my parents, but I haven't seen her for many years. She still lives in Seoul, I think. A nice old woman, really. Actually, I called her my aunt when I was growing up. We've lost contact, I think."*

*So there was no Young Song here. I had visited all the parks and most of the bars in this sailors' town before learning she couldn't have been here. Obviously there could have been no sign of her. Intellectually, I knew that she couldn't be here. But what does intellect really have to do with this trip? It has surely been a mistake, and I should think about going home.*

*So I took my leave of the Camden-Cho kid. That was easy enough: he could make a life well enough without me. To suggest otherwise was to violate his Oriental sense of independence.*

*But the memories.... Last night I found the picture frame that Young Song had given me, and from it she had smiled at me for years...until My Dear Ex found it. No one else would have cared. No one else would have had or wanted access to my old Army duffel bag in the attic. Or would have wanted to destroy the picture.*

*Life goes on.*

# Chapter Sixteen

"What time is it?" asked Camden as they left the confines of the post and crossed into Hoo Am Dong.

"Five of seven," answered Beaumont.

"I told Young Song we'd be there at seven—and we'll just make it."

"Good. I told Ai Ja to come at seven-thirty."

"That makes good sense," Beaumont said sarcastically.

"It does unless you expect me to spend my last few days in Korea at the movies with you."

"Which means that Kim and I should get tired of waiting for Miss Choh and go off to the movies without you."

"Something like that. You're not as dumb as you look."

"And what time can we get back?"

"Give me a couple of hours."

"What if she has other ideas?"

"Then we'll be a half-hour late to the movies."

"Plus five minutes for the old college try. Are you going to tell her your departure date before or after the main event?"

"Sometimes, Bo, I think I underestimate you."

"Everyone does," Bo answered. "And now, won't you come into my parlor?"

They went into the empty shop room, were scanned from the hall by a child as they removed their shoes, and went up to Young Song's room. Her door was partly open, and the two stepped quickly inside. Beaumont slid the door shut behind them.

"Good evening," called young Song. "We are waiting for you." She rose to meet them.

"Hi," said Beaumont. He put his arm around her, but she moved away immediately. He knew he should have known that self-respecting Korean people didn't show affection in public or in front of others: shame.

"Hello, Miss Kim," said Camden, and he received a bow in return. It had seemed to become a logical way to greet.

"I am sorry. Do you not see my cousin-sister, Miss Choi?" asked Young Song.

"Good evening, Miss Choi," said Beaumont.

"Good evening, GI," she replied to him with an effort. Then she made a respectful gesture toward Camden, who acknowledged it.

"Now that we're all here, the whole family can go out to the movies. 'Movies are better than ever' I hear," Beaumont laughed, quoting the current filmland slogan.

"Excruciatingly funny, Bo!" Camden exclaimed. I don't need blind dates."

"Miss Choi not wish go PX for eating. So Miss Choi and Miss Kim eat at Korea restaurant."

"Now or before?" asked Beaumont. Verbs without tenses really hampered communications, he knew anew.

"Already," said Young Song.

"That was very thoughtful," said Camden.

"What else have you done?" asked Beaumont.

"We have discuss. Thing," answered Young Song.

"Miss Kim and me—we discuss many thing as happily friend," said Miss Choi. "Please be seat," she added, and the men did so. Would it be a game of who's in charge?

"What did you talk about?" asked Beaumont, his irritation beginning to rise.

"Many thing," Young Song said. "We discuss Shakespeare movie 'Pfft' at Myungbo Theatre. Remember, last week?" She made a sword thrust of remembrance. "Also *La Traviata*."

"I remember. What else?" Beaumont.

"We discuss secretarial school."

"What else?" Beaumont, again.

"We discuss maybe soon you go back to United State." She hesitated. "*Kwaenc ansumnikka?*" It didn't matter.

"*Sayang-ch'i masipsio,*" Beaumont replied without conviction, and Young Song knew that despite the words, it did indeed matter.

"Will you, also, travel to the United State soon?" Miss Choi asked of Camden.

"In about eight days," he answered.

"I am sorry," said Young Song into the silence.

"Troop ship seven day. Also three week," said Miss Choi.

"That doesn't mean I'll be on it," lied Beaumont. He swore under his breath because he had learned only yesterday about he troop movements. The Korean grapevine was unbeatable.

"No, GI?" As if to say "I can be convinced."

"I guess we're all sorry that I'm going," said Camden.

"Perhaps we must now to go to the movie," said Young Song to Beaumont. "Perhaps not happily friend must discuss this thing."

Beaumont laughed aloud. "You're magnificent." He then attempted to pull her close to him, but she drew away.

"I'm sorry," said Young Song quietly. "Friend must not to see." She sat at a distance.

Hers was a perpetual innocense, and both men felt it.

Beaumont stood up. "Shall we go?" Taking her wrist, he helped Miss Kim to her feet. "We don't want to be late."

"Miss Choh come, yes?"

"She's not here yet," said Camden. "You'll miss the movie. Hurry. We'll follow in a few minutes."

Young Song took a coat from a glassed wardrobe. She turned to the pair still seated on the floor. "You perhap be away when we return. Good night." She turned, picked up Beaumont's shoes, and carried them into the hall for him.

To Miss Choi he said, "Mr. Camden will stay with you until Miss Choh comes...if she comes." He hesitated. "Maybe something happened," said Beaumont. "See you at the post at seven-thirty-five, Chas," said Beaumont from the doorway. "They've remade all our plans." To Miss Choi he said in his best form, "*Annyong-i kesipsio.*"

"*Annyong-i kasipsio,*" she said pleasantly.

Beaumont slid the door shut. Amost immediately Young Song shoved her head through it again. A crush of words in her language brought a single word in reply from Miss Choi. "They must to lock the door," said Young Song, and she led the way downstairs.

The pair within the room heard the street door slam behind the others. Avoiding his look, Miss Choi turned her attention into the room, which was generously furnished with various things Western, although not in matching suite: a chair; the glassed wardrobe, which more or less separated the bed from the rest of the room; a bureau with a crown of cut glass bottles; a radio; a record player; somewhat fancy curtains. It was a relatively large room, by Korean standards, but far too small for a gaggle of strangers.

Camden lifted a stack of records from the turntable, reset the automatic changer, and switched on the machine. A ballad began to play, and he tuned it into the background. Love music was not appropriate for sitting with Miss Choi. They both recognized that. Then, recognizing that the situation was not the best test for her, Miss Choi decided that she had forgotten something and needed to leave.

"Must to hurry," she said as she put on her street coat. "Must much to hurry." She scurried out, banging doors behind.

Camden lay on the bed, shoes on, to get a few minutes of relaxation while he could. He listened to the Korean records, which contained more wail than an American pop song but were nonetheless interesting to listen to. But he'd had the Kim Sisters' imitation of American records for more than a year, in which time had stopped; and he didn't need more. Eight days to home. It seemed like forever...less one day nearly gone.

Abruptly, Miss Cho, Ai Ja arrived, accompanied by the hallway child as a guide.

"Is correct, this place?" she asked humorously as she entered.

"It's correct if you know the person here," he answered.

She sat in a plush chair, which probably seemed home-like to her, although foreign to Miss Kim, Young Song. How different were the backgrounds of the girls, and yet they were caught up in the same type of liaison, he felt. Well, actually not. But he could dream, couldn't he?

"Where Miss Kim?"

"At the movies. I told you the wrong time. I'm sorry. Did you want to go to the movies? We still can if we hurry."

"If you like," she said listlessly.

"What's wrong?" he asked.

"Not wrong. Okay."

He knew that she knew that he was surely leaving. But how could the subject now be broached? They made idle conversation for a time...nothing that needed to be discussed, certainly. It wasn't even a test for her limited but ever-improving English. Another Korean ballad began to play. He lighted a small lamp and turned out the electrical bulb overhead.

He knelt before her chair and took her face between his palms. She looked down on him. Her stroked her cheeks and traced the hairline behind her ears. He ran his hands along her neck and fingered her throat. She look at him less than hostilely, he thought. Time passed. Quickly or slowly. He didn't bother to look at his watch—it didn't matter. Finally, her reserve spilled, and he blotted it with gentle hands and kept it for his own. She placed her hands on his wrists, slipped her thumbs under the cuffs of his shirt, and bruised the sinews. She stretched her hands along his arms, kneaded his shoulders, and slipped a hand inside his shirt when a button gave and admitted a tentative hand.

After a time of tracery, he moved his hand dragging it from her waist to remolded her firm breasts in the press of his fingers, and rested again at the small of her neck. He drew her head forward, leaned to meet her, and exchanged a kiss. She gave him her eyes and he gave her a kiss.

Then he stood against her hold, scooped her from the floor, and settled her on the bed. He lay beside her, and they caressed and explored each other with lengthening runs of quick hands. Then he put aside her clothing and his own and created a woman.

They lay together for uncounted time, until even their untuned ears caught the repeat and repeat of the last record in the stack. It was an American melody.

"What song is that?" she asked after humming its melody. "It is very beautiful."

"It's called *All the Things You Are*. It's very old—older than I am."

"Can you sing it?"

"I can't sing. It's horrible, my voice."

"Never, I forget," Ai Ja promised.

"Me neither. That is our misfortune," he promised in return.

"I do not understand."

"Neither do I," he confessed.

After a time he roused himself from the bed, dressed, and gathered apparel for Ai Ja. When she had dressed, Ai Ja went to the record player, switched off the machine, and took the top record from the stack. She read the label and returned the disk to the rack.

"Are you ready?" Camden asked.

She nodded, and they went into the hall. Carefully Ai Ja snapped the padlock into the latch. At the bottom of the stairs, they slipped into their shoes and then into the street.

They got into a taxi, and with his hand shielding her face from the passers by, went north toward her home.

They borrowed the Hoo Am household again for the whole of an afternoon when the weekend arrived. They talked of his going and of her visiting America. And with the chosen record playing repeatedly in the background, they commingled new feelings and became other beings. They were spent with the day, and they left without awaiting the arrival of friends.

Without warning Choh, Ai Ja was back that day. Unexpectedly she burst in on an evening of Kim, Young Song and Beaumont and railed in her language. She sat in a dark corner with her face averted so they could not see the bruises.

"Miss Choh father very angry," Young Song explained after Choh, Ai Ja had ceased to talk. "You must to bring Mr. Camden to this home, please."

Beaumont went out immediately. He hurried south on Hoo Am Dong, and when he reached the military reservation, turned into the Signal Corps compound. From there he telephoned the unit and reached Camden by messenger to the barracks.

Fifteen minutes passed before the two met at the foot of Hoo Am Dong.

"He beat the hell out of her," Beaumont replied in answer to an inquiry. "You might have to go over to her house sometime. Not now. Now she's at Young Song's. He probably threw her out."

"All I need right now is to get into a fight. It'll take me five years to get out of this country. We'll work it out another way. I have to."

"If you like I can say I couldn't find you...."

"I can't abandon Ai Ja to this."

Worldlessly after that they walked to Young Song's house. Beaumont remained behind as Camden went upstairs. Camden rapped on the door, and Young Song slid it open to admit him.

"Bo is waiting for you downstairs," he said, and Young Song went out.

Miss Choh didn't look at him, and when he greeted her, she didn't answer. It was serious beyond words.

"I'm very sorry," Camden said after a time.

"Thank you. Everything now happily," she said. "Thank you for sorry."

"Can you go home?"

"Never."

"We'll fix it up."

"What mean *fix?* Already we complete. Father." There was no animation in her features or voice.

Camden sat on the end of the bed and tried not to watch her. Finally she went to the record player, selected one and put it on the spindle. "Do you forget this song?" she asked. In a moment the melody of *All the Things You Are* assaulted them.

"No, I won't forget it."

"You not go United State, Charl. You must to employment at OEC."

"That's not possible."

"Is possible. I know. Is possible."

"In two days I go to Inchon. After three days I will be on the ship."

"You not go. You must to take care of me. You not go." Her voice was rising in pitch and intensity. "You not."

He crossed toward her and put his hand on her shoulder. She grimaced and beat his hand away.

"Now I street girl. Thank you."

"Shut up with that kind of talk."

"True. You go away. I be street girl. No father. No house. I find soldier."

He grabbed her shoulders and shook her.

"Take hand off!" she shouted. "You lousy, GI. Lousy GI. Everybody tell me. I not believe. Is true."

"I love you very much. I was very happy."

"You. Not Miss Choh! You go United State, GI," she shouted. Then she bolted to the record player, seized the single disk, and smashed it on the bureau. I *hating* you."

A word from the movies, no doubt. He felt humiliated for having thought of such trivia now. He bent down, picked up a piece of the recording disk. He tossed it in his hand and then slipped it into his pocket. "I will never forget."

The gentle gesture stunned her. Then she came alive with an anguish that welled from her core. She threw her arms around his neck and rested her whole weight upon him. Her entire body cried against him. He carried her to the bed and sat her on the edge. She fell back and lay still.

"Charl, she said after minutes, "Not go without me. Not leave me."

"I love you very much," he said.

He bent down to kiss her, and she crooked an arm around his neck. When he straightened up, she was raised with him. He lowered her again.

"I'm sure you can stay here tonight," he said. Miss Kim is your friend. Tomorrow I will bring you some money, and we'll find a place for you to stay for a few days."

"That not important," she said quietly. As an afterthought she inquired, "You love me?"

"Very much."

"I not think so." She relaxed her hold.

Camden pushed away from her, turned off the light, shed his uniform and went back to her. She took him in quickly and with desperation, needing his firmness. Violently it was over. He smoothed her garments and brushed his fingers through her hair. Then he was up and dressed.

"Tomorrow," he said. He lighted the lamp and went outside.

As Camden crossed into the street, Beaumont called. He had been waiting. They met almost in the center of the street: three of them; none knowing exactly what needed saying.

At Camden's question, Young Song said, "Miss Choh stay this home. We happily friend."

"I'll be back in the morning," Camden said to either. I can give her enough money to get by until her father has quieted. Why did this have to happen?"

"Getting quiet could take a while," Beaumont said. "He's hinted at knowing before."

"It's all I can do at this late date."

Beaumont shrugged. "If I can help...I'll see you tomorrow," he said to Young Song, and a gentle push started her toward the house. When she was inside the gate, Beaumont and Camden set out for the post.

"They say that Caesar were ambitious," said Beaumont after a fair time.

"And grievously hath Caesar paid for it...with his military credit card."

"Your credit is still good there," Beaumont observed.

"It's just that the payments are somewhat steeper than expected." They passed the sentry box at the top of the long incline and moved into the post proper.

"Dr. Choh is right," said Camden after a time. "At least on the surface this alliance between Ai Ja and me seems as shoddy as any in the country. And I'm not even sure that even Ai Ja knows that the difference exists...and that we know it."

"Did you promise to marry her?"

A long pause. "More or less. Before."

"Then try giving her assurance instead of money. She'll keep it longer."

"Presto-chango. Besides, look who's talking."

"That's your problem, Pal. I never promised mine."

111

## Chapter Seventeen

"Only one minute. Sit, please."

Dr. Choh went back into his office, leaving the soldier in the anteroom. Beaumont sat for a time, grew restless, and began to browse the spines of the countless books that lined the small case near the entry. There were many written in Japanese, numerous more in Chinese, and several in English. Some Korean, of course. One was the recent gift from the elder Camden to the elder Choh; Beaumont picked it up and leafed through. Already there were notations and markings in the margins. Dr. Choh was dedicated.

"Also," said the doctor, returning, "I wish to know—is book gift or payment?"

"A gift," said Beaumont immediately. "I have no doubt. Neither should you."

Dr. Choh ignored his assurances. "If we give nothing in return—it is gift. Some person—surely it was not this person—gave my daughter. Therefore it is payment."

"If someone as knowing as a doctor could say such a thing, I have no doubt, it is in jest."

"This person cannot jest you my daughter."

"If you have suspected for a long while, why didn't you object sooner?"

"Certainly. I know. Each time Choh, Ai Ja and Mr. Camden met at tea room or restaurant, I know. Each time she come home sorry. Perhaps this American person should respect Korean person. He was her teacher. I wish to believe all proper it should be."

"My friend Camden did respect your daughter. He does respect her."

"Mr. Camden took my daughter to his bed to be prostitute. For that she is sent away."

"Perhaps Mr. Camden loves your daughter."

"Perhaps all soldiers love all prostitute. They return to United State. To show love. Now Mr. Camden go back to United State. Choh, Ai Ja is here...this not same thing?"

"Two people must love, Dr. Choh, and nobody knows why or how well. How can you change that?"

"In your country, perhaps. In Korea only one woman for have, make love—maybe nobody. Still are baby. Choh, Ai Ja now fear that. We do not live like American movie. Choh, Ai Ja belong to me. Only this person give her away. Mr. Camden think he buy my daughter with medicine? That is insult!" The doctor spoke his words with great force, and yet quietly. His calm was beginning to leave him. "Mr. Camden not welcome here. Nevermore."

"Mr. Camden is gone, now. You can relax. He left money to rent Miss Choh a house. Now he can keep her well for a time...until he can act properly."

"Like a prostitute."

"Or Miss Choh can go home to her father's house—like a dutiful daughter."

"This no more her house."

"You have made a great mistake."

"Only I am Korea person. You not know."

"Mr. Camden wishes to marry your daughter."

"He not marry her. How I believe?"

"Believe it because I am telling you."

"You ask too much from this humble person."

"You ask much of me—to believe what you say and what your friends have told you. Should I not believe my American friend, Jerome, instead?"

"Do you visit a Korean girl, Mr. Beaumont?"

"Yes."

"You love her?"

"I am fond of her."

"You love her?"

"Probably not."

"Is she prostitute?"

"No."

"And when you go away—what?"

"I am now sending her to secretarial school." She will be able to obtain a better job than when I first met her."

"Better job. For that you take our women? She is of the family of the Ancient One. Perhaps it be better to leave her with her father."

"Her father was at home when I first visited her house. Her mother was there. Her sister. Her brother. Her cousin. It was business.

"Shame-shame."

Beaumont shrugged. "Some things are necessary. They are not the fault of the soldier. They are life after war. Who benefit? Not us!"

"I sorry to hear. Not mistake me," said Dr. Choh. "I know is necessary because of Korea government. Also I know soldiers need women. In whole world is big army men and small army women. Korea people do not like. I not angry for that. I angry for be sometime friend—sometime stranger. Mr. Camden cheat me. Now he is stranger."

"And I?"

"Perhap you also. We know soon."

"How will you know? I am going home soon, like all soldiers. I do not wish to marry anybody."

"You make promise. To me. To Kim, Ki Yu, who is the Ancient One. To many person. Now you must help. I will know. Then you be friend or stranger."

"We call that blackmail."

"I understand word. Now you are mistake. I wish help from true friend. Blackmail from enemy." He thought for a moment. "Perhap now we blackmail enemy even for help."

"I have promised to try to help. I will try. But you must remember that I am not doing this thing for myself," Beaumont protested. "I am doing it for all Koreans. I will do it most of all for the Korean girl I keep. You call her prostitute, but she can help her family. Will they take help from a prostitute? Will you?"

"If I must."

"But you will not take your own daughter into your house again."

The doctor was silent for a time. "Send her to my house," he said. "For you I do this, Mr. Beaumont. "Not Mr Camden. Now I have repay for any medicine. We are complete."

"We are not complete if Choh, Ai Ja is not yet welcome in your house. It is not finished yet. Not complete," Beaumont persisted.

"Perhap in time she welcome. Now only she sleep my house. Is enough. For you I do."

"All right. We're quits. If I help, we're friends; if I don't help?"

"Then we are stranger."

"That's fair enough." Beaumont bowed to acknowledge the agreement, but he received no courtesy bow in return.

"When will you travel to United State, Mr. Beaumont?" asked the doctor.

"In exactly one week, I'll leave for Inchon." Everyone knew the name of the sea harbor for Seoul. "Then we'll sail a few days after that."

"Certainly I meet with you again."

"Possibly not," said Beaumont. "I'm sorry if we do not."

"That not important now. Therefore you must take this thing. He left the anteroom and returned almost immediately with a packet of papers. "Last time, when Ancient One speak with us, Mr. Lim told you about this thing. It is book that tell Korea people that they be punish if talk about Administration when travel." He handed the papers to Beaumont.

Beaumont thumbed the pages. They were ordinary sheets of coarse paper stock bearing oversized characters in the Korean language. The edge was stapled.

"Inside," said the doctor, "I have written what means all words. Never you tell who gave you this thing."

"I asked several of my sources about the Ancient One's fable. Everybody here seems to know about Rhee and the original provisional government that dismissed him for corruption."

"Everybody who *old* Korea people know. Child, not know. That why can be no history book permit in Korea. No true. If America people not know, now must to learn, sure. Will die, the White Deer."

"Even if we are strangers, Dr. Choh, you can trust me for silence. I promise not to jeopardize you or your friends. Because we are friends—you and I—there is no danger."

"I believe you, Mr. Beaumont.... Thank you tell honest for Miss Kim. All, already I know."

"Thank you, Dr. Choh."

"Send Choh-*sonsaeng* to her father."

"Right away. Thank you. You will be surprised. Goodbye."

"For all time—goodbye."

"For a brief time——goodbye," corrected Beaumont.

"We know soon."

The doctor smiled a seldom smile and paid the courtesy of a slow and proper bow. Beaumont returned the courtesy and left.

# Chapter Eighteen

From their house the pair rode north on Hoo Am Dong to the junction at Nam San—South Mountain. The driver stopped for a moment while Young Song pointed out yet again the statue of the President, who artfully proclaimed the independence of the city while giving it little.

Independence from the Japanese. Not yet from the Americans, not yet. Beaumont declined to walk up the long flight of stairs to the base of the monument. He motioned to the driver, and the taxi rolled down the incline that bridged a flat of tented dwellings at the foot of Nam San. In a moment they passed the slum at South Gate market and rounded Nam Dae Mun gate. The creatures on the swayback gate never seemed to tire of sunning themselves in electric suns. No one else in Korea seemed to have that luxury.

They turned up Tae Pyung Ro, and as they neared Duk Soo Palace, drove into Jung Dong, a narrow corridor that made its way among the diplomatic quarters. In a few minutes they had reached one of the office buildings into which the OEC had spilled.

"You're sure you remember all the things I told you?" he asked as the taxi pulled into the graveled lot.

"Yes, I remember," she answered. Then, as she followed Beaumont out of the car she added, "You think they like me to work here? Sure?"

"Of course I think so." He paid the fare, and as they started up the stairs of the brick building, the taxi pulled away. "Do you have the application blanks?" he asked once more.

"I am sorry. I already tell you—yes."

"All right. I'll wait for you outside.

"You go inside and get the job! Good luck." He kissed her forehead and let her into the building.

Young Song found the receptionist, presented her papers and asked to see S. Martin Jerome.

"Have you been seen at the employment office at Eighth Army compound?" asked the receptionist.

"No," Young Song answered, "but Mr. Jerome tell my friend that I must to come and see him."

The receptionist made a call, explained the circumstances, and hung up. "He will see you in just a few minutes. Would you care to sit down." It was not really a question. She pointed out a bench, and Young Song sat. A Korean guard glanced her way occasionally but said nothing. Before long the receptionist took a call and directed Young Song to a room on the second floor. She went upstairs and found the number. A gentle rap brought no response, and after a moment she repeated the knock—once, tentatively. Miss Moon opened the door and greeted Young Song in their tongue. She motioned toward a chair, and Young Song took it.

"I'll be with you in a moment," said S. Martin Jerome from across the room. "I believe your name is Kim, isn't it?"

"Yes, Sir. My name is Kim, Young Song."

"And I invited you to come here?"

"My friend told me you wish to see me."

"Who?"

"GI Mr. Beaumont."

"All right."

S. Martin Jerome turned his attention back to his secretary. He selected several papers and gave instructions. As she took her place at her typewriter, he spoke up again.

"I might have to give Miss Kim a typing test, Miss Moon. Would you use the typewriter in the other office? I'll call you when I'm finished here."

"Yes, Mr. Jerome," said Miss Moon. She went out.

"Now, what can I do for you?" asked Jerome as he pushed his chair away from his desk and dropped his hands to saddle his stomach.

"I wish to be a secretary," answered Young Song.

"Can you type?"

"Yes, Sir."

"Fast?"

"Thirty word each minute. More."

"Where are you learning?"

"At secretarial school."

"Isn't that expensive?"

"Yes."

"Do you have that kind of money?

She was puzzled at the colloquialism. "No, Sir."

"Well, then, how can you go to secretarial school?"

"My brother help me."

"Is he in the Army?"

"Yes, Sir."

"You don't have to say *Sir*. We're not in the army. Is your brother in the American Army?

She was openly distressed as she answered, "He not longer in the Army. He at home."

"Very good. So you're available once again."

"Yes, Sir. I can employ very soon."

"There's a little bit more to it than that." He took a sheet from his desk. "Let's see you put this draft of a letter in final form. Can you do that?"

"Yes," she said. "I can to do that."

117

"Good. Then go ahead."

Young Song sat down at Miss Moon's desk and set a sheet of letterhead in the carriage. She counted spaces very carefully and then began to type. As she worked, the door opened. She was careful not to look up, but the voices distracted her. She stopped typing but started again as soon as she caught herself.

John Lim had come into the room. He dropped a sheaf of papers on his own desk and sat down. In answer to his name he got up again and joined Jerome at the latter's desk.

"I'm afraid you're making the young lady nervous, John. Why don't you go and get a breath of fresh air—or do some library research? You'll probably be gone at least a half hour."

John Lim exchanged a long look with S. Martin Jerome. Then he went out of the room and down the stairs. He nodded to the guard, and then, taking a cigarette from his pocket, stepped outside. Even outside there was no freedom from the office.

"You have been here before, I think," John Lim said to Beaumont after he had lighted his cigarette. "Upstairs. Is she your friend?" Beaumont nodded. "Does Mr. Jerome know that?"

"I don't know—I think so." Which answer was proper? "I'm afraid I've forgotten your name. Mine is Beaumont. I'm sorry."

"That does not matter. My name is John Lim." His diction was essentially faultless without being flawless.

They shook hands.

"Do you have a lawyer in your near-family?" asked Beaumont.

"My uncle is a lawyer," answered the young Lim. "Do you know him?"

"I have met *one* lawyer by your family name. But whether he is your uncle, I don't know."

"Possibly it was my uncle. Of course there are many lawyers named *Lim*. It is a very large clan...Korean style.

"Our conversation would seem to make that so."

"Our conversation?"

"Your uncle's and mine."

"I understand." He thought for a moment. "He has very interesting ideas."

"So has this man whom I met. And he probably has a good deal of information besides. It rather surprised me."

"Information travels very fast in Seoul, you know."

"I've found that out. After a moment without conversation, Beaumont asked, "How soon will Miss Kim be finished."

"She was typing a letter when I came downstairs. I did not wish to disturb her. It will not be very long before she is finished with the letter. Perhaps you would wish to be there."

"Thank you, but I don't want to push."

"Then why do you not wait inside? They are in Room 207. It is more comfortable inside. There is a bench near the door of 207."

"It's cooler out here, I think. And fresher. I don't mind standing. But thanks, anyway."

"Very soon she will be finished with her letter. Perhaps you would want to be inside."

John Lim snuffed out his cigarette and went inside. After a time Beaumont followed. He took a seat on the bench and avoided the glance of the receptionist. He listened, and from time to time caught a phrase that rang with what he thought was Jerome's tone. He settled himself for a long wait until Young Song had finished her first test.

"You have definite possibilities, Miss Kim," said S. Martin Jerome as he inspected her first letter. Then he unsettled himself from the desk and walked across the room. He dropped his bulk on a leather couch that filled the wall behind the door. "How soon are you able to start work?"

"I can start employ next week," she said.

"And what about your evenings? Sometimes our late hours has us meeting in unusual places.

"I do not mind to work hard," she answered.

"Why don't you come over here and sit down? Be comfortable, and we can have a friendlier chat."

Young Song sat cautiously at the far end of the long couch.

"So your brother has gone home from the Army now. That means he and you are now unemployed, and you have to make your own way for a while, doesn't it? Have you had other jobs before?"

"This my first employ. I graduate secretarial school."

"I'm not sure we can use you here at OEC. But of course we cannot make that decision overnight. I have to talk it over with several of the other men. Then we might get together—just the two of us—and talk about it." He tried to put his hand on her knee, but she pulled away. "Someplace quiet," he continued. "When are you free?"

"I can wait here. I do not mind."

"Of course you don't. What about an evening?"

She thought for a moment. "Perhaps. If it is necessary. I can to wait now. I do not mind."

"As I said, we cannot make that decision overnight. You cannot wait. Others might want to interview you. Evenings, okay?

She thought for a moment. "Possible. If it necessary."

"I think it might be necessary.... You look like a real class act in those clothes, Miss Kim. Is that a gift from your Army brother?"

"A Korean tailor made my dress."

"What's it made of?" He slid his hand across her shoulders.

"It is made of solid color fabric," she said with authority, having studied the labels.

"You know all the answers, don't you?"

"I study at secretarial school."

"But that isn't where you learned all about the birds and bees, is it?" He rubbed her shoulder and put a finger her hair.

"I not understand this word." She pulled away.

"Sure you do. Jobs are hard to get. So they go to the people who do most to please. It's simple."

"I be very please for to do OEC employ."

"Would you?" He got up and shot a small bolt on the door. Immediately he was back. He sat close to her, and she inched away. He laughed. "All the broads play hard to get. It's worse here than in the States."

"Please. Do not," she said as he took her hand.

"I'm not going to hurt it," said Jerome. He laid her hand on his inner thigh and clapped his own hand over hers. With his free hand, he touched her hair.

"Please. Do not!"

"You knew what you were in for. Student, he said. You're only his moose." He leaned over and tried to kiss her, but she ducked away. "Don't be so goddamn stubborn," he said. "It won't get you anything but fired. And you're not even hired yet."

She tried to stand, but he held her fast against the back of the couch.

"Do not!" she said, frantically.

"Do you want a job or don't you?" He tried to touch her breast and, failing that, tried to undo a hair bun.

She wrenched, and several buttons tore free. "Bo!" she shouted as loudly as she could manage. "Help me!"

He clapped a hand over her mouth. "Shut up!"

She grabbed his hand and tried to pull it away from her face, but he held tight. She tried to bite but failed. Then she scratched his arm, and he cursed her.

Then someone tried the door. It rattled. Jerome jumped up. Then there was a heavier weight against it.

"Bo!" she shouted again.

The weight hit the door again, and the small catch broke. Beaumont was inside, and without a word he put the whole force of his body behind his fist.

Jerome fell against the book case. I didn't touch her," he shouted. Then he tried to roll from a kick loosed at him. The boot caught him in the ribs, and he lost his wind.

Beaumont grabbed Young Song's arm. "Get downstairs," he said. "Go!"

She started to run, and he followed close behind. As they reached the stairs, the guard appeared at the bottom. Beaumont passed her on the stair and took her arm as she reached the first level. Young Song hesitated, and Beaumont took her shoulders and pushed her forward. The guard spread his arms to halt them. A harsh Korean command sounded, and the guard whirled to find John Lim upon him.

"I tried to tell you," Lim said as they passed. "But Americans don't want to understand." Then he told the guard to forget everything because nothing had happened and started up the stairs. On the avenue, Beaumont hailed a taxi. He put Young Song inside. "Go to our house. And stay there. Do you have money?"

"Yes. I have money."

"Then go. Don't worry...*Ka-seyo*," he said to the taxi driver.

At the command, the taxi driver moved off. Beaumont called another taxi and went another way.

"Did you catch him, Lim?" asked Jerome frantically.

"Catch whom?" asked Lim in return.

"That goddamn soldier."

"I saw him as he went out the door. I did not see him before the time I heard running. I was outside. Smoking."

"Where's the guard?"

"Elsewhere, I think. There was no time to see anything."

Jerome rubbed his jaw. With a handkerchief he lifted blood from the nail cuts on his arm. "I wouldn't hire his moose; so that bastard clipped me." He went to his phone. "What's his name? I'll get him good."

"I do not know him."

"He was here a couple of weeks ago."

"I'm afraid I do not remember."

Jerome took up the handset and jiggled the switch. "Get your record book and give me the name of every soldier that's been in this place during the last month. Fast!" He hung up. "If that bastard thinks he's ever going home, he's got another guess coming."

"It is surely better not to make trouble."

"I'll make more trouble than ten guys can handle. Just who in the hell does he think he is—taking a swing at me!"

"That is most unfortunate," said Lim, pointing at the nail marks. "She, too?"

"Find his name, Lim. You know who he is."

"I do not know."

"Then go downstairs and help Carol find it!" He shuffled papers. "That Kim bitch called him something. Bowman, maybe. Try the post locator. Well, go!" he shouted.

Lim went quietly out of the room and down to the receptionist, quietly reminding the guard, as he passed, that the guard had seen and remembered nothing. Then he smiled and set industriously about *not* finding a name.

# Chapter Nineteen

As she admitted him to the waiting room of Dr. Choh's office, the servant said brokenly, "Doctor—soon." With that she had exhausted her English-conversation vocabulary. When Beaumont pointed to the telephone, she made a shrug and went off, returning almost instantly to grant an unspoken permission with a gesture.

Beaumont dialed and waited. He heard a busy signal and hung up. He waited, dialed again, and hung up. After a longer wait, his call went through.

"*Yo bose-yo*" Beaumont answered the clerk. "Karl Kauffmann." Momentarily, Kauffmann answered. "Karl...Gordon."

"How are you, Gordon?"

"I'm not sure yet. Problems. Listen. I need a favor."

"Of course. What is it?"

"I've just had a fight with S. Martin Jerome at the OEC office. I took Young Song—a Korean friend—there to get a job. He made a pass at her. I bopped him."

"Why did you not tell me? I could find work for her to do in my shop."

"That would be an imposition."

"And this is not?...What is it that I should do?"

"Do you know anybody at OEC who could convince Jerome not to make a Federal case out of this?"

"Nobody at OEC can tell Jerome anything. But possibly I can notify the foreign news correspondent who is here. If he knows both sides of the incident, surely Jerome will see the wisdom of caution. Where are you now?"

"I'm at Dr. Choh's office. I told you about him. I'll stay here for a while. I think it's best not to go back to the post until I know what to expect."

"Expect not too much. There are other people who can embarrass Jerome if he gets the MP's after you."

"I could be an imitation hero, Karl, and sit around the post waiting. But I think I know Jerome. If this goes as far as a court martial—me against an OEC officer—my chances are slim. And if it goes to a Korean court, I'll be around six months or more—waiting."

"I don't know why it would go to the Koreans. This is, after all, an American incident in an American office."

"But Young Song is involved—a Korean national."

"Maybe so. I'll get after the news services. And, Gordon—" but he was cut off.

"I can get some money if you need to buy silence in other places," said Beaumont. Use his methods against him."

"I'd rather not do it that way. We'll try to work it through the newspapers."

"Don't expect too much of them. After all, no one has shown much interest in your information yet. There's an old phrase linking discretion and valor. It just might apply to this situation."

"You're very stubborn. We'll see how things turn up. If nothing else seems to work quietly, I'll see his Korean-born wife. She's his passport here. But it's close to being over for you, and she might not be interested. But it could clear things. If necessary."

"Thank you, Karl."

"I have done nothing, yet. I'm sorry I can think of nothing definite now. Give me the doctor's number. I won't be able to find it in the book."

Beaumont read off the digits. Repeating them, Karl hung up after the briefest farewell. At once he picked up the receiver and dialed. He reached the hotel switchboard at the Bando Hotel and asked for the bar.

"There's an American newspaper man around the hotel," Kauffmann said to the barkeeper. "Is he there?"

"Possibly. You will wait, please."

Kauffmann waited impatiently while the handset was dropped on the counter. Then it was lifted.

"Sanders talking—World-Wide."

"This is Kauffmann. You told me to call you if ever I got a line on something."

"Sure thing, Kauffmann. Good to hear from you. What's happening?"

"Plenty of things that you've never heard about before. Starting with the Americans here and ending with a few Koreans.

"Let's just pick on one group at a time."

"They're all mixed up in this together. Or is that too complicated an arrangement for your readers?"

"Did you call to give me information or to make wise cracks?"

"Whichever will do you the most good."

"Try information."

"A soldier assigned to Seoul has uncovered some very uncomplimentary information about apparently crooked deals between some of the people at OEC and a few of the Koreans who have been receiving large loans just before intentional bankruptcy."

"Can he document any of that information?"

"As much documentation as anyone can use."

"And what else?"

"Also the man found out that jobs are being sold to Korean civilians. To the men, for cash. To the women, for whatever they can get in trade."

"I've heard that. Rumors, apparently. According to the OEC. I don't know anyone that it happened to, personally. What does it have to do with the soldier?"

"He tried it out. He took a Korean girl over there for a job, and one of the men tried to get at her. Right there."

"And did he?"

"They had a fight. The soldier and the OEC man."

"So two guys had a fight over a broad. This is for the international news wires?"

"The fact of it—shouldn't that be?"

"Look, Kauffmann. I don't need you to tell me how to turn a trick. I've been around the Far East for quite a while."

"Surprising, isn't it—to be so bold? Behold the newest conquerors. Well, I'm not going to give you a handout on it, but if you want to get the jump on something that's going to hit hard, I suggest you get moving."

"As soon as I finish my drink."

"Certainly everything else can wait."

"What's the name of the soldier?"

"Beaumont. He's from Ohio. Heart of America. Sharp boy. Knows government. Knows a lot about this one, too."

"I get my news straight from the Presidential Palace."

"Now that you mention it, I recall. In case you want something accurate for a change, I'll put you in touch with this Beaumont. The corruption around here would fill a year's columns for you. Worthwhile columns."

"And lose me the contacts I need to survive."

"You'll be too big to touch."

"Dreamer. What do you want out of this?"

"Beaumont's safety."

"Who's the man at OEC?"

"Martin Jerome. Do you know him?"

"Yeah, I know him—who doesn't? He's one of my best sources. Dedicated man."

"If that's a value judgment, it's not worth much more than any of the others you've made in the past few years. Why don't you dig up some real news, Sanders? Why don't you *dig?* You could turn up an honest story once in a while."

"Sweetheart, when the world decides it wants an honest news story, I'll learn how to write one."

"One more thing. There's going to be political trouble over here. You might start preparing the people back home for it. It's not going to be great for the U.S. prestige."

"Take it up with the U.S. State Department, Kauffmann. I only work here."

"As you like. But before you leave the country again, try to find time to walk around the block. It's good background for any story. You know: starvation, misery, abandoned half-breed children, corruption, sex."

"Kauffmann, next time you find a story, do me and yourself a favor-jam it!"

"One would think you don't appreciate one of your best sources. But, *natuerlich*, you've been drinking."

"Remind me to buy you a drink sometime. In exchange for the story of the century—a triangle! And I'll bet it isn't even nearly love."

"I found him at the bar," said Kauffman later to Beaumont. "As I expected. We have him guessing. He doesn't know at all what's really happening here. Of course, that's not unusual for him. But this time he *knows* he doesn't know—and that *is* unusual. With luck, we'll provoke him."

"Good. Maybe you'll straighten him out."

"If he has any sense at all. I certainly told him enough.

"What about my mess?"

"I can't be sure he'll do as I suggested."

"Don't get yourself involved too far. I'm on my way home, but you'll be here a while."

"So might you, you know. I shall manage. But now I must walk over to your embassy. I have friends there. I shall sound very disturbed about this *international incident*. They should be very anxious to quiet it before it has the Korean press shouting for blood. You'll probably get off with just a polite warning. But I'm going now, before they close. If they don't hear now, it might be months."

"You'll get yourself run out of this country."

"If this works your way, I don't mind. Magda likes Japan more than here, anyway. Is there any problem at your end?"

"None. Dr. Choh is tied up with a patient. Which is good, because there's really nothing for him to bother about."

"Very well. I'll call you again there." Both handsets dropped into the cradles.

Beaumont turned back to the book with which he'd been trying to occupy himself and then put it aside as the doctor came in.

"You could not be expected again," said Dr. Choh. "Forgive, my patient was so long here. It was a charity patient. I told she this medicine brought here by so and so and so, who are American soldiers."

"You're very thoughtful.... But I don't want to bother you. I stopped by to use your telephone. I took the liberty while you were busy."

"You are fortunate is telephone today. Few day ago somebody steal—cut out from window for to sell in black market. I must to buy new telephone." He recognized without resentment that Beaumont was not interested in the telephone. "Perhaps you tell this person why you come here today."

"I didn't want to go back to the post until I had finished some personal business downtown."

"Business for OEC, perhaps?"

"You know already?" Beaumont was not truly surprised at the grapevine. "It's really not much. It'll be settled in an hour."

"Perhap you do not wish for tell this person."

"I took Kim, Young Song to OEC to get a job. Martin Jerome tried to take advantage of her. I was not too gentle with him. It'll be okay. I hope."

"For you, perhaps. For Miss Kim, perhap not." He selected a number from a personal book and dialed, talking briefly. To Beaumont he said "Mr. Lim of OEC worries." Then he dialed again and talked to Ahn, Yu Man. There was an exchange of courtesies in their language, followed by rapid discourse on the part of the doctor. He answered several suggestions, and then he became persuasive. Then he was argumentative, then conciliatory, and agreeable. He hung up. Certainly you know Miss Ahn of the conversational English class."

*Certainly*—it was one of his favorite words. "We had met at her family's house all winter."

"Her father, we talk. He is elected National Assembly—important person. I tell Mr. Ahn you are in difficulty who was his daughter teacher...he was sorry. I tell him there was Korean student girl problem at OEC...he very angry. I tell him you send her to school...he say was expect. I tell him soon you go home. He say *maybe*. Korean law very strict. I tell him you and friends smuggle medicine for this person charity patient. Now he help. Now we must to call Chung, Kyung Tae, who is Ministry of Justice. Important person. Mr. Ahn said will be difficult. Chung, Kyung Tae wish OEC loan. Must not to fight with OEC people."

"Do you know Chung, Kyung Tae?"

"When young men, we very friends. Then was Ie, Sung Man form government. Chung, Kyung Tae join.This person say to him many terrible thing. Now we stranger, but he will do this thing. I know. Last time party for conversational English class his daughter—his house. First time angry. Perhap we not be strangers more.

"Chung, Byung Mil—is she his daughter?"

The doctor nodded. "Of course. Many politic children in conversational English class. If politic, are wealthy. Dr. Choh, Tae Man is smallest man." he said effacingly. But truthfully...

"Likely, the biggest man around..."

Dr. Choh dialed and held through a circuiting to Chung, Kyung Tae. As before, the conversation started quietly and built in intensity and volume. There was a barrage of harsh sounds, followed by an imperious declaration and silence. There were only a few more words before the conversation was ended.

It was Chung, Kyung Tae who ended the talk. He was angered and hurt by the doctor's familiar impudence. Abruptly the doctor's friend shouted, "*Ani-yo!*" No! He hung up and went to the window. He stood for some time looking down over the wall into the garden of Chang Duk Palace. He decided to take the chance. Finally he took up the telephone and called for S. Martin Jerome.

"Chung, Kyung, he said as Jerome answered.

"Hello, Chung. Good to hear from you, although I don't have any definite word for you yet on the project."

"This is other matter. I would like to see you this afternoon. With Ahn, Yu Man of the Legislative Assembly. How soon will you be able to see us?"

"I'm very busy right now. I have a man in my office, and I must go down to the main Army post before the end of the afternoon. What about tomorrow morning?"

"This afternoon. Important," said Chung with finality. "We will be there in one hour."

"All right. But we'll have to make it short."

"When discuss, as you wish. Goodbye." said Chung.

Martin Jerome heard the receiver click off. "Goodbye to you, too," he said as he put down his handset." Then he turned back to his visitor. "Now, where were we?"

"We were discussing the philosophy of reason," said Sanders of World-Wide News.

"Oh, yes. We couldn't possibly hire all the moose these soldiers would bring in here if we let it be known that we hired that way. Unfortunately, neither of them was willing to take *no* for an answer. I have the bruises to prove it."

"That isn't their version."

"They have to justify some pretty rash action. But they'll get that chance as soon as I see the Provost Marshall and get a few papers signed."

"Were there any witnesses to the attack? On you, I mean."

"No. Unfortunately. My office mates happened to be away."

"What do you think of this Beaumont?"

"Well..." Jerome forced a laugh. "His moose told him all sort of weird tales about graft and corruption and made him feel like a real hero to set the world right. We've seen his kind before."

"And if graft and corruption should turn out to be fact?"

"My job is building the economy. We don't meddle in the internal affairs of the country."

"Exactly how are internal affairs doing?"

"Coming along fairly well, all things considered. There are complaints, of course. But the *outs* always have nasty things to say about the *ins* in any country. I wouldn't worry too much about it."

"Do you get along with the *ins* around town?"

"Like peas in a pod. It's a rewarding job. I move in government circles. It has a pace all its own. You know the feeling. You can't say you aren't impressed by your own access to some of the most influential men in the Far East."

"I hadn't given it much thought."

"Maybe not," said Jerome. "Maybe you should. It might keep you from wanting to rock the boat. Otherwise, where would your "news" come from?"

"And a sensational article would certainly rock the boat around here, would it?"

"It might. But only until the real facts are known, of course. Then you'd be in an embarrassing position. Everyone here would have lost confidence in your ability to see the news as it *should be seen*. News might become scarce. No news—no job. And you must admit that my friends and I have been generous in the past. Why give up a good job for one sensational story?"

"If it worked that way."

"It would."

"And if the Korean press takes up the story?"

"I'll take care of that. We have a statement prepared in case their press inquires. They probably won't even hear about it. This is a matter for the American military. Just state the facts—I've given them to you—and you'll have a happy future with Korean news sources."

"I'm going to give some space to the political scene," said Sanders.

"Don't be too willing. The State Department has a preferred version, you know. And you're living on a U.S. passport, whether or not your boss is foreign. Besides, there's no way to explain why you haven't written earlier about things around here if they're so bad. Either you admit to being totally misinformed in the past, or you do a now-it-can-be-told expose—based on the uncorroborated story of a love-sick soldier."

"I guess that's the way it shapes up."

"How else could it? You have a job worth keeping. By the way, why not try to say something nice about the American civilians working over here? You, know, we work hard under less than luxurious conditions. We sacrifice the comforts of home and accept hardship conditions. We're really dedicated people…. Oh, once in a while we might make mistakes," he said expansively. "…but they're honest mistakes. They get distorted in the telling over here. Put in a good word, will you? It'll help a lot."

"I write news, not public relations copy."

"This *is* public relations. For you." He glanced up as a rap sounded at the door. "Come in, he called.

Chung, Kyung Tae and Ahn, Yu Man came inside, directed by a clerk who knew their importance.

"Hello," said Jerome. "I didn't know you were so close. He shook hands with each and then introduced Sanders, whom they recognized by name.

"We have seen your articles," said Mr. Ahn. "They are very good. No one in the government could possibly take offense. Naturally we have had difficulty in the past. Other political people have not been so wise. Some take offense."

"Thank you. I try to be objective." He understood the hint and made a mental note to follow up.

"Objectively you could tell your readers that we need more small industry," said Chung.

"And that means a bigger aid budget for Korea," said Jerome. "By the time we build the large and necessary plants, there's little money left for other things needed by the economy."

"That's a quaint way to express it," said Ahn.

"That's an unusual expression for a Korean," said Sanders. "We rarely hear the word *quaint* over here."

"I learned it in Minnesota," Ahn replied.

"I don't want to interrupt your little visit, Gentlemen," said Jerome, "...but I am very short on time. Saunders, I'll talk with you another time."

Right," said Sanders with an air of distraction. "Do you have a card?" he asked of Ahn.

"Certainly," said Chung, and both Koreans produced one; they exchanged.

"Well, so long," said Sanders, and, waving, he went out.

"To what do I owe the pleasure of your visit?" asked Jerome as he went back to his desk.

"To an incident with a Korean girl this afternoon," said Ahn, Yu Man bluntly.

"Word certainly gets around. But she really didn't do me too much damage, and so I shouldn't complain, I suppose." Clearly the matter was about to leave his hands.

"On the other hand," said Ahn, using the idiom with gusto, "she might complain. Can you imagine what the Korean press would do with that? Very dangerous situation."

"She has nothing to complain about. She came here to get a job without going to the personnel center first. She didn't qualify. I refused to hire her, and her soldier friend decided to be a hero in front of her."

"We are helping you, please. You must to listen."

"That is an excellent version for the press," said Ahn, Yu Man. "As a matter of fact, I do like to know this. Subsequently, however, we might have to discuss the incident in the Legislative Assembly. It can further our request for a Status of Forces Agreement. That is very important to all Koreans."

"That's a distortion of fact."

"Clever distortion of fact is the key to political success," said Ahn. "I'm sure my colleagues would agree to that. In that process, your version would not be very important to them."

"The soldier teaches conversational English to our own daughters," said Chung. "Teachers try to protect and help their pupils, I'm sure. Even if that is not wise each time."

129

"If you cannot prove that she is—or is not—his pupil," said Ahn... He left the sentence hanging, but the thrust was clear. "Therefore, we would like to avoid any harsh measures against him if possible."

"We are helping you," said Chung again. "You must to listen."

"This could be an unsavory thing," said Ahn. "You would be at the root of it, of course. Your wife could discover, and wives do not believe in husbandly innocence. There could be other complications. And the American embassy would blame you for new Korean jurisdictional demands. That is not enviable, Sir."

"He's a troublemaker. And if he gets by with it this time, he'll try it again somewhere else. I think it's my duty to pin him down since we have him now."

"We do not have him, Sir. We have only your claim, their explanation, and...rumors that are also not savory." Ahn said the last few words with an air of triumph. The two had probably succeeded in weaving their web of intrigue. "Could you explain an international incident to your Washington office?"

"I'm not going to be blackmailed into anything." Jerome.

"We wish only cooperation for avoiding problems between our nations," said Ahn. "We can make it so."

"And if I see things differently?"

"Then we will have to bring charges against you because that would be very popular with the Korean people. And even possibly against other persons in this office. Rumors...you understand. They might come to nothing at all...but they must be examined by the Korean public."

"I see. Well, this kind of pressure is probably going to be reflected in less cooperation in all things. That's a consideration for you, Chung." He leaned back as if casually. "If you know what I mean."

Chung and Ahn exchanged a long glance.

"I have already made these considerations," said Chung. "That soldier help the children of many important Korean. Not possible to say terrible thing to many father in government. If I must to suffer for help you—okay. Is worth," said Chung. "You my friend."

"I'm delighted to hear that," said Jerome, realizing defeat.

"You have a complaint at the office of the Provost Marshall," said Ahn. "Please cancel the order. It was a simple mistake, yes?"

Jerome hesitated and then picked up the phone. He asked the operator for the section chief. "This is Jerome again. That soldier came back and apologized. Possibly I was a little hasty. Is it too late to forget about the whole thing?...Good. Internal harmony seems much better. Sorry I bothered you at all. But we had to make our point.... So long." With an unpolished flourish, Jerome hung up. "Gentlemen? More?"

"Very intelligent you cooperate," said Chung. "Let us help you. Very intelligent."

"I believe you have application papers for the young lady," said Ahn. "May I see them?"

Jerome decided against shuffling papers and handed the application blanks to Chung, Kyung Tae, who slipped them into his pocket. Her name went with them, as did the proofs.

"I certainly hope that this little event doesn't mar our future relationships," Jerome said to Chung.

"I think not so. Happily we help you."

So that would be the official version if one were needed. Okay. They had won. But was fighting this worth possibly losing all his current and future power?

"I think it prudent that the soldier leave the country as soon as possible. You could arrange that as your anger," said Ahn. "You have many friends."

"I don't remember his name," said Jerome. Possibly it was true. Possibly it was go-along. "I suppose I could."

"Perhaps you could do that now. While we are here to help you."

Jerome nodded, and as Ahn, Yu Man reached for the telephone, he slid the instrument closer to Jerome. Ahn verified a number written on a slip of paper and dialed. "We have arranged, Doctor, that the soldier shall not be bothered by the Military Police. Mr. Jerome very kindly wishes that." In English. Jerome himself confirmed grimly.

Ahn held up the handset. "We are grateful for your assistance," said Dr. Choh to all.

"Naturally we must insist that the soldier cannot discuss incident with no person before he leaves Korea. That is fair to Mr. Jerome, is it not?"

"Assuredly, he will not."

"If so, you must answer for it."

"I have not fear," said the doctor. "He is a substantial person. He knows all thing in Korea. We can trust him."

"Good day, Doctor," said Ahn, Yu man.

Dr. Choh grinned as he set down his phone. "It is all arrange, Mr. Beaumont. There be no difficulty with Military Police. Now you have obligation."

"Thank you, Doctor."

"You must not to discuss this day with any person until after you leave Korea. Better never."

"That's not too much to ask."

"I am pleasure you agree."

"Well, we're no longer *quits*, are we? I owe you. More medicine?"

"Korean people are *quits*, you say, only before Japanese war. Perhap never more."

Beaumont slipped his cap from under his belt, and, before leaving, offered a slow, deep bow to the doctor.

*"Annyong-i kesipsio*, Choh-*Sonsaeng."*

"*Annyong-i kasipsio*, Beaumont-*Sonsaeng.*"

Then they bowed with great decorum to each other. By careful watch, Beaumont permitted the doctor to terminate the courtesy. It was proper. He turned and went out.

In the thoroughfare, he found a taxi and directed the driver to an address on Cho Ro. He went into a shop that identified itself as the Geneva Trading Company. Personal thanks to Karl. He was back in moments, directing the car to turn into Hoo Am Dong and to the Post.

# Chapter Twenty

Karl is not here, Gordon," said Magda Kauffmann as she admitted him to their home. "Of course we were not expecting you this evening. But *wilkommen.*"

"I didn't expect to be here. But last night I received special orders to go back home immediately. Somebody has arranged military airspace. I'm flying out in the morning And no troop ship! It couldn't be better."

"I shall be happy for you, Gordon...or shall I cry to see you go? I am not sure, so quickly does it happen. *Ach*, Karl. *Wo bist du?"* Where are you? To Beaumont: "You cannot go if he doesn't say goodbye. You are his son."

"I can't stay, Magda. I have to go."

"But a minute. Karl surely will be here."

"I phoned the shop nearly an hour ago. He wasn't there. That's why I took a chance on coming here."

"And so not coming to see me?" she said with mock indignation and laughed. "He is possibly paying a bribe to someone to stay in business longer? *Nein. Ach.* Everybody does but not my Karl."

"I wanted to thank Karl especially for helping me out a couple of days ago. He told you what happened, didn't he?"

"Yes. Karl tells me everything."

"He said that if necessary he would talk to his friend, Jerome's wife. Now that shouldn't be necessary now."

"*Gut.*" Good.

"They are countrymen, she and Karl. She was born here, but her other people are Austrian. People say her family owned much property here. Karl knows if that is so. That is how Rhee is so powerful. When the Japanese went out, the government took all things and gave them to political friends. Now everything Rhee does is perfect. Now the politicians are all wealthy. A clique."

"I can't say I'm surprised."

"More. When other Korean people lost papers during the Korean War, the Korean government confiscated their property and gave it to friends, too. Now those friends own Korea—together with OEC's wife. She is Korean-born, yes, but part Austrian—I said. Karl tells everybody he is Swiss. It is not true. It is not good if everybody knows that he knows that woman. He must then leave Korea, to be so powerful, this stranger. I am glad you are free. I worry for Karl. I worry for you, too. Always I worry...worry, Karl says."

"You've been worried about me since the first time we met. My mother would really appreciate you."

"We are all the same, mothers." She caught his expression of surprise. "We had a child, Karl and I."

"I didn't know."

"Karl is very private." She breathed deeply, as if considering. "We do not talk about it. Some things are good not to remember."

Beaumont sat on the arm of the sofa beside her. He waited, and after a few seconds, she began to talk again. She seemed detached from her thoughts, as if conversation were possible only because she was not involved.

"That is the reason Karl tells you all these things about the corruption here— because we had a child. You are his child grown tall and strong. And a father wants to help. But he forgets that you are still a child, too. Changing governments is not the work of children, Gordon. I am afraid for you when you go back home."

"Don't be, Magda. I'll be fine."

"We were living in Bern, my husband and I. Karl went back to his native Austria when the war turned bad. He had to fight, he said. And when the war was over, I took our child to Austria to meet him. It was difficult, but he would not return to Switzerland, where we are citizens. Karl told you about his sister in the United States. That is not the reason he tells you. The reason is an accident with American soldiers, and our child was killed. Karl was like a wild man. For a month—two months—he didn't eat or sleep. Then he began to forgive. And he forgave and forgave and forgave. But never forgot. He still cannot prove to himself that he has forgiven. That is why he tries to fix things with the Americans. The Americans wanted to pay us an indemnity for our child. With money they try to do everything. Karl was furious. Now he sees that you Americans are still trying to pay with money—to solve with money. You lose money, yes. You have plenty. All over the world, you are losing prestige. Of that you cannot have too much. Power, yes. But you are losing the hearts of the Korean people. Without the hearts of people, you have nothing. Karl wants to change that. Perhaps he will; perhaps not, and he will die while changing and forgiving. With every fine American he meets, it is the same. There are only a few who care, but always he tries. I am afraid for them. They will be torn apart. Governments are vultures. They pick flesh for their own needs and leave bones for monuments But still we honor them with wars."

"Maybe we have fought the last of them."

"Already you are losing your next war in Asia. That is why Karl fears for you. Here, as in China, you are on the side of deceit and hypocrisy. We were there, Karl and I. Perhaps you don't know and must be told. Karl is telling you. Korea is telling you. Somebody must change it, Gordon. I am sorry if it must be you—for you will be torn apart. Your friends here, too. There are many lies to protect."

"Our way is different, Magda. Change is possible."

"Because you are young you say that. Because you are young you will try. I am sorry for you."

"I was young when I came to this country. Now I feel very, very old. You needn't worry."

"*Fuehrt gottbegnadet*, Gordon." Go in God's grace. Then she went to the door. "Now you must go before I cry. Karl does not permit me to cry. He says it gains nothing." She touched his sleeve.

"Tell him goodbye."

"Yes, yes; of course." She kissed his forehead.

"*Auf wiedersehen*, Magdalein."

"*Auf wiedersehen, Meiner Kleiner.*"

The door was closed behind him without resolution. He refused to see her in a window and started down the steep and twisting road to the foot of Ie Tae Wan. It was dusk, and the last glow from the sun oversaw the lifting of the heat. At the foot of the hill he found a taxi. He directed the driver to Hoo Am Dong and sat back to watch the night run promiscuously after the sun. At Hoo Am Dong he counted out a fare, overpaid to end an argument with the Driver's Second, and bounded into the building. He caught off his shoes with hardly a change in gait and mounted the stairs. Silently he pushed the door aside.

"*Nanun tansinul sarang hamnida*," he said to the figure on the floor. I love you very much.

"Hello, GI," she said without turning.

"Where's Young Song?"

"*Opse-yo*," said Miss Choi. Gone.

"That's what you said last time."

"I say again. *Opse-yo.*"

"You'd better tell me where she is."

"Nevah hoppen, GI."

"I'll pull her father's house apart."

"She not she father house."

He gripped her shoulder. "Then where is she?"

"You hit me? Okay. Is not first time GI hit me. Okay. Hit me. Okay."

She didn't really care. He loosed his grip on her shoulder and sat beside her. Finally, he asked again, "Where did she go?"

"Away. She not wish see you."

"Why?"

"She love you, GI."

"That's ridiculous. I told her many times, I'm leaving."

"You don't know she heart. Miss Kim Number One Heart hava. Number One."

"I know all about it."

"She fraid same-same Miss Choh. Miss Kim cry, cry, cry. Nevah time say goodbye, Miss Kim say."

"Is Young Song at Miss Choh's house?"

"Nevah hoppen I tell you."

"I think most of this is your fault."

"Maybe so, GI. You not know."

"I want to say goodbye. I have some money for her."

"She not want your money, GI."

"You Number Ten Heart, I think, he said.

"First day time, I Number One Heart. *Kasuk* GI make me Number Ten. Now I same-same whore girl."

"I told you not to use that word!"

"*Kasuk, kasuk,*" she repeated in defiance.

"All your life you're going to be a whore-girl. Don't you care?"

"What I can do?"

"Stop talking like a whore-girl, for one"

"Okay, you say. Not possible, I do. Everybody know."

"Miss Choi, I want to see Young Song."

"Why you want? Only you hurt her."

"I want to tell her that I love her very much."

"Why you not marry with Miss Kim?"

"That's not what I mean."

"You not love Miss Kim. She same-same whore-girl you think. I know. GI all same-same."

"Didn't you have a steady GI once?"

"Kurae!" No! "So I know. Hava Number Ten GI for steady me. Catchee now all time Number Ten GI. Nevah hoppen Number One GI catchee Miss Choi."

"We've got to find her a job."

"She catchee job *mo sukosh.* No sweat, you."

"I want to see her."

"You want catchee Miss Kim I know. Whatsa matter, GI? Hot pants hava yes?"

None of your goddamn business."

"You hot pants, I catchee you. Two dollah. All same thing. Catchee short-time. Go back post." She thought. "No hurt Miss Kim." She stripped her blouse.

He stood up, and she did likewise.

"Hot pants? You catchee me." She shook her shoulders, and her breasts rolled.

"Lookee, I. Hot stuff. You like?" Firmly she set her hands on the sockets of his hips. With deliberation she brought her hands sharply together at his genitals, insinuatingly.

"A whore-girl does that, Miss Choi." She had known she could hurt him more, and he hurt her in return.

"You not want catchee me?"

"Not a whore-girl."

"All time GI say that!"

She clenched her fists on his genitals, and he jumped with pain. He swung at her without wanting to hurt but she fell to the floor, maybe intentionally. Maybe not.

"Okay," she said. "Not first time GI hit me. All time Catchee Number Ten GI. Number One GI nevah want catchee me. Miss Choi whore-girl. Talk whore-girl. *Kasuk...kasuk...kasuk!*" Then she sat up. "Why you not catchee me? You Number One GI. You Number One. I want. Why you not catchee me *presento?*"

"Forget it. I not want catchee whore-girl."

"You do. For me. Please, GI. Number One American. Then I no more whore-girl."

"It's a great act, Choi."

"I say true. I want you. Here." She clutched her belly. "Please. Is first time Miss Choi say 'Please, GI, catchee me.' Is first time. Other time for eat. Please." She padded across the floor on her knees. "You catchee me now. Please." Skillfully she undid his belt buckle.

He turned away and picked up his shoes.

With a shrill cry she lunged at the bureau, grasped a bottle, and threw it at him. It tore through the paper panels of the door.

"Why you not do me this thing?" she cried. "One time Number One GI catchee me. Please. I not hurt you."

"What about Miss Kim?"

"She nevah know. I not tell her. Promise."

"If I do you this thing, will you take care of Young Song for me?"

"Promise. Nobody catchee Miss Kim. Sure."

As he crossed to her he took his handkerchief from his pocket. He scrubbed the mascara from her eyes and the abundant lipstick from her face. That is for whore-girls," he said. "Never more you do that."

"You catchee me now?" she asked apprehensively.

"I catchee you now."

She whirled and walked to the bed, shedding clothing as she made her way.

"Choi!" He caught himself. "Miss Choi, put that blouse on." He got only a stare in return.

"Put it on,' I said."

She put her arms through the sleeves of her blouse and covered her bare breasts.

"Now those."

She stepped into her panties.

"Whore-girls do that. Tonight you are Number One Lady. I will do that."

"Yes?" She stared in wonderment as she backed onto the bed. She saw him take a packet from his shirt pocket. He turned out the light, and she heard him shed his clothing. Then he sat beside her on the bed. He raised her shoulders and removed her blouse.

"*Ch'oum...ch'oum,*" she said as he caressed her face and neck and breasts: first time. She raised her buttocks from the mattress and slid her panties away.

"*Chuse-yo,*" she said as he joined her under the cover: Someone honored gives to me.

Convulsively they honored and were honored.

"My name Choi, Han Il," she said as he drew away.

"How do you do, Miss Choi, Han Il," he said with great decorum. "My name is Gordon Beaumont. Bo, not 'GI'."

"Please to meet you, Mr. Beaumont-Bo," she replied.

He covered her, dried himself, and dressed.

"You Number One Heart hava," she said.

"You're Number One yourself. We say 'a little rough around the edges?' No more you catchee Number Ten GI. You understand?"

"*Iae hamnida,*" she said. No, definitely. She was immensely pleased with her new status.

"If you see Dr. Choh," he said as he went toward the door, "tell him to add another chapter to his books on psychotherapy. I surely would, if I could."

"Okay, you say," she said, having no idea of his meaning.

"And tell Miss Kim that I love her very much."

"I know. I tell her. Sure."

"*Annyong-i kesipsi-yo.*" he said.

"*Annyong-i kasipsi-yo,*" she said; and then, with conviction, "You Number One Heart, GI."

He waved and went out. He was in Hoo Am Dong and well into the military compound before he decided who it was who had arranged the farewell. To use or to be used seemed all the same in practice. But which role was his, really? He shrugged, went into the barracks, and went directly to the showers. Tonight was comfortable, unlike the many freezing days with false temperatures reported in the *Stars and Stripes* paper. So little could be believed in all Korea....

*April 17<sup>th</sup>*

*It's no longer seen in the streets, but some of the horror and wearing poverty of the old city life and even military life here has come back to him almost live in the thoughts and dreams. Will it go away, ever?*

*It was a mistake to come here. He had planned to give the search about thirty days, and already this was pushing six weeks' visit. It's foolish to think she might be here. Or that he might find her, if she is still here. Would she be waiting? Why? And if not waiting, then why had he come? He found the empty picture frame in his duffel bag and set it on the tiny table. Empty. The twin phoenixes perched calmly still...just as regal as in the royal pavilion.*

*Okay, he'd come. The time is spent. The money is spent. Even he felt spent. Well, he supposed, he could hold out a little longer without going too much more deeply into debt on behalf of a brainstorm; but the Western style accommodation costs here. He decided to give it another few days. Maybe a week. But no more. No Young Song—no stay! It's time to pack it up and go.*

*Damn! Why had he come? Or why had they not left together, long ago? Why life?*

# Chapter Twenty-One

When the single cannon shot jarred the Eighth Army camp into morning activity, Beaumont had nearly finished dressing. He slipped into his clothes and jacket as the barracks lights flashed on, draped his cap into place, and went down the road to the assembly area. He remembered the traumatic first-morning shot, when brand-new arrivals were never warned that the cannon shot was *not* a warning that the North Koreans were visiting again, although expected. That provided the month's humor for the thirty or more guys housed in that Quonset hut. Very funny! Sure. Just like the rumors about some massacre at No Gun Ri. Had we really done that?

Already a handful of men from nearby barracks had assembled in the road awaiting roll call. Surly men pushed out the door behind him and fell into a sleepful line, trailing shirt-ends and boot laces. It was a rag-tag assembly—the usual. It was very difficult to make dumb procedures enjoyable. Besides, no one was ever reported missing if someone else knew that they had planned to sleep *out* that preceding night.

Four hundred mornings had begun this way, relieved only by R&R trips to Japan and regular leave. And now, by excusing him from reveille during his last days there, the military had unwittingly stolen his last chance to imitate a soldier. He laughed. To muster *in a military manner* was the phrase used in the handbooks. More aptly they were phrase books, he knew, since the principles were intended more for recitation than application.

*I shall walk my post in a military manner*...that was in the phrase book, too. He walked unhurriedly up the hill toward the mess hall, reaching it just as the musters released several hundred men behind him. Half of the men went back to bed, against known regulations, *in a military manner*.

Beaumont dipped his metal tray into the kettle of boiling water and walked through the kitchen service line. He avoided the chipped beef masquerading as breakfast and settled for bread toasted on one side by a conveyer-belted heat machine, cherry jam scooped with a long-handled marmalade spoon, and finished with a spotted orange. Brackish coffee swilled the taste of tinned milk from his palate, and he was through eating. It would be difficult to miss this when home.

He dropped the orange into his pocket as he slid the tray into the clipper room. Once outside, he walked behind the mess hall and passed the orange through the fence to a band of urchins moping there daily at meal times. They were more likely to sell the oranges and rolls than to eat them, but anything would help. Passing oranges this way was an offense, he knew; humanity was made offensive in the name of war. But rationalizing war was the politicians' game, not his. How could he set priorities for others in their predicament? And how sad this country, he felt.

He started back down the hill to the barracks. It was going to be hot. The air was clear and the huts atop Ie Tae Wan already shimmered in bad air. Foul air. The mood was foul. Memory of an over-long year was foul. That thing called government was foul as it sat upon the shoulders of the people of Korea. Political Korea was foul to the senses of Asia. A family of nations had staged a foul travesty on democracy. China applauded. Once more Beaumont shared the disgust of the Oriental world for the trappings and values of the West.

He reached the barracks and drew his duffel bag out from under a cot. He shook hands with people he's never likely to see again and went down to the orderly room. Surely the truck to Kimpo airfield would be *late—in the military manner*—and for the first time in over four hundred mornings he really didn't care. After nearly fifteen months of waiting, departure didn't matter. There were so many things still to be done...places to be visited...people to be known. Somehow, he felt, the elongated year had cheated him. And already he was only three days from home. Only hours from the States. Hallelujah!

Military records in hand, he went outside to wait. Three days to the States. Maybe he'd go through Hawaii. Maybe direct. It wasn't his choice or need to know. By boat it would have been three weeks of transfer time. Thanks be to S. Martin Jerome, who was a kind of demi-god and could arrange such things.

Almost on schedule, the truck arrived. "All set, Papa-san," said Beaumont to the Korean civilian driver as he threw his duffel bag into the lock box under the canvas cover. After a moment's hesitation, he pitched a smaller canvas grip of shaving gear and under garments into the holding box. Small things tended to be ripped off by thieves when the truck stopped at intersections...well, he could buy more. Then he jumped into the cab with the driver. "Kimpo-*Ppalli-ppallyi ka sipsio.*" To Kimpo, quickly, please.

"No sweat," said the driver amiably, and to prove the stamina of the antiquated equipment, he ground the transmission. The truck was waved out of the main gate of the post and rolled quickly to the traffic circle. They made an abrupt turn and headed toward the Han River. The outdoor market they passed was writhing. Women trundled the streets with babies bound in scarves to their backs as they apportioned time to the shops and the open market stalls. Older children, probably dirty from the year before, played at the edge of the road. One or two who hadn't yet learned distaste called out the only words of English they knew. Invariable they knew *GI* and *okay*; the latter described nothing in their lives.

The truck was blowing up dust storms with its speed, and the smell of waste and excrement in the gutters and open drainage canals outside the central city clung to the nose and clothes like honey. Flies were everywhere about. And people. Indistinct and enduring people: whores waved; old men looked after the truck and sometimes waved; young men looked after the truck and then spat.

Beaumont was relieved to be making the trip alone. Except for an occasional unsatisfactory exchange with the driver, there was silence—it was a fine variation from Camden's departure, he remembered. Camden had joined thirty men in a convoy to the ship at Inchon. The two had shaken hands amid others' talk of Home and Mother and Copulation, and How Horrible This Place Is. The loudest voice tended to prove the most feeling. That chaotic departure had been a chore. He was reminded that no word had come from Camden since returning home. But, then, Camden was probably still on the ship. Word never came regularly from the departed. Leave-taking in Korea had the finality of death about it. Most of these faces would never be in front again.

At the bridge, they stopped. An accident had displaced traffic into one lane. A sound came from the back of the truck, and instantly Beaumont leaped out. A young man dropped out from under the canvas cover. It and the lock had been cut. He had a canvas grip in one hand and the duffel bag in the other. Beaumont lashed out at the man as he rounded the back of the truck, catching him behind the ear. The boy hurled the lighter grip to friends nearby, but it missed, and all ran. Beaumont threw the bags back into the truck and climbed into the cab. They started off again.

When his immediate anger had died, Beaumont said to the driver, "That bag has enough good stuff for the black market to rejoice. They'd all have had a good meal from it."

The driver looked at him and smiled. Slicky boys were a part of life and probably the finest retribution for the GI's, the driver probably thought, although he wouldn't say so. Besides, counting the blow that Beaumont had landed on the thief, there had been honor for both sides in the incident. It could be forgotten.

"My name is Gordon," he said after a bold laugh at his companion's unspoken attitude. "What's yours?"

"Chung," answered the driver.

"Do you like this job."

"Before war, I study be engineer."

"Do you like this job?"

"No sweat." Why should he jeopardize it?

"Do you have babies?"

The driver held up all the fingers of one hand. He was paid about twenty thousand Hwan each month, Beaumont knew. It was about forty dollars at the legal rate but was worth little more than half that in purchasing power on the open market. The economy ran on black market rates. So civilian employees of the U.S. were penalized to maintain the pretense of monetary stability that the economic advisors proclaimed. Such was diplomacy. Probably since the world's beginning.

Such was Korea: hunger, disillusion, disparity—the lot of Asia until the Age of Promise. Beaumont counted them mentally. Promise of food. Promise of shelter. Promise of jobs. Promise of freedom. Nothing had worked, and there was bitterness for the cruel prank of the smiling liberators. Poor Miss Kim had to stay behind. Well, it couldn't be helped. Unless....

Beaumont closed his eyes as they headed into the puffy, hilly, countryside, composed of rounded mountain humps more tired than even he. He rolled the window tight to keep the gravel road mostly outside the cab. Dirt and noise and pounding. There was a taxi near the gate. Trolleys squealed. Taxi horns blared. People ran. Peddlers hawked, and the destitute urinated in the concourse of the Rail Terminal Office. All of it was happening together. Push, steal, lie for survival and what else? Nobody laughed. It wasn't funny. He closed his eyes against the offensive images.

Then he opened his eyes, just as they passed an old man peddling a bicycle. The old man's beard nearly touched the wheel of the bicycle as he rode hunched over the handlebars so the long A-frame carrier strapped to his back just cleared the rear wheel. Beaumont heard the old man cough as the dust overcame him. He faltered, and the bicycle fell from under him. The old man shook his fist and turned away. Simply another lesson in power.

"Remember us with gratitude," said Beaumont to no one in particular. "And God damn us!" They rode into the airfield. Soon Korea was behind.

# Chapter Twenty-Two

He re-read the letter another time:

September 2, 1961

Dear Gordon:

I am sorry I did not wish to correspond with you while were are separately. Miss Choh correspond to inform me her father now wish you to return to your home in Korea. She does not speak of Charles. Of course I will not be at your home, but you are welcome to live there. I will be happily met can we visit as friend.

Your love,
Song

She had enclosed a photo of herself in a black frame inset with mother-of-pearl in the form of a pair of phoenixes with exaggerated tails. That was the ancient symbol of royalty, and I'd seen it often at the palaces. And she smiled her sweetest smile ever. She pleased him greatly by using only her second given name—that simple act showed great favor and family—style intimacy. It was not the letter of a woman who did not wish to see him, he was sure. He looked back over the note, and its bookish phrasing brought a smile to his face. Young Song was evidently a secretary to a Korean executive. Precision in the English language didn't matter. Her style had changed, certainly, and her English was much improved. But her plurals still didn't exist. He went to his desk, took a packet of letters out of a drawer, and slipped the new letter under the rubber band. Then he slipped the band off and fanned the packet. There were seven pieces. The first was from Young Song, too, he noted. It was dated July 1, 1958—only days after he'd left Seoul. How very quickly the years were fleeting. He unfolded the letter and read yet again:

Dear Gordon,

As you wish I do no longer think about you and your Korea home. Sure it was not difficult, and therefore I thank you for your kindness. If your future wife will allow, please write to me a letter sometime. I will be happily to know you are safe in the United States.

Goodbye.

Your love,
Young Song

He couldn't remember what his reply had been, although it must have been almost as brief and as bare of emotion. And she had placed a final-S. He returned the only other one of her letters to its envelope and took up the next communication. It was a reply to his own letter of apology and farewell:

> Seoul, Korea
> July 26, 1958

Esteemed Teacher:
   Naturally we understand that many important things remained here before Mr. Camden and you could return to your homes in the United States.
   Thank you very much for the fine conversational English lessons. We suggest that you return to visit with us soon.

> Very truly yours,
> Conversational English Class

They had all signed it, in both the Korean characters and Roman alphabet. He laughed aloud. Their letter had followed the best model of their language texts for spacing and verbiage. And they had even contrived to use a phrase from the classroom: *Suggest something, Mr. Lee,* Beaumont heard himself say that day in the living room of Miss Ahn's house.   But why laugh? He himself was forgetting how to write even the few common words captured in that book. It was all very real, and he reminded himself with a start to contact Camden. Then he found the only word he'd had from cousin-sister Miss Choi. He couldn't read the postmark, which had blurred in a rain. But he remembered that the note had arrived during the fall of 1958, after he'd sent a gift to Young Song:

Dear Bo:
   Miss Kim now happy she job.   She not need money.   She say I not tell you she cry you go States.   Same-same I cry.   I meet Number One GI now.  He Kentucking person. Sahgent.  Maybe I marry with him.

> You friend all time
> Choi, Han Il

And even she had honored him with use of her own personal names.   They seemed to remember him.   Still, half a year had passed before the next letter had arrived with the doctor's acknowledgment of Beaumont's few newspaper articles.

> Seoul, Korea
> March 25, 1959

Dear Mr. Beaumont:
   We are pleasure that now you have newspaper writing about Korea. Perhaps now will change American thing. We are regret if nothing more

is for to do, and we are thank for help. Now we must to work in Korea. Korea is sad country now. We hope better.

We hope also you having good health. Here is everyone also good health.

Sincere friend,
Dr. Choh, Tae Man

So he was pleased, the doctor. How unusually fine. And rare. No word of Miss Choh. Well, surely the doctor did not blame him for the escapades of Camden and Ai Ja. He would have to write to Camden and see how things really were between them.

And there was still another letter concerning the news articles:

Seoul
April 4, 1959

My dear Gordon—

We are both surprised, Karl and I, that you have been able to do anything at all, especially these articles. *Wunderbar!*

We cannot blame you that you have become discouraged with the American press. Surely you must not blame yourself if the newspapers no longer have courage. And if those who should heed you only ignore—remember, as Karl says, the ability to ignore others is the great hidden asset of the powerful—don't be discouraged.

Karl and I are proud of you, for you have not allowed yourself to be buried. We cannot know what you plan for your future. Do not permit us to lose contact, for you are welcome wherever we are.

God bless you,
Magda and Karl

He lost contact.

And still another half year had passed before Dr. Choh had sent him news of the Korean revolution. Not that it had been ignored in the American press. Rhee was gone. Finally:

Seoul, Korea
October 31, 1960

Dear Mr. Beaumont:

We have traded a jackal for a jackal.

Sincere friend,
Dr. Choh, Tae Man

Except for Young Song's own last letter, the last of the group's letters was also from the doctor:

Seoul, Korea
July 16, 1961

Dear Mr. Beaumont:

Perhaps now new administration can give to Korea people first freedom for fifty year. We must to work very hard but happily. Also we must to have teachers who know what is freedom who can help us. Now is my friend Mr. Ahn and Mr. Chung sorry for past and wish honest people for talk about government. I have educate them about you are teacher for government things. If you wish come to Korea now is new Junta. Perhaps will you meet government people and sometime will teach at Seoul University. Is good position.

The Ancient One is very pleasure with your newspaper writing long ago. He said perhaps you help for changing, now American people are know better. Please soon answer me who is a friend.

Choh, Tae Man

Without his title, Dr. Choh was leveling the playing field. And even Young Song had repeated the invitation. He collected the envelopes, set them in order, and banded them. He located a pen and paper and began a letter to Young Song. Then he crumpled the paper. She could wait a week longer—what a surprise if he would greet her with a kiss. He put away the packet of letters and turned to packing.

In less than a week he was ready to depart. As he was riding to the airport, he thought again of Camden, and as soon as he was ticketed, he made a telephone call.

"Chuck, this is Bo," he said as Camden answered the operator's inquiry. "I know it's late, but I'm afraid that this can't wait until the morning. How are things?

"Great. But where are you?"

"At the airport—at home. I don't have much time before we hit Chicago for transfer. Could you meet me? I'm flying to the West Coast to pick up an overseas flight."

"You can do that from here."

"No. I'll explain. Just meet me."

"Home? Here?"

"O'Hare International."

"Big place. Where? When?"

"How about the International terminal? Nine-thirty tonight."

147

"You mean I should miss my TV programs just for you? Okay. If you can stay over at all, stay with us."

"No. I'm making connections for Tokyo. Thanks. I'm going back to Korea. The revolution—you know. To help if I can."

"You're out of your mind—it's a revolution."

"Half of this country—and my family—agree with you. Not to fight. But I'm going over. So if you have a message or a folding green gift for Miss Choh, Ai Ja—"

"She's here. At school."

"Thanks for telling me."

"I wanted to see how things would work out. You know, the cultures are so very different."

"Did they work out?"

"She won an art scholarship and spent a year at drawing. Now her medical illustrations are paying her way through med school. She's determined to go back to Korea. That's everything for now. How's Young Song?"

"Stubborn. A couple of letters. But we're not really in contact. I'll tell you about it if you meet my plane."

"Sure. I'd forgotten that planes were the topic."

"Great. I'm still in Ohio. Be at the International terminal in about two and one-half hours. I'm sorry it's so fast—I haven't had time to plan."

"I know how it is.... Sure." He paused. "How much time do you have?"

"Two hours is what they plan. I don't expect to be late. Weather's good."

"See you there."

Beaumont went out to the ramps.

In Chicago, Camden knew he would be early and would order himself a beer when he reached the airport. He tried to think of reasons why he shouldn't be surprised by Beaumont's decision. He thought of none but reminded himself that he still didn't know the duration of Bo's Korean visit. That would make a difference in what he thought—but it was in fact a surprise. Quickly he showered and dressed. Deciding against a shave, he splashed shave lotion on his face and went out to his car. He drove uneventfully along the expressway that linked the downtown to the O'Hare Airport. That had been part of a boon-doggle, too. There was something new abuilding every time he passed. But by the time he had parked a long distance from the terminal, he was no longer early. It was a long walk to the terminal.

They met wordlessly and without ceremony and let a reluctantly-released handclasp convey personal regard. When the flight gate had been reconfirmed, the two went to a cocktail lounge and selected a table against a distant wall.

"What about Ai Ja?" Beaumont began.

"She's at the University of Minnesota. They have a teacher-exchange program with Seoul University. That gave her the idea. Another year to be a teacher really doesn't bother her. Then another few years for studying medicine. She'll be here a while, I'm sure. After the revolution, emigration laws were relaxed. For students they're almost nothing now. And here she is."

"I'm surprised that her father let her come over. He'd written me a couple of times, but he never mentioned that she was here."

"He let her accept the scholarship on condition she not contact me," Camden said. "And she didn't—at first. But when I'd addressed enough mail to Korea, the good doctor wrote me that she'd left his house. She'd previously hinted at plans. Phone calls to Minneapolis did the rest. It's not hard to find a name like hers in the telephone directory. I just went up to see her. A few weeks ago."

"Why didn't you call me?"

"You know. She was too much on my mind."

"Is it working out?"

"Seems to be. She came down to stay with my family. All of which is respectable, as she sees it, because I don't live at the family home any more."

"What a girl! How'd she fare with your family?"

"*Veni, vidi, vici.*" Wryly he added, "It's a beautiful icing, but will the cake go stale? Sometimes I'm afraid of that. Sometimes I think it could work out. Sometimes I don't know what to think."

"And what does Ai Ja make of it?"

"Before long she'll graduate as a teacher. Then she's going back home before med school. I don't know why, other than to wear herself out *doing good* for her country. When General Park's military junta took over the country, she thought that Korea had found its potential. The junta seems to have made a good start. I hope it won't turn into just another power party. But you know the history there. It would take a miracle.

"It seems to us that the junta cleaned up the Rhee-Chang jackals, but Dr. Choh doesn't agree. More manipulation?"

"Probably. Do you think there actually was a Communist plot in Chang's planned administration, as General Park claimed?"

"Nothing is what was claimed; so I doubt it," said Beaumont. "I think we've simply been pegged, and they know how to push the hot buttons. The junta simply coated the power pill with *State Department's* favorite flavor: communism. And we're willing to swallow it."

"I kind of hoped we'd go along with the junta," said Camden, "until they suspended the country's constitution. Then I began worrying about them."

"Why? The junta couldn't be worse than Rhee. Their constitution was a farce. Rhee's security laws made our John Adams' Alien and Sedition Acts look like a boy scout code. Dictators are dictators. Too bad we think we need them in order to succeed. At least there's hope for genuine reform from this government—or the next one. It's got to happen. Eventually."

Maybe that's wishful thinking. But you have a lot of information, Bo. Why didn't you ever get around to using more of it?"

Because our vaunted "free press" was afraid. Countless refusals.They accused me of looking for publicity for myself. They demanded that I name the sources—which I couldn't possibly do, even though I might use a pseudonym for myself. Well, I tried. Several of the major city papers and all of the wire services told me that they were reluctant to tangle with *State*. They even asked whether I was really looking for a good job. How's that for covering cowardice? Anyhow I did publish the articles you saw in the Minnesota paper. They were as provocative and libelous as the editor dared print. They had some Congressional attention, but nobody challenged them. Unless you count a special section in a New York paper a few weeks later to present the status quo, PR style. It plumped for Rhee and his official version.

"Any results?"

"Attention and excuses. No real action. I suppose that's ultimately why I didn't continue. What for?" He thought for a moment. There were maybe some indirect results. Independent editorials had appeared in one or two other papers. Even Sanders turned out an intelligent story or two—based on mine. "There's hope for some of the other correspondents if they'd quit hob-nobbing with the power structures and start collecting facts. But even if they investigate, will their publishers come alive?"

"The U.S. was lucky in Korea," said Camden. "If only the Communists had been free to operate, they'd have paid lip service to the revolt against Rhee. That would have made us a a pro-Rhee enemy of the people, and we'd have been pushed out of the country immediately after." He thought for a moment. "Maybe we should have been."

"Crediting the Communists with a really brilliant political maneuver they hadn't really engineered. It's a very common world pattern. Will we ever act against the pattern, and can the dictators?"

"*State* doesn't see anything except as past history, highly glossed. Anything else is bad for business. Pardon me—*national security*." There was a generous silence before Camden continued. "What are you going to do over there?"

"I really don't know. A few years ago, I'd probably have had an answer. I'd have said I was going to *change* things. Now I'm just going to look around...fill myself in on the past three or four years.

"I'll expect you to reform the junta."

Beaumont laughed heartily with Camden. Humor or nerves? he wondered.

"I'll tell you whether the junta needs to be helped or overthrown," Bo said. There's a possibility that a movement will build outside Korea. I hope we're going to be on the deserving side, for a change. Then there's Dr. Choh to worry about. I don't know what he plans for me...but I also don't know whether he and his friends are safe now if I want to visit them. I have to be careful what I say— anything that could identify them. I'd never forgive myself."

"He was waiting for the Ancient One's *difficult things* to happen. Now maybe they have in fact happened, Camden offered. "Do you remember?"

"Yeah. I remember. And they make me regret that we ever stopped working on our end. We could accomplish so much for freedom if our government would act instead of pose."

"What should we have done, do you suppose?" Camden asked.

"We should have made it more uncomfortable for our own government to sit still.

"And it's not polite to say *we*. That's Oriental indirection. I get the meaning."

"Well, it's probably time to take a chance. Americans have tried just about everything but *reality*. Let's try that next."

"They're calling your flight for check-in. Want to be on that plane?"

Camden called for the check, and in minutes they were well down the ramp. If you did miss the flight, I could feel much more justified in my own having done nothing practical since we came back. A couple of petitions—you know— to keep Ai Ja happy with her politicking."

"At least you're keeping Ai Ja safe. That counts for much with me. She'll go home with warm regard for us Americans. We need a lot more of that."

They reached the loading gate, and Beaumont took his place in the check-in line.

"When you get back to the Land of the Morning Calm," Camden began, "...say hello to Young Song for me. You do intend to see her, don't you?"

"I suppose...yes, definitely! Judging from the paucity of letters, we haven't been close, of late. Also she's independent now with her new job, and so it'll be different. It's strange, but regardless of the help I gave, I also helped to corrupt. Corruption in a corrupt country. Call it simple internal practice, I guess: Young Song and I have lived the relationships of our two countries. Freaky."

"Statutory rape with fanfares...but if you lie a little, you can make the whole affair sound very touching. You can even be a hero over cocktails. Nobody expects perfection from soldiers. That follows the pattern of diplomacy, too. Don't think about it too much."

"Sometimes I think it's you who should go back there," said Beaumont. "I talked. You did things. The medicine and instruments were your idea."

"It still is. Sent occasionally in my father's name with his brief note so Choh can't refuse. You wrote those articles. You tried."

"Enough mutual admiration. What did we do—really? As individuals or as a nation, we did only little things. Money is little—it doesn't *cost* emotionally. I guess the Koreans are rebuilding despite our ineptness; and if democracy should happen—despite us—our theoreticians will claim great credit!"

151

"And go on to destroy some other country in the name of freedom via the helpful American people," Camden finished. "*State* and everybody else involved had better hope that the American people never do learn exactly what is happening overseas.... You know the U.S. agreed to partition Korean to get Russia into the war. China was only doing what Russia was afraid to do after the war. Weren't we the true aggressors acting the role of hero?"

"I can't argue that. Do you remember," Beaumont began slowly, "when the Ancient One told us that the jackals slew the White Deer of freedom and brought *an amber doe, rutting and making the sounds of life* into the government chambers?"

"I remember, although not the exact words, like you."

"Maybe the Korean people will turn a buck loose in those chambers—even without our help—and even without our help the rutting amber doe might drop a white fawn. Wouldn't that be neat?"

"Sloppy sentimentality," said Camden. "Go and sleep it off, will you?"

They both heard the final gate call for boarding.

"Do your damnedest, Bo" said Camden as the other man readied himself to board the plane. Soon it would blink away. "Even to accomplish something—anything!—that should shake us up. Then, who knows?"

Another handclasp, and Beaumont moved past the gate and into the brisk night air. Camden went back to the waiting rooms and started to go outside He turned and climbed instead to an off-limits observation deck outdoors.

The wind toyed with the night, and the people were moving in it. Then he realized that the plane that was Bo's was sealed; nothing was what it seemed. The plane taxied onto a runway. The motors harumphed, lest anyone think them not equal to the task, and the plane committed itself to the air.

Soon Camden heard nothing more. It was over. For how long?

*All those years ago, when Camden had seen him off at the airport, he hadn't been allowed into the country. So either then or now, he really couldn't speak of his search to Dr. Choh, who had never approved of the liaison, or to the doctor's friends, who never should have known, although they surely must have. Jeffrey could hardly be news to his own grandfather. Were any of them alive? Should he continue resolutely to search or to ask their help? He couldn't do that, either.*

*So he was becoming discouraged and ready to return to the States when he received a telephone message from Jeffrey Camden. It said very simply and without explanation that his adopted "aunt," Mrs. Kim, Young Song, could be found at the White Deer Tea House on many nights. Bless you, Jeffrey! It's so logical, and so little did he think of the possibility of communicating through you.*

*He tucked the picture frame into his jacket pocket; she would be sure to remember that. Of course he went there immediately...and nightly for a week after that. Finally she came in. After all the false hopes dashed and the innocent women previously accosted, he was hesitant. But this woman had something of the face and much of the walk he remembered of Young Song, and he decided to chance it.*

*"Kim-Sonsaeng," he said quietly as she passed. "Nanun tansinul sarang hamnida." I love you very much, he called after her. Certainly he didn't expect her to be the young beauty he remembered. Jeffrey had said she was a nice old woman; that didn't really register until he saw that she was an old nice woman.*

*She whirled in astonishment to face the fool who would say such words in public. There was no look of recognition.*

*"I am Gordon." Misshapen and old, too, he admitted to himself.*

*"Oh, hello." she said coolly. "I am the wife of Sergeant Milton Anderton."*

*He knew that the no-longer-pristine women tended to marry old American sergeants who didn't demand too much in the way of perfection. Her voice, after all these years, was well modulated—almost unaccented. Damn it! What should that matter now?*

*"It is very nice to see you." There was little hint of truth, and she didn't continue the chatter.*

*"Would you have tea with me? I've come back to see you."*

*"I am sorry." Crashing silence! "We had a moment, a long time ago. It was business. I understand."*

*Business was a phrase he knew he had used with Dr. Choh. Was it an accident of usage or the after words of a forgotten conversation transmitted from father to daughter in anger, and then to Young Song in confidence? It could be either, if the two young women had remained friends, as in fact (for Jeffrey's having called her aunt) they must have.*

*"I have not forgotten you."*

*"That is nice. What I sold you I cannot buy back. Why have you come?...But it is very nice to see you. Goodbye."*

*She turned and, without hurry, said something to an elderly Caucasian in civilian clothes who was just entering. Both of them went out together. What was her explanation to that Caucasian man, other than headache...or maybe a-friend-of-a-friend whom she didn't like...or instructions to a tourist? Or not worth any explanation at all?*

*What is Bo's explanation to Korea?*

*"Young Song," he said to no one. "I am sorry!"*

*And then he went home.*

*J.T.* —

    *Who knows?  Forget it?*

*M.W.*

Richard Cavalier

<u>Our Failures in Korea --</u>

# Glittering Public Buildings Cover
# Failures in Reconstructing a Nation

(Gordon Beaumont recently returned to this country after more than a year in the Far East, including a number of months in and about Seoul, Korea's capital. In a series of three articles beginning today, he relates his impressions of post-war Korea and its successes and failures in presenting democracy to an a r e a dominated by the Commun i s t drive. — Editor)

**BY GORDON BEAUMONT
as told to Pete Vanderpoel**
ONLY A SHORT WALK north of Nam Dae Mun — South Gate, portal to the ancient walled city of Seoul — rises the war-gutted masonry of Cho Ong Chung, the capitol building constructed during the Japanese occupation.

It dominates one of Seoul's major thoroughfares, Taepyong-no. Within a fan-shaped sector of the city bounded by Nam Dae Mun a n d Cho Ong Chung lies the central business district.

As I walked at will among this district's meandering streets and alleys, I could not help but be struck by the industry of the Korean people.

They have reconstructed, refurbished, and rehabilitated a district ravaged by war only a few years ago.

There is almost a surfeit of life in the streets. Violent wa r n i n g horns on motor cars patterned after jeeps, careening motor buses and rumbling trolleys — all are scrambled into an awesome traffic pattern through which d o d g e pedestrians and ox carts. And close at any point is a street peddler hawking his wares in haunt i n g chants.

As do nearly all in their first hours, I found Seoul quaint, as only Americans can apply the word. And I noted that the restoration of the administrative and cul t u r a l center was the reality often reported here and invariably assign e d newsreel footage.

—o—
**Smug Feelings**
IN BRIEF, WITH a feeling of self-satisfaction for my American share in the progress, I made my obeisance before the facade of a once-broken nation.

War is never far from S e o u l. Fewer than 50 miles to the north is the arbitrary boundary w i t h

which diplomats of conflicting political ideologies have pulled a nation in two pieces.

Across this boundary rain charges and counter-charges of aggressive and provocative acts which fill newspapers and radio reports. and so the war which divided a country now provides the Republic's major cohesive influence.

Korean adults display a marked reticence to discuss war, post-war conditions or politics.

They do not share the American addiction to indiscriminate discussion of internal affairs. Rat h e r, their polite conversation reflec t s good taste and fierce nati o n a l pride

—o—
**Fear Quiet Voices**
BUT THERE IS another reason for their reticence, a reason often found in a totalitarian state. Fear. For anti-administration sentime n t is often interpreted as pro-communist politics in Korea.

But among the youth of the city can be observed an impatient, feverish dedication to the liberation of North Korea, an attitude which signals their political orientation.

The political fashion of the day is termed democracy.

Yet the long-considered views of the people of Korea can not be learned in a day, or even in a month. For that reason, I smile at the compromising, often ill - informed reports of non-resident U.S. governmental or news agency representatives whose observat i o n s appear to be formed within a few minutes' walk about the Bando Hotel and an hour's talk around its bar

The Korea which a distinguished visitor or superficial observer sees — or is shown — is a far cry from the Korea which a resident knows.

During his short stopover, the distinguished visitor is taken into the gracious custody of the city's administration to be wooed with pleasant conversation, c o r d i a l thanks for past assistance, a n d presentation to the President of the Republic of Korea, Syngman Rhee.

Few persons are not won — and effectively detained. Seoul's reputation for sincerity and savior-faire is embellished by glib pronouncements of the newly-departed guest.

I wa neither limited by time nor detained with formalities, and so I began to look.

Without purpose or plan I began to see the tourists' Korea. And that meant Chang Duk and Duk Soo palaces, the residences of the last reigning dynasties in Korea. Both are somewhat refurbished a n d present in a few acres a panorama of East contrasted with West.

Across palace gardens and retaining walls, the city sprawls with abandon. Department stores, public office buildings and the Bando Hotel (plush by Korean standards) provide easy landmarks to t h e unpracticed eye.

Museums, libraries, schools and universities dominate the reaches of Seoul, and the rebuilding of these properties provides what employment exists.

Watching private buildings arise in the central business district, I knew that private fortunes have been accrued in the brief t i m e since the Korean War, for these structures do not generally qualify for economic aid.

—o—
**Somebody Has Money**
AND, ALTHOUGH FEW, if any, private fortunes survived the Japanese occupation and the Korean conflict, (Korea was virtually untouched by World War II) wealth is nevertheless in evidence.

I saw fine houses in the vicinity of the capital building and East Gate. Movie theaters are striking examples of contemporary architecture. Their unusually well-appointed interiors and their number belie the shortage of materi a l s and capital encountered by more worthy projects.

By teaching English in these houses — by direct contact with people who comprise the upper economic strata — I learned t h a t wealth is almost surely a concomitant of political prominence in Korea.

But if one's interest in the country is genuine, he turns from the pleasant aspects of central Seoul city to the realities of the metropolitan area.

Metropolitan Seoul numbers almost 1,700,000 persons, the majority of whom cohabitate in squalor only a few steps from the city's respectable main streets.

Next: Koreans' Korea.

# Our Failures in Korea-

HEADLINE:  Glittering Public Buildings Cover  Failures in
Reconstructing a Nation

(Gordon Beaumont recently returned to this country after more than a year in the
Far East, including a number of months in and around Seoul, Korea's capital.  In
a series of three articles beginning today, he related his impressions of post-war
Korea and its successes and failures in presenting democracy to an area
dominated by the Communist drive. – Editor)

(February 26, 1959)

BY GORDON BEAUMONT
As told to
PETE VANDERPOEL

**ONLY A SHORT WALK north of Nam Dae Mun-South Gate,
portal to the ancient walled city of Seoul-rises the war-gutted masonry of
Cho Ong Chung, the capitol building constructed during the Japanese
occupation.**

It dominates one of Seoul's major thoroughfares, Taepyong-no.  Within a
fan-shaped sector of the city bounded by Nam Dae Mun and Cho Ong Chung lies
the central business district.

As I walked at will among this district's meandering streets and alleys, I
could not help but be struck by the industry of the Korean people.

They have reconstructed, refurbish, and rehabilitated a district ravaged by
war only a few years ago.

There is almost a surfeit of life in the streets.  Violent warning horns on
motor cars patterned after jeeps, careening motor buses and rumbling trolleys—
all are scrambled into an awesome traffic pattern through which dodge
pedestrians and ox carts. And close at any point is a street peddler hawking his
wares in haunting chants.

As do nearly all in their first hours, I found Seoul quaint, as only Americans
can apply the word.  And I noted that the restoration of the administrative and
cultural center was the reality often reported here and invariable assigned
newsreel footage.

Smug Feelings

IN BRIEF, WITH a feeling of self-satisfaction for my American share in the
progress, I made my obeisance before the façade of a once-broken nation.

War is never far from Seoul. Fewer than 50 miles to the north is the arbitrary boundary with which diplomats of conflicting political ideologies have pulled a nation in two pieces.

Across this boundary rain charges and counter-charges of aggressive and provocative acts which fill newspapers and radio reports. And so the war which divided a country now provides the Republic's major cohesive influence.

Korean adults display a marked reticence to discuss war, post-war conditions or politics.

They do not share the American addiction to indiscriminate discussion of internal affairs. Rather, their polite conversation reflects good taste and fierce national pride.

### Fear Quiets Voices

BUT THERE IS another reason for their reticence, a reason often found in a totalitarian state. Fear. For anti-administration sentiment is often interpreted as pro-communist politics in Korea.

But among the youth of the city can be observed an impatient, feverish dedication to the liberation of North Korea, an attitude which signals their political orientation.

The political fashion of the day is termed democracy.

But the long-considered views of the people of Korea cannot be learned in a day, or even in a month. For that reason, I smile at the compromising, often ill-informed reports of non-resident U.S. governmental or news agency representatives whose observations appear to be formed within a few minutes' walk around the Bando Hotel and an hour's talk around its bar.

This Korea which is distinguished visitor or superficial observer sees-or is shown-is a far cry from the Korea which a resident knows.

During his short stopover, the distinguished visitor is taken to the gracious custody of the city's administration to be wooed with pleasant conversation, cordial thanks for past assistance, and presentation to the President of the Republic of Korea, Syngman Rhee.

Few persons are not won-and effectively detained. Seoul's reputation for sincerity and savoir-faire is embellished by glib pronouncement of the newly-departed guest.

I was neither limited by time nor detained with formalities, and so I began to look.

Without purpose or plan I began to see the tourists' Korea. And that meant Chang Duk and Duk Soo palaces, the residence of the last reigning dynasties in Korea. Both are somewhat refurbished and present in a few acres a panorama of East contrasted with West.

Across the palace gardens and retaining walls, the city sprawls with abandon. Department Stores, public office buildings and the Bando Hotel (plush by Korean standards) provide easy landmarks to the unpracticed eye.

Museums, libraries, schools and universities dominate the reaches of Seoul, and the rebuilding of these properties provides what employment exists.

Watching private building arise in the central business district, I knew that private fortunes have been accrued in the brief time since the Korean War, for these structures do not generally qualify for economic aid.

### Somebody Has Money

AND, ALTHOUGH FEW, if any private fortunes survived the Japanese occupation and the Korean conflict, (Korea was virtually untouched by World War II) wealth is nevertheless in evidence.

I saw fine houses in the vicinity of the capital building and East Gate. Movie theaters are striking examples of contemporary architecture. Their unusually well-appointed interiors and their number belie the shortage of materials and capital encountered by more worthy projects.

By teaching English in these houses-by direct contact with people who comprise the upper economic strata-I learned that wealth is almost surely a concomitant of political prominence in Korea.

But if one's interest in the country is genuine, he turns from the pleasant aspects of central Seoul city to the realities of the metropolitan area.

Metropolitan Seoul numbers almost 1,700,000 persons, the majority of whom cohabitate in squalor only a few steps from the city's respectable main street.

Next: Koreans' Korea.

Richard Cavalier

# Visiting Americans Rarely Pay Visits To the Sidestreets of the Little People

By GORDON BEAUMONT
as told to
PETE VANDERPOEL
(Second in a series of three articles on present-day Korea)

THE KOREA OF the sidestreets is the Korean's Korea.

Countless alleys branch from major streets such as Nam Dae Mun Ro, Ul Chi Ro and Chong Ro and disintegrate into the dirt of overcrowded quarters.

It was mid-winter. I walked through a confusion of passages amidst the most offensive sights and odors I have ever experienced.

In a supposedly "recovered" area I encountered families living under a canvas or huddled into a shack constructed of scrap wood, cardboard boxes or sheet metal carried from a U. S. Army installation.

Scantily-clad children tumbled in aimless games through gutters running with raw sewage. From time to time a child was called away to an over-populated, under-supplied house which afforded scanty protection from the elements.

Then it was summer, and unwashed urchins fought with flies for chunks of meat or fish. The atmosphere was fetid.

Korea has no sanitary system, no water system and an electrical service so rudimentary that much of rural Korea lacks even the civilizing effects of electricity.

### Rains Flush Sewers

THROUGHOUT THE country garbage is committed to drainage canals which carry off the summer monsoons.

More often than not human wastes are collected overnight in special containers and are hauled away as fertilizer, a timeless practice. And so contagious disease becomes epidemic during summer months.

While I spent the free hours of several months surveying the Seoul area I acquired the friendship and confidence of several informed Korean nationals.

Through them I obtained many of my earliest answers to questions not easily answered in a nation where one speaks little of the language.

Through long, direct conversations I came to understand much of the cynicism, hostility and even contempt with which Koreans regard Americans.

I had assumed that much of the overcrowding of Seoul was a direct results of refugees' push into the city. I reasoned that some portion of American economic aid should have been turned to housing the 1,700,000 bodies. It was not.

### No Shelter For Them

TODAY ONLY SEVERAL settlements constructed under UN-KRA shelter displaced Koreans. These I found — all things considered — admirable quarters, but too few to serve a nation.

Remember that the masses of the East can probably never be properly quartered, as we envision housing. The U. S. contribution to the problem appears to be promises and much building material, a good portion of which is said to have been turned to private use and gain by early Korean administrative agencies.

The hovels of today's Korea were originally pieced together as temporary shelters by the people, who put childlike faith in the promises and rumors of promises made by American and United Nations forces.

Because this country was essentially evident in the Korean campaign and subsequent negotiation with the Communists, it is the U.S. which took and now bears the brunt of resentment which has developed in the people in recent years.

A shrug of the shoulders conveys the Korean's concept of American aid. He has benefited only from the direct transfer of funds from America's sons to Korea's daughters.

### Crimes For Profit

PROSTITUTION AND theft are rampant in Korea. Several correspondents have already presented the bald facts for their sensational value. None has mentioned that these two methods of sustenance are the sole source of income — either direct or indirect — of thousands of jobless Koreans.

I looked for American-built hospitals. None carry this country's name. The U. S. Forces' contributions to innumerable clinics about the country is unknown or overlooked.

At the same time, a hospital project begun by a Scandinavian nation is now known and discussed as the Swedish Hospital, although a large portion of its material aid will come from the United States.

Food. It can be found in shops, but not everyone has the money to buy. While there is hunger in Korea—an abundance of it—CARE packages, stolen in transit or sold by recipients, are on sale in major department stores.

### For Those Who Pay

DOMESTIC CIGARETS and cosmetics and other high-profit commodities are available at their price; shops and stalls in the market areas carry American-made consumer items in plenitude.

Nearly all were stolen from U.S. military supply points or started toward black market channels by American personnel. But just enough legal imports arrive to make identification and recovery impossible.

Prices, of course, are exorbitant. Yet the very presence of quality American goods defeats small Korean enterprise, which cannot compete effectively at any price.

These are realities of Korea today. Whatever the American contribution, it has little aided the common people. Their lot has changed little since the war, charts and graphs in diplomatic offices to the contrary.

And if practices of both Korean and American agencies remain unchanged, so also will the lot of the Korean people through all the years of promise.

NEXT: Tangled policies.

160

# Our Failures in Korea

HEADLINE:  Visiting Americans Rarely Pay Visits To the Sidestreets of
the Little People

(February 27, 1959)

By Gordon Beaumont
as told to
Pete VANDERPOEL

**THE KOREA OF the sidestreets is the Korean's Korea.**
Countless alleys branch from major streets such as Nam Dae Mun Ro, Ul Chi
Ro and Chong Ro and disintegrate into the dirt of overcrowded quarters.

I was midwinter. I walked through a confusion of passages amidst the most
offensive sights and odors I have ever experienced.

In a supposedly "recovered" area I encountered families living under a
canvas or huddled into a shack constructed of scrap wood, cardboard boxes or
sheet metal carried from a U.S. Army installation.

Scantily-clad children tumbled in aimless games through gutters running
with raw sewage. From time to time a child was called away to an over-
populated, under-supplied house which afforded scanty protection from the
elements.

Then it was summer, and unwashed urchins fought with flies for chunks of
meat or fish. The atmosphere was fetid.

Korea has no sanitary system, no water system and an electrical service so
rudimentary that much of rural Korea lacks even the civilizing effects of
electricity.

Rains Flush Sewer

THROUGHOUT THE country garbage is committed to drainage canals
which carry off the summer monsoons.

More often than not human wastes are collected overnight in special
containers and are hauled away as fertilizer, a timeless practice.  And so
contagious disease becomes epidemic during summer months.

While I spent the free hours of several months surveying the Seoul area I
acquired the friendship and confidence of several informed Korean nationals.

Through them I obtained many of my earliest answers to questions not easily
answered in a nation where one speaks little of the language.

Through long, direct conversations I came to understand much of the
cynicism, hostility and even contempt with which Koreans regard Americans.

I had assumed that much of the overcrowding of Seoul was a direct result of refugees' push into the city. I reasoned that some portion of American economic aid should have been turned to housing the 1,700,000 bodies. It was not.

No Shelter For Them

TODAY ONLY SEVERAL settlement constructed under UNKRRA shelter displaced Koreans. These I found-all things considered-admirable quarters, but too few to serve a nation.

Remember that the masses of the East can probably never be properly quartered, as we envision housing. The U.S. contribution to the problem appears to be promises and much building material, a good portion of which is said to have been turned to private use and gain by early Korean administrative agencies.

The hovels of today's Korea were originally pieced together as temporary shelters by the people, who put childlike faith in the promises and rumors of promises made by American and United Nations forces.

Because this country was essentially evident in the Korea campaign and subsequent negotiation with the Communists, it is the U.S. which took and now bears the brunt of resentment which has developed in the people in recent years.

A shrug of shoulders conveys the Korean's concept of American aid. He has benefited only from the direct transfer of funds from America's sons to Korea's daughters.

Crimes For Profit

PROSTITUTION AND theft are rampant in Korea. Several correspondents have already presented the bald facts for their sensational value. None has mentioned that these two methods of sustenance are the sole source of income-either direct or indirect-of thousands of jobless Koreans.

I looked for American-built hospitals. None carry this country's name. The U.S. Forces' contributions to innumerable clinics about the country is unknown or over-looked.

At the same time, a hospital project begun by a Scandinavian nation is now known and discussed as the Swedish Hospital, although a large portion of its material aid will come from the United States

Food. It can be found in shops, but not everyone has the money to buy. While there is hunger in Korea-an abundance of it-CARE packages, stolen in transit or sold by recipients, are on sale in major department stores.

For Those Who Pay

DOMESTIC CIGARETS and cosmetics and other high-profit commodities are available at their price; shops and stalls in the market areas carry American-made consumer items in plenitude.

Nearly all were stolen from U.S. military supply points or started toward black market channels by American personnel. But just enough legal imports arrive to make identification and recovery impossible.

Prices, of course, are exorbitant. Yet the very presence of quality American goods defeats small Korean enterprise, which cannot compete effectively at any price.

These are realities of Korea today. Whatever the American contribution, it has little aided the common people. Their lot has changed little since the war, charts and graphs in diplomatic offices to the contrary.

And if practices of both Korean and American agencies remain unchanged, so also will the lot of the Korean people through all the years of promise.

NEXT: Tangled policies.

Richard Cavalier

## Our Failures in Korea –
# Mishandling of American Funds Viewed As Result of Plain Theft or Collusion

**BY GORDON BEAUMONT**
**as told to Pete Vanderpool**
(Last in a series of three articles on present-day Korea.)

POOR PUBLIC relations might be cited as a reason that no accurate concept of the American role in developing Korea's economy has emerged since the Korean War.

But widely divergent views of the Korean people and their American counterparts point to the fact that differences are based on something far more substantial.

During the years of hostilities —and for one or even several years following the armistice — disbursement of huge sums was adequately explained in terms of logistics and strategic repair.

But since 1956 — an arbitrary date — military aid has become a more constant and easily-defined expense. It is no longer possible to accept vague references to the war as an accounting for the millions of dollars still going into Korea.

And it is millions — for 1958 alone, appropriations totaled $2.2 million.

The Office of the Economic Coordinator for Korea (OEC) is the sole distributor and principal auditor of all American aid grants. Since June, 1958, that agency has also assumed the same control over what funds might be appropriated by the United Nations.

**Avoid Accusations**

I HAVE READ various publications of the OEC. Aside from a declaration of admirable goals, they include several artistic graphs and several pages of pointless statistics —BUT they in no way offer specific information to counter or disprove disparaging remarks and charges of profiteering made by Korea's people.

It is not difficult to put a certain amount of faith in the Korean grapevine, which is now and has been spreading word of government waste and mismanagement of American aid.

Grapevine reports are credible because it has proved an able network — faster and surer than newspapers and more accurate than the partisan radio.

The system is a phenomenon perfected over centuries of communication, its success culminating in its announcement of the arrival of atomic arms at Inchon harbor almost simultaneously with the receipt by the UN command of an official, classified document reporting the shipment.

**Press Had Details**

THE KOREAN PRESS released the grapevine story immediately, a full day before the UN announcement, which then became confirmation.

When such incidents were consistently repeated, I began to put credence in the undocumented reports of responsible individuals who could distinguish between fact and rumor.

I began to question fund dispersal in Korea when these responsible persons talked of waste and mismanagement of American aid,

which totals $1.3 billions between fiscal years 1954 and 1958, inclusive .

I mention several reports of special interest. Each has been corroborated by a European businessman, very much in a position to know, who is still in Korea and must remain nameless.

1. Only 96 of 300 enterprises which received aid grants are completed and in operation today. The remainder either failed or remained incomplete because The entrepeneur went "bankrupt." Successful ventures enumerated in reports under "Project Assistance" headings are almost doubled by failures, which are grouped under "Non-Project Assistance" headings.

2. A glass factory was constructed which produces such a poor grade of flat glass that a Japanese pane was substituted for presentation to president Syngman Rhee on his official inspection of the plant March 18, 1958.

3. A bran oil processing plant of such excessive capacity was constructed that the entire castor bean crop of Korea can be processed in a week's time. Cost: Three - quarters of a million U. S. dollars.

**Too Much Caustic**

4. TWO CAUSTIC SODA plants were constructed, either of which can produce enough caustic soda to meet the present and foreseeable needs of the country. Justification for the duplication: strategic value in event of war. Location: Side by side in the primary target area of Inchon harbor. Combined cost: $1,750,000.

These examples might well indicate questionable judgment alone. But in the two instances below, I recognize the beginning of a disreputable trend — multi - million - dollar federal projects being transferred to private control at great loss to the Korean government, a veritable gift to influential individuals:

1. In April last year the ROK government accepted bids on a fertilizer plant still under construction after more than three years.

Total cost of the plant is estimated at $33,336,000, including a supplementary allotment of $2,788,000 in February, 1958.

Bid conditions: Open bid against the working capital required ($10 million); minimum bid, one quarter that amount.

2. A dam and hydro - electric plant (favored project of the OEC) is quietly being readied for similar transfer to private business. Statistics on cost were refused me by the OEC reports officer, Vaughn Mechau, who speaks for OEC chief m Warne.

**Accidental Information**

I LEARNED OF the proposed transfer of this dam quite by accident in Mechau's office. The discovery resulted from my direct challenge of OEC policy based on pertinent material such as I have related in this article.

By Mechau's admission, the organization is not qualified to review engineering specifications

which accompany proposals in request for loans. Because a sufficient number of bona fide engineers is not available, the "engineering" staff is buttressed with individuals whose major qualification is their willingness to pretend.

In Mechau's words, OEC will "take what we can get" among employes. What OEC can get includes a host of young Army personnel or unsuccessful career soldiers, both totally unprepared to discharge obligations of such responsibility.

Recognizing OEC incompetence, in January, 1957, the U. S. government retained as consulting engineers the firm of Smith, Hinchman, Grylls Associates, Inc., New York.

The firm's chief consultant in Korea — Chester W. Clarke — refused to approve such ventures as the bran oil and caustic soda plants, and was found to "obstruct" the disbursement of funds.

OEC raised so much pressure in agitating for Clarke's replacement that a company vice-president arrived in Korea in March last year to deliver this ultimatum: The Korean office would operate as a rubber stamp for OEC or Clarke's resignation would be necessary.

I spoke by telephone with Clarke just before he left Korea. Today he is associated with the engineering division of Chrysler Corp.

**Business Maneuver**

ANOTHER OEC downfall — it does not command cooperation of the banking organizations of Korea. Consequently, a legal "bankruptcy" maneuver has created a number of private fortunes in recent years.

This is possible because OEC requires that applicants have a current bank balance equal to 20 per cent of the requested loan, if granted.

But engineering firms regularly make 24 - hour loans of such amounts to their clients, the head of a foreign engineering firm which works exclusively with OEC-associated projects told me.

The 24-hour loans which cover the 20 per cent OEC requirement are deposited, a bank statement is obtained, the account is closed.

On the strength of a single deposit statement, OEC makes its loans. Many go to individuals who claim a "business failure" well in advance of receipt of the OEC loan. No cash is recovered, of course.

I should like to think that OEC is unaware of the practice. If it is not, it is open to embarrassing questions.

Collusion is an ugly charge, but it is on the lips of the man in the Korean street who discusses OEC. And these discussions have been carried into the diplomatic corps of nations of the free world. Only

the American people are unaware that their country's prestige is draining away with their dollars. Korea is America's example of democracy in the oriental world. Without confidence in their administration — with disillusion in America — the Korean people speak out for democracy.

I hear only muted voices.

164

# Our Failures in Korea-

HEADLINE:   Mishandling of American Funds Viewed As Result of Plain
Theft or Collusion

BY GORDON BEAUMONT
AS TOLD TO PETE VANDERPOEL
(Last in a series of three
articles on present-day Korea.)

POOR PUBLIC relations might be cited as a reason that no accurate concept of the American role in developing Korea's economy has emerged since the Korean War.

But widely divergent views of the Korean people and their American counterparts point to the fact that differences are based on something far more substantial.

During the years of hostilities-and for one or even several years following the armistice-disbursement of huge sums was adequately explained in terms of logistics and strategic repair.

But since 1956-an arbitrary date-military aid has become a more constant and easily-defined expense.  It is no longer possible to accept vague references to the war as an accounting for the millions of dollars still going into Korea.

And it is millions-for 1958 alone, appropriations totaled $2.2 million.

The office of the Economic Coordinator for Korea (OEC) is the sole distributor and principal auditor of all American aid grants. Since June, 1958, that same agency has also assumed the same control over what funds might be appropriated by the United Nations.

Avoid Accusations

I have read various publications of the OEC. Aside from a declaration of admirable goals, they include several artistic graphs and several pages of pointless statistics-BUT they in no way offer specific information to counter or disprove disparaging remarks and charges of profiteering made by Korea's people.

It is not difficult to put a certain amount of faith in the Korean grapevine, which is now and has been spreading word of government waste and mismanagement of American aid.

Grapevine reports are credible because it has proved an able network-faster and surer than newspapers and more accurate than the partisan radio.

The system is a phenomenon perfected over centuries of communication, its success culminating in its announcement of the arrival of atomic arms at Inchon harbor almost simultaneously with the receipt by the UN command of an official, classified document reporting the shipment.

Press Had Details

THE KOREAN PRESS released the grapevine story immediately, a full day before the UN announcement, which then became confirmation.

When such incidents were consistently repeated, I began to put credence in the undocumented reports of responsible individuals who could distinguish between fact and rumor.

I began to question fund dispersal in Korea when these responsible persons talked of waste and mismanagement of American aid, which totals $1.3 billions between fiscal years 1954 and 1958, inclusive.

I mention several reports of special interest. Each has been corroborated by a European businessman, very much in a position to know, who is still in Korea and must remain nameless.

1. Only 96 of 300 enterprises which received aid grants are completed and in operation today. The remainder either failed or remained incomplete because the entrepreneur went "bankrupt." Successful ventures enumerated in reports under "Project Assistance" heading are almost doubled by failures, which are grouped under "Non-Project Assistance" headings.

2. A glass factory was constructed which produces such a poor grade of flat glass that a Japanese pane was substituted for presentation to president Syngman Rhee on his official inspection of the plant March 18, 1958.

3. A bran oil processing plant of such excessive capacity was constructed that the entire castor bean crop of Korea can be processed in a week's time. Cost: Three-quarters of a million U.S. dollars.

Too Much Caustic

4. TWO CAUSTIC SODA plants were constructed, either of which can produce enough caustic soda to meet the present and foreseeable needs of the country. Justification for the duplication: strategic value in event of war. Location: Side by side in the primary target area of Inchon harbor. Combined cost: $1,750,000.

These examples might well indicate questionable judgment alone. But in the two instances below, I recognize the beginning of a disreputable trend-multi-million-dollar federal projects being transferred to private control at great loss to the Korean government, a veritable gift to influential individuals:

1. In April last year the ROK government accepted bids on a fertilizer plant still under construction after more than three years.

Total cost of the plant is estimated at $33,338,000, including a supplementary allotment of $2,788,000 in February, 1958.

Bid conditions: Open bid against the working capital ($10 million); minimum bid, one quarter that amount.

2. A dam and hydro-electric plant (favored project of the OEC) is quietly being readied for similar transfer to private business. Statistics on cost were refused me by the OEC reports officer, Vaughn Mechau, who speaks for OEC chief William Warne.

Accidental Information:

I LEARNED OF the proposed transfer to this dam quite by accident in Mechau's office. The discovery resulted from my direct challenge of OEC policy based on pertinent material such as I have related in this article.

By Mechau's admission, the organization is not qualified to review engineering specifications which accompany proposals in request for loans. Because a sufficient number of bona fide engineers is not available, the "engineering" staff is buttressed with individuals whose major qualification is their willingness to pretend.

In Mechau's words, OEC will "take what we can get" among employees. What OEC can get includes a host of young Army personnel or unsuccessful career soldiers, both totally unprepared to discharge obligations of such responsibility.

Recognizing OEC incompetence, in January, 1957, the U.S. government retained as consulting engineers the firm of Smith, Hinchman, Grylls Associates, Inc., New York.

The firm's chief consultant in Korea—Chester W. Clarke—refused to approve such ventures as the bran oil and caustic soda plants, and was found to "obstruct" the disbursement of funds.

OEC raised so much pressure in agitating for Clarke's replacement that a company vice-president arrived in Korea in March last year to deliver this ultimatum: The Korean office would operate as a rubber stamp for OEC or Clarke's resignation would be necessary.

I spoke by telephone with Clarke just before he left Korea. Today he is associated with the engineering division of Chrysler Corp.

Business Manuever

ANOTHER OEC downfall-it does not command cooperation of the banking organizations of Korea. Consequently, a legal "bankruptcy" maneuver has created a number of private fortunes in recent years.

This is possible because OEC required that applicants have a current bank balance equal to 20 per cent of the requested loan, if granted.

But engineering firms regularly make 24-hours loans of such amounts to their clients, the head of a foreign engineering firm which works exclusively with OEC-associated projects told me.

The 24-hour loans which cover the 20 per cent OEC requirement are deposited, a bank statement is obtained, the account is closed.

On the strength of a single deposit statement, OEC makes its loans. Many go to individuals who plan a "business failure" well in advance of receipt of the OEC loan. No cash is returned, of course.

I should like to think that OEC is unaware of the practice. If it is not, it is open to embarrassing questions.

Collusion is an ugly charge, but it is on the lips of the man in the Korean street who discusses OEC. And these discussions have been carried into the diplomatic corps of nations of the free world. Only the American people are unaware that their country's prestige is draining away with their dollars.

Korea is America's example of democracy in the oriental world. Without confidence in their administration—with disillusion in America—the Korean people speak out for democracy.

I hear only muted voices.

# Failure to Pinpoint Foreign Aid Waste Affront to Public, Boon to Our Enemies

EDITOR'S NOTE: Sev e r a l weeks ago The Tribune published a series of articles by Gordon Beaumont and Pete Vanderpoel on the waste in our mutual security program in Korea. That series has since come to the attention of the Committee on Foreign Affairs (see letter in adjacent Town Crier column). Today The Tribune prints another article by the same authors expanding the subject.

**By GORDON BEAUMONT**
**As told to**
**PETE VANDERPOEL**

During the past several wee k s many American newspapers have published stories of a s p e c i a l House committee's f i n d i n g s of waste and theft in the American foreign aid program

Citing a need to withhold unfavorable propaganda from Russia, our agencies gallantly decline to "name names.' They claim that to remain "cooperative" with foreign governments involved in mismanagement of our funds we m u s t play at naivete.

After carefully considering my impressions and observations in touring many areas of the F a r East, I state unequivocally that the reticence of the House committee is intended more to h i d e from the American people t h e bungling of American econo m i c missions than to protect our economic "allies."

It is an almost indisputable fact that each instance of aid fund mismanagement is a direct consequence of the failure of an American representative to discharge properly the obligations of his office.

Neither is the claim to be "withholding information from Russia" valid — at least not in so far as it purports to relate to the Far East.

I have seen a British intelligence report which graphically described conditions in Korea. Such a report is periodically circulated to embassies of all countries of t h e British Commonwealth There is little reason to believe that such routine dispatches are protected as secret documents by the countless offices receiving them. Similar reports are prepared by agencies of other UN countries keeping token forces in Korea.

Furthermore, throughout the day Radio Pyongyang and Radio Peiping warn the millions in free and controlled Asia that corruption and moral decay are concomitants of democracy.

**Convincing Claims**

The Communists' most convincing arguments: (1) mismana g e ment in nearly every country receiving foreign aid; (2) the current administration of the Republic of Korea.

We are defenseless. The f i r s t point is a matter of record even in this country. As for the second — the government of the Republic of Korea is morally destitute and is rapidly transforming itself, while we watch, into a dictatorship.

Democracy in South Korea was patterned after the political theory of the United States of America and was nurtured under laboratory conditions. Its failure is our failure in our most serious undertaking — propagating democracy.

**American People Uninformed**

Because of the narrow outlook of some men prominent in our foreign affairs, the American people —and they alone in the entire free world — are ignorant of such conditions. Our paternalistic government has attempted to rear its citizenry unaware of their true status, much as a misguided parent might try to educate a child by shielding him from life's realities.

I have heard bitter accou n t s from many disillusioned Asians. They once had hope for and with America, but too often they experienced a "justice" m a d e to serve the ends of their own nationals in office; too often these ends were won with the knowledge and-or assistance of inept a n d sometimes dishonest American economic advisers.

**Voice of the People**

In Seoul, a doctor claimed that there was no such blatant dishonesty before American money was pumped into the country. (I found Orientals to be far more honest and direct in all respects than the majority of their Western counterparts.)

In Yokohama, a banker asked me cynically whether economists in the US were as adept at juggling facts and statistics — and bank accounts — as those in Korea and Japan.

In Hong Kong an exporter told me of his sale and shipment of thousands of air mattresses and tennis balls to an Asian nation as "logistic materiel" paid for by American taxes.

A British engineer who had represented his firm in several Far Eastern and Near Eastern countries told me flatly it is his organization's policy to work exclusively in countries receiving American economic aid.

Nationals AND AMER I C A N S were amassing sizeable personal wealth, as he explained it, so why not a legitimate organization — his company — too?

On Okinawa, a taxi driver asked me whether we believed that American's really came to that island to serve their country.

**Aid to the Rich?**

In Manila a shopkeeper o n l y shrugged when the topic of American aid was broached. "I h e a r about it," he said. "It builds more hotels for the rich."

In Macao, an innkeeper stated "perhaps communism is bad, but America hasn't shown me a n y thin better."

These comments by the people perh aps should not be accepted as entirely accurate. Neither should they be dismissed as having no basis in fact.

Whatever their validity, the observations indicate unquestionably that our representatives do n o t command the respect or trust of the people among whom they work. Their mission is therefore impaired, if not made impossible of accomplishment — they are best recalled.

**Key to Our Failure**

Perhaps this is the key to our consistent failures: we've offered money and talk — our most abundant exports — administered with little intelligence and less ability.

Impressions I gained of many Americans to whom we've entrusted our recovery plans remain offensive.

I recall two American women working for a government agency in Korea. Camp-followers who'd found their way onto an ICA payroll, they called foul names after a Korean prostitute competing with them for American officers in a hotel lobby.

**Ill-Considered Talk**

I remember overhearing affairs of the American embassy d i s cussed on Seoul's streets by two attaches wandering about with unkempt wives and ill-mannered offspring.

At another time an emba s s y clerk confided his promotion to vice-consul served solely to p r e serve his place on the payroll during a personnel shuffle.

Few Americans serving w i t h government agencies or various military organizations over s e a s have qualities to recommend them as domestic servants, much less as civil servants and representatives of the American people.

During my long year's r e s i dence in the Orient, I was often made ashamed of their behavior and frequently had occasion to apologize for that behavior.

**Showed Real Respect**

Possibly to compensate for these affronts to the intelligence and integrity of the people of the Far East, I made a point of showing courtesies to foreign nationals I met. I spoke a few words of their language when I could and showed genuine respect for their persons and customs.

With astounding frequency my conduct drew this terse observation: You do not act like an American! I have never encounter e d another phrase which at once so sincerely compliments and so thoroughly humiliates as does that.

Despite my comments, I believe it would be irresponsible for Congress MERELY to cut foreign aid appropriations. Congress must also correct the practices of our agencies abroad, for malpractices are the cause and not the result of our economic fiascos overseas.

Properly disbursed, half the foreign aid funds will vastly increase the accomplishments of the present program.

It is entirely within Congress' purview to demand that only intelligent persons of integrity be allowed to represent America abroad — to oversee the distribution of the large sums of money which turn the heads of small men.

If the Asian nations conceive of Americans as a mercenary, crude and shallow people, they see us as our governmental representatives have shown us to be.

169

Richard Cavalier

# Must We Remain Quiet?

HEADLINE:  Failure to Pinpoint Foreign Aid Waste Affront to Public,
Boon to Our Enemies

(April 17, 1959)


By GORDON BEAUMONT
As told to
PETE VANDERPOEL

**During the past several weeks many American newspapers  have
published stories of a special House committee's finding of waste and theft in
the American foreign aid program.**

Citing a need to withhold unfavorable propaganda from Russia, our agencies
gallantly decline to "name names." They claim that to remain "cooperative" with
foreign governments involved in mismanagement of our funds we must play at
naivete.

After carefully considering my impressions and observations in touring many
areas of the Far East, I state unequivocally that the reticence of the House
committee is intended more to hide from the American people the bungling of
American economic missions than to protect our economic "allies."

It is an almost indisputable fact that each instance of aid fund
mismanagement is a direct consequence of the failure of an American
representative to discharge properly the obligations of his office.

Neither is the claim to be "withholding information from Russia" valid-at
least not in so far as it purports to relate to the Far East.

I have seen a British intelligence report which graphically described
conditions in Korea.  Such a report is periodically circulated to embassies of all
countries of the British Commonwealth. There is little reason to believe that such
routine dispatches are protected as secret documents by the countless office
receiving them. Similar reports are prepared by agencies of other UN countries
keeping token forces in Korea.

Furthermore, throughout the day Radio Pyongyang and Radio Peiping warn
the millions in free and controlled Asia that corruption and moral decay are
concomitants of democracy.

Convincing Claims

The Communists' most convincing argument:  (1) mismanagement in nearly
every country receiving foreign aid; (2) the current administration of the
Republic of Korea.

We are defenseless. The first point is a matter of record even in this country. As for the second-the government of Korea is morally destitute and is rapidly transforming itself, while we watch, into a dictatorship.

Democracy in South Korea was patterned after the political theory of the United States of America who was nurtured under laboratory conditions. Its failure is our failure in our most serious undertaking-propagating democracy.

American People Uninformed

Because of the narrow outlook of some men prominent in our foreign affairs, the American people-and they alone in the entire free world-are ignorant of such conditions. Our paternalistic government has attempted to rear its citizenry unaware of their true status, much as a misguided parent might try to educate a child by shielding him from life's realities.

I have heard bitter accounts from many disillusioned Asians. They once had hope for and with with America, but too often these ends were won with the knowledge and/or assistance of inept and sometimes dishonest American economic advisers.

Voice of the People

In Seoul, a doctor claimed that there was no such blatant dishonesty before American money was pumped into the country. (I found Orientals to be far more honest and direct in all respects than the majority of the Western counterparts.)

In Yokohama, a banker asked me cynically whether economists in the U.S. were as adept at juggling facts and statistics—and bank accounts—as those in Korea and Japan.

In Hong Kong an exporter told me of his sale and shipment of thousands of air mattresses and tennis balls to an Asian nation as "logistical materiel" paid for by American taxes.

A British engineer who had represented his firm in several Far Eastern and Near Eastern countries told me flatly it is his organization's policy to work exclusively in countries receiving American economic aid.

Nationals AND AMERICANS were amassing sizeable personal wealth, as he explained it, so why not a legitimate organization—his company—too?

On Okinawa, a taxi driver asked me whether we believed that Americans really came to that island to serve their country.

Aid to the Rich?

In Manila a shopkeeper only shrugged when the topic of American aid was broached. "I hear about it," he said. "It builds more hotels for the rich."

In Macao, an innkeeper stated "Perhaps communism is bad, but America hasn't shown me anything better."

Such comments by the people should not be accepted as entirely accurate. Neither should they be dismissed as having no basis in fact.

Whatever their validity, the observations indicate unquestionably that our representatives do no command the respect or trust of the people among whom they work.

Their mission is therefore impaired, if not made impossible of accomplishment-they are best recalled.

### Key to Our Failure

Perhaps this is the key to our consistent failures: we've offered money and talk-our most abundant exports-administered with little intelligence and less ability.

Impressions I gained of many Americans to whom we've entrusted our recovery plans remain offensive.

I recall two American women working for a government agency. Camp followers in Korea who'd found their way onto an ICA payroll, they called foul names after a Korean prostitute competing with them for American officers in a hotel lobby.

### Ill-Considered Talk

I remember overhearing affairs of the American embassy discussed on Seoul's streets by two attaches wandering about with unkempt wives and ill-mannered off-spring.

At another time an embassy clerk confided his promotion to vice-consul served solely to preserve his place on the payroll during a personnel shuffle.

Few Americans serving with government agencies or various military organizations overseas have qualities to recommend them as domestic servants, much less as civil servants and representatives of the American people.

During my long year's residence in the Orient, I was often made ashamed of their behavior and frequently had occasion to apologize for that behavior.

### Showed Real Respect

Possibly to compensate for these affronts to the intelligence and integrity of the people of the Far East, I made a point of showing courtesies to foreign nationals I met. I spoke a few words of t heir language when I could and showed genuine respect for t heir persons and customs.

With astounding frequency my conduct drew this terse observation: You do not act like an American! I have never encountered another phrase which at once so sincerely compliments and so thoroughly humiliates as does that.

Despite my comments, I believe it would be irresponsible for Congress MERELY to cut foreign aid appropriations. Congress must also correct the practices of our agencies abroad, for malpractices are the cause and not the result of our economic fiascos overseas.

Properly disbursed, half the foreign aid funds will vastly increase the accomplishment of the present program.

It is entirely with Congress' purview to demand that only intelligent persons of integrity be allowed to represent America abroad-to oversee the distribution of the large sums of money which turn the heads of small men.

If the Asian nations conceive of Americans as mercenary, crude and shallow people, they see us as our governmental representatives have shown us to be.

Richard Cavalier

# Return From Devastati

## Cities Rising From Ashes Of Late War

### Population Gains Helping Economy

Like the fabled phoenix, the cities of Korea have risen from the dormancy of Japanese occupation and the ashes of war to acquire fresh stature and vitality.

All but one of southern Korea's major cities is on, or fairly near, the western and southern coasts. The exception is Taegu, inland and on the east of the Korean Peninsula.

In order of population, these cities are Seoul, 1,800,000; Pusan, 1,040,000; Taegu, 488,000; Inchon, 321,000; Kwangju, 233,000; Taejon, 173,000; Masan, 130,000; Chonju, 124,000, and Mokpu, 114,000.

**Cities Were Stagnant**

During the Japanese times, these cities were far smaller and, except for Japanese-owned and operated trading and light industrial companies, comparatively stagnant commercially. In fact, by 1945 Japanese owned 85 per cent of all property in Korea; the Koreans were virtual tenants in their own land.

Following Japan's World War II defeat, Korea lapsed into confusion. But Japanese acquisition and holding of properties in Korea was ended.

Under the American Military Government that followed, the country was mainly concerned with reforming the economy. It had to shift overnight from one integrated with Japan's to the economy of an independent state. For a long time there was economic chaos.

**Almost Hopeless Task**

To bring viability out of this dislocation seemed an almost hopeless task — h n the Russians

President Syngman Rhee

## U.S. Amity Hailed By President Rhee

### By President Syngman Rhee

On behalf of myself and of the Korean people, I extend our warm good wishes to the people of the United States.

Koreans regard Americans as their best and closest friends. This has come about not so much because you have helped us—although that assistance has been crucial to our survival—but because we have come to know and admire the American people so much. We like them as people and as friends. In our country, they have created a great reservoir of good will for the United States.

While we still face the problem of unifying the countr

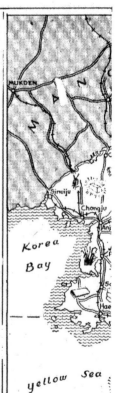

Legend —
IRON
COAL
GOLD
BARLEY
RICE
RYE
SOY BEANS
WHEAT
TOBACCO
SILK
COTTON

YORK **Tribune** KOREAN SECTION

Section **11**

IARCH 29, 1959

SIXTEEN PAGES

# on: *The Story of Korea*

## An Ancient Culture And a Modern Ally

### Aid Restores War-Torn Economy, Maintains a Bulwark of Freedom

By Walter Briggs

SEOUL

The Republic of Korea considers itself America's closest friend and ally.

This is a consequence of likemindedness and the dictates of history. Koreans and Americans can get along together. They think alike, even though the United States is far more advanced in technology and democratic experience.

Historically Korea was brought out of its isolation by American influences. But before that isolation, caused by the war-like intentions of its neighbors, it had created a civilization which was famous in the Orient and had sent scholars abroad at the request of foreign rulers.

For nearly 2,000 years, Korean dynasties had encouraged the arts. As early as 600 A. D. a 100-volume history of the country had been compiled. With Korean development of movable type and the creation of a new alphabet in the fifteenth century, many books were published on such varied topics as medicine and agriculture, geology and astronomy, music and military science. In those days more than 800 musicians were attached to the court. There were so many dancers that they "seemed like a cloud." Painting, ceramics, lacquer ware and sculpture attested to the interest in many phases of cultural achievement.

#### Japanese Rule

It was impossible to carry on much of this creative activity during the Japanese occupation period of forty years, a painful experience that left scars but no newspartitions. Ko

## A New Law To Attract Investment

### Policy Mapped By Legislature

Foreign investment should be the lifeblood of Korea's future economic development—to the mutual profit of the investor and the Korean people.

Because of the Japanese occupation from 1905 to 1945 and the devastation of the Korean War, Korea has had extreme difficulty in accumulating investment capital. Opportunities are numerous. The only stumbling blocks are money, efficient management and technical know-how.

Mineral resources require exploitation. Industrial prospects are unlimited, including such diverse areas as petroleum processing, ceramics, textiles, fishery development and various specialties, such as handicrafts. Technical co-operation is needed and will be welcomed.

A liberal foreign investment

*Richard Cavalier*


The Town Crier—Headline  Korean Wastes Verified


By KEN ALLEN

NOT TOO LONG ago, *The Tribune* published on this page an exclusive report of unsavory conditions in Korea with reference to waste of taxpayers' money. Quite frankly, editors in this newsroom were somewhat skeptical of the facts related by Gordon Beaumont.

The series was published mostly on my say so. I argued that U.S. taxpayers' money was involved and *Tribune* readers had a right to know how it was being wasted. Furthermore, Beaumont was writing about things in Korea that paralleled what I had learned in other Asian countries.

Today *The Tribune* publishes another Beaumont article on this page. I have intercepted a letter that you ought to read along with that Beaumont article. The significant thing for me in this letter is the rather calm tone Mr. Morgan uses. He refers to "shortcomings" when I would prefer "corruption;" he says "less efficient" when I would say "dry land piracy."

But he does admit the Beaumont facts, which is important. This gives you opportunity to make up your own words!


Dear Mr. Beaumont:

I have gone over with interest the clippings enclosed with your letter of April 9 referring to the situation in Korea. Several of the shortcomings of the program which you describe have been confirmed by information developed by the Committee on Foreign Affairs. In a few instances you mention situations which are new to us, and we will make inquiries concerning them as rapidly as we are able to do so.

The Committee on Foreign Affairs is in the midst of its consideration of the Executive request for authorization of additional funds for the continuation of the mutual security program. The problems which confront the Committee are difficult. Even though we recognize that the operation of the mutual security program in Korea has been less effective than it should have been, it does not follow that the answer is for the United States to pull out of South Korea and allow that area to fall into the hands of the communists.

There are severe limitations on what the Congress can do to legislate greater zeal, prudence and ingenuity on the part of the Executive Branch. Presumably some curtailment of funds would make those responsible for operating the Korean program more careful in what they do, but there is no way that the

Congress can assure that the money it cuts out would be wasted and that the remainder would be well spent.

There are a number of aspects of the program of which the Committee has become aware during its investigations that indicate the desirability of modifications of ICA operating procedures. We are bringing pressure to bear to produce such changes. There have been a few discernible results already.

I appreciate very much your interest in this matter and the information contained in your articles.

Thomas E. Morgan
Chairman
Committee on Foreign Affairs
House of Representatives

## About the Author

Richard Cavalier has traveled in more than forty countries and has seen both the many actual happenings of the world andalso the sanitized offical versions given in many places.

Cavalier is also the author of an ESL how-to text, *Practical Word Power,* that helps volunteers to tutor classes of up to ten adult, middle-competency students in learning the dictionary key to pronunciation. He also has three how-to business books on group communications coming in the Winter of 2002.

Printed in the United States
1143300005B/148